MAGGIE CHRISTENSEN

The Restaurant in Pelican Crossing

Cover and interior design: J D Smith Design
Editing: John Hudspith Editing Services

Dedication

To Jim, my soulmate.

Also by Maggie Christensen

One

It was a mild winter morning in the Queensland coastal town of Pelican Crossing, the sky a brilliant shade of blue and the sea sparkling like diamonds.

Poppy Taylor wiped away a tear as she watched Scarlett walk across the white sand towards the flower-covered arch beneath which her bridegroom awaited her. How she wished Jack could be here to share the day. He had been gone for five years now, and never a day went by without her missing him.

Scarlett was her youngest, and the last of Poppy's three daughters to marry. She had always been the wildest of the trio and her father's favourite. How he would have loved to see her on this special day as she married the boy she'd known all her life, the son of Jack's best friend.

Cam had been a good friend to Poppy too since Jack died, helping her organise all the paperwork involved in keeping the restaurant going, and listening to her problems. It was strange to think that when Scarlett and Lachlan were married, they'd all be one family. It didn't seem so long ago they'd all been young together – she and Jack, Cam and Gail – swimming on this very beach, their whole lives ahead of them with no thought of what the future might bring.

Poppy pulled her mind back to the present just in time to hear the celebrant declare Scarlett and Lachlan husband and wife. The young couple turned to each other and kissed as if they were the only two people in the world. Then the sounds of the music Scarlett had chosen floated across the beach, competing with the squawking of the seagulls and the hum of the guests' conversations as they began to chat now the ceremony had concluded.

The official part of the event which had been planned so carefully, anticipated for so long, was over, and it was time for the guests to make their way to *Crossings*, the restaurant across from the beach Poppy and her husband had taken over what seemed like a lifetime ago. Together they had renovated and extended the fish restaurant her parents established when she was a young child. What had begun life as a small fish restaurant was now, thanks to Poppy's efforts, touted as one of the best restaurants on the coast, having been featured in several foodie magazines as well as the popular television programme, *Weekender*.

'It went well.' A gentle hand touched hers.

Poppy turned to the man sitting by her side. Cam's familiar face smiled back at her, his eyes crinkling with pleasure. 'It did. They're a lovely couple. I'm glad it worked out.' There had been a few occasions over the last couple of years, when it had looked as if the wedding might never take place, when her headstrong daughter had seemed intent on destroying the love of the young man who was now beaming at her proudly.

'She's a beautiful bride, almost as beautiful as her mother. I remember when you and Jack married. It seems like yesterday.'

'You were best man,' Poppy remembered. She also remembered how, at the last minute, she'd had cold feet, wondering if she was making a mistake, if she'd chosen the wrong man. But it had been a happy marriage until Jack had been taken from her – the freak accident which should never have happened. He should have been here today to give Scarlett away, as he had her two older sisters.

Her mind went back to that day five years earlier.

It was a glorious day, the sun sparkling on the ocean just like today, and one Poppy had been looking forward to. The renovations had finally been completed in the restaurant she and Jack had taken over from her parents ten years earlier and tonight was their opening night. She had spent the day ensuring everything was ready for the big event to which all their friends plus the mayor and the town's leading residents had been invited. She couldn't wait to see their reaction to Crossings *as the new restaurant was to be called.*

The only fly in the ointment was that Jack had decided to spend the afternoon out sailing in the small boat he and his dad had built many years ago, before both his parents passed away. It was the anniversary of his dad's birthday, and something he always did on this day each year. It was just unfortunate they had also chosen this day to launch the new restaurant. But he'd promised to be back in plenty of time, and Jack always kept his promises.

It was one of the things which had attracted her when they'd met as teenagers. Unlike many of his peers, Jack, while always the life and soul of any party, invariably kept his word. That and the fact he was the best-looking boy around. For several years, they went around in a foursome, Poppy and Gail, Jack and Cam. Then she and Jack had become a couple, got engaged and married, followed a few years later by Gail and Cam.

Over twenty-five years later, they were still as happy as they had been on the day they married, only a few months after Jack had got down on bended knee on the beach and asked her to be his wife. She fingered the necklace Jack had given to her on their silver wedding anniversary. The two figures hung on a gold chain, the gold woman and the silver man in an embrace. When Jack fastened it around her neck and kissed her, she'd vowed never to take it off, and she hadn't. Now their three children – all daughters – were grown, the older two married, and they might soon become grandparents. It didn't seem possible. How quickly time had flown.

Poppy had set out her outfit for the evening on the bed – a long silver gown which flattered her curvy figure, which Amber, her oldest daughter, had helped her choose, and she was luxuriating in a hot bath scented with a concoction her youngest daughter, Scarlett, had given her for Christmas, when she heard someone at the door.

Cursing Jack for forgetting his key again, she stepped out of the bath and pulled on a towelling robe before heading downstairs to answer it. The two-storey house, built on top of the cliff to take in the view was another dream come true. She and Jack had had such fun finding the site, choosing the design and arranging the builders. It had been a wonderful spot to raise a family and, now only Scarlett was at home, they could look forward to living there right into their old age.

'Jack,' she began when she opened the door. But it wasn't Jack standing there in his old shorts and tee-shirt, a lopsided grin on his face.

'Cam?' she said, peering behind him, expecting Jack to be there.

'Poppy, can I come in?'

It was only then she noticed the serious expression in his eyes. Her heart lurched as a feeling of dread engulfed her. Where was Jack? Pulling her robe up to her neck, Poppy led him inside to the living room which looked out onto the ocean. She took a seat, embarrassed to be caught in her robe.

'I'm sorry, Poppy. It's Jack.'

Poppy stared at him, bewildered. What was he talking about? What had Jack done now? When he was younger, Jack had got up to all sorts of stunts, but since he become a married man and a father, he'd left those days behind him.

'He's...' Cam cleared his throat. He blinked. 'There's been an accident... the boat...'

'Where is he? Is he in hospital? I need to go to him.' Poppy started to rise. The restaurant opening could wait. She needed to be with her husband.

'No, he's... Oh hell, Poppy, there's no easy way to say this. Jack didn't survive.'

From somewhere in the distance, Poppy heard someone scream, not realising it was her.

Everything went black.

When she came to, Amber, Megan and Scarlett were bending over her.

'Thank goodness, Mum. We thought we'd lost you too,' Megan said. All three of her daughters were in tears.

Poppy peered at them. Her eyes blurred. What were they doing here? What was she doing in the living room in her bathrobe? Then she remembered. Was it true? 'Your dad,' she said.

'Oh, Mum!' Her daughters put their arms around her. 'Uncle Cam called us, and we came at once. We couldn't believe it at first. Dad's such a good sailor. It was a freak accident, the boat...'

'Stop! I don't want to hear.' It was bad enough to have them confirm her hazy memory of Cam's words. 'Where is...?'

'Uncle Cam went off to cancel this evening. We didn't think...'

'No.' Poppy couldn't imagine facing everyone, knowing... It hit her again, more forcibly. Jack was dead. She'd never see him again, never feel his arms around her, hear his bad jokes, listen to him tell her how much he loved her.

'Oh, Mum!' Amber, Poppy's oldest daughter, the one she could always count on to know exactly what she was thinking, pulled her into a warm hug. 'Dad would have loved to be here. But we can't be sad on Scarlett's big day.'

'You're right. I just had a moment. I'm fine now.' Poppy blinked away the tears.

'Mum!' It was Scarlett's turn to hug her mother, the girl who'd always been her baby, a baby no longer, but a young woman with a husband and a life of her own.

'Aunt Poppy.' Lachlan hugged her too. 'My two favourite women.' The two families had grown up so close together; she'd always been Aunt Poppy to Lachlan, as Cam and Gail had been Uncle Cam and Aunt Gail to her three girls.

'Congratulations to you both,' she said, teary again, but this time they were tears of joy. She couldn't have wished for a better husband for her daughter, even if he was about to whisk her off to Canberra where he worked in an architectural practice, designing homes for the residents of Australia's capital city.

'Ready?' Cam asked, offering her his arm as they followed the young couple across the road to where Poppy's staff had been preparing the wedding feast.

Today, the restaurant was decked out for the wedding, The door and windows of the hundred-year-old, two-storey building had been given a fresh coat of ocean-blue paint that gleamed in the sunlight, and gorgeous twists of bougainvillea adorned the wrought iron balconies on the upper level. Inside, the main dining room had been rearranged to provide several long tables, a space for the small group of musicians, and a tiny dance floor.

When Poppy and Cam entered, they were greeted by her staff offering congratulations and bearing trays of sparkling wine and canapés, all carefully prepared in the restaurant kitchen. They were soon surrounded by friends and relatives offering their congratulations too. The only person missing was Gail, Poppy's old friend – Cam's ex-wife and Lachlan's mother. She'd be devastated to miss it.

'How is Gail?' Poppy asked Cam when they were finally seated together at the top table. Lachlan had just started high school when Gail had told Cam she'd fallen in love with one of the women she taught with. Although apparently devastated, Cam had agreed to divorce her, the shock tempered by Lachlan's decision to remain living with his dad when Gail and Judy, her new partner, chose to move to New South Wales. The two women were now married, and Judy was currently undergoing chemotherapy for stage four breast cancer.

Cam shook his head. 'Not good,' he said. 'We'd been hoping Judy might be well enough to attend the wedding, but…' he shook his head again, '… Gail felt she couldn't leave her. Lachlan said he understood.'

'I'm so sorry.' Poppy touched his arm gently. She admired the way Cam had coped with the situation, both when Gail left and when they received the news of Judy's illness. Gail had been Poppy's best friend, growing up together here in Pelican Crossing. Her decision to leave Cam for Judy had been a shock to her too, but she'd come to accept her friend's new partner when she realised how happy they were together.

'Mum?'

Poppy turned to Scarlett with a smile, and for the rest of the meal, she was caught up in the excitement of the wedding feast and the ensuing speeches, during which Cam managed to make everyone laugh with his anecdotes of Scarlett and Lachlan growing up together.

All too soon, it was time for the bridal couple to leave, then for the celebrations to wind down.

Poppy and Cam found themselves alone in the centre of the restaurant, the staff having a well-earned break in the kitchen to enjoy their own meal before clearing up the tables and returning the room to normal.

'You look tired. Glad it's over?' Cam asked.

'Yes and no. It's been a hectic few weeks but worth it to see Scarlett so happy. I'm so pleased she and Lachlan are finally married.'

'You'll miss her.'

'Yes.' Poppy sighed. Scarlett had been a big help with the restaurant, taking responsibility for all the publicity as part of her PR business. Now Poppy would have to hire someone else to take on that role. Until now, she'd delayed making another appointment but knew she couldn't put it off much longer. She'd miss her daughter at home too. While Scarlett had spent a lot of time travelling around, darting from one part of Australia to another promoting *Crossings* and her other clients, she'd always regarded Pelican Crossing as home, regularly returning to the large house Poppy and Jack had built on the high cliff overlooking the town.

'You wouldn't consider moving?'

Poppy looked at Cam in surprise. He knew how much she loved

her home, how many memories were tied up inside its four walls. But his words reiterated something Amber had said only a few days ago.

'Now we'll all be gone, Mum, what are you going to do rattling around in that big house? Wouldn't you be happier in one of those townhouses they're building opposite the marina? It'd be handy for the restaurant, and you'd be able to walk everywhere.'

Poppy had dismissed her daughter's suggestion, replying that she and Angus, the West Highland Terrier she'd bought after Jack died, were perfectly all right where they were. But the idea had taken root. It would be lonely with Scarlett gone.

'Not really,' she said, trying to dismiss the image of the empty house that awaited her.

'Well, give it some thought. I've never regretted downsizing when Lachlan moved to Canberra.'

'It was different for you.' Poppy tried to laugh it off. It was different for a man.

'Hmm. Well, I should go now. Take care and make sure you have a good rest. Catch up tomorrow for breakfast?' Cam put an arm around her and gave her his usual kiss on the cheek, the friendly gesture she'd become accustomed to over the years.

'See you then,' she said, watching as he walked out of *Crossings*, her heart beating a little faster than usual. Today, for some reason, perhaps due to the wedding, her emotions were closer to the surface than usual, and she missed Jack more than ever.

Two

It had been a good wedding, and the young couple looked so happy.
Cam sighed as he poured himself a glass of brandy before gazing out at
the harbour. He hoped their marriage would be happier than his had
been. It had started well, even though it had seemed he and Gail had
only drifted together because their best friends had become a couple.
But the news she had fallen in love with another woman had been
a shock, made him feel inadequate as a man. It had taken him some
time to become used to it, to be able to meet her and Judy without
feeling resentful, without wondering where he'd gone wrong. But, for
Lachlan's sake, he'd done it, and the three were now friends. He just
wished there was something he could do to help the two women in
their current situation.

His phone rang.

'How was the wedding?' Gail asked as soon as he answered. 'I'm so
sorry we missed it.'

'Lachlan knows you'd have been there if you could.'

'I hope he does. I spoke with him this morning to wish him and
Scarlett well, and they plan to stop by on their way back to Canberra
after the honeymoon, but it's not the same as being there.' There was
a tear in her voice, one that had been there almost every time they'd
spoken in the past few months.

'How's Judy?'

'Much the same.' Gail sighed. 'The doctor says it's only a matter of
time. Oh, Cam, I don't know what I'm going to do without her.'

Cam felt helpless. If she had been there, he'd have given her a hug, but there wasn't much he could offer from so far away. 'You'll let me know if there's anything I can do.'

'Thanks, I will. I don't know why you're so good to me, Cam. I don't deserve your kindness.' She sniffed.

'I'll always be here for you, Gail. You're Lachlan's mother, and we had some good times together.'

'You're right. We did. And we made Lachlan together. I can never regret that.'

There was silence, then Cam said, 'We did well there.'

'More thanks to you than me, I'm afraid. It was touch and go for a few years, but we're good now.'

'Mmm.' Cam remembered how bitter Lachlan had been when Gail left. It had taken him most of his high school years to recover from what he saw as his mother's abandonment of him and his dad, even though he'd had the option of going with her. Cam was glad common sense had prevailed. Gail was going to need both of them when Judy's time was up.

'Now, tell me about the wedding,' she said, injecting a brighter note into her voice.

The remainder of their conversation was taken up with Cam describing the ceremony and the following celebration.

When the call ended, he picked up his brandy again and drained the glass, contemplating how fate dealt some terrible blows, first Jack's death, now Judy's illness. He recalled how he had railed against it when Gail left him too, but that faded compared to the loss of the life of a loved one. He rinsed his glass, set it on the draining board and headed for bed.

*

Next morning, Cam was glad he was meeting Poppy for breakfast. Sunday breakfast together was a habit they'd developed over the years. It had started long before Jack's death when the two families met every Sunday morning to share the week's news. When the children were little, they'd head to the beach with a picnic, then as they grew older and found their own amusements, the four – then three – adults preferred to enjoy a more grown-up breakfast in the café opposite the marina, where they could while away a few hours putting the world to rights.

For the past five years, it had only been Cam and Poppy. He was glad they'd continued the tradition. It was something to look forward to when everything else in his life was in a mess.

Arriving at *The Blue Dolphin Café* before Poppy, Cam took a seat at their usual table overlooking the ocean and gazed out at the rows of boats and yachts sitting in the large marina, gleaming in the sunlight. Pelican Crossing was a jumping off spot for people who wanted to explore this part of the coast and the islands offshore. From its humble beginnings as a fishing port, it had become a mecca for yachties from all over the world and was now on the tourist route for many international travellers, while still managing to retain its unique ambiance.

Like Poppy, Cam had grown up here and had never wanted to live anywhere else, despite the fact the town had changed over the years. It was older than many of the other communities along the coast and some of the original buildings were still standing. Many, like *Crossings*, had been renovated in recent years.

He ordered a coffee, and sat back to enjoy the view, smiling when he saw Poppy hurrying towards him. The sight of the small, curvy, blonde woman never failed to bring a smile to his lips. Poppy hadn't changed much from the girl who had filled his teenage dreams, till it became obvious she preferred his best friend. He'd accepted her choice and started dating Gail but had never forgotten those heady days when he hoped he might have a chance with her.

'Morning, Cam.' Poppy leant over to give him a kiss on the cheek, before taking a seat. 'How's your head this morning?'

'I'm good. I paced myself yesterday. You?'

'I'm good too. I didn't want to disgrace myself at my daughter's wedding. Not like…'

Cam chuckled, remembering how Jack had overdone the alcohol at both Amber and Megan's weddings. He had always enjoyed being the life and soul of the party. He guessed that was one of the things Poppy had loved about him. Cam was dull by comparison, too conventional for someone as lively as Poppy was then… still was. 'Let me guess,' he said, when Poppy picked up a menu, 'eggs benedict with a skinny cappuccino.' It was the breakfast she'd ordered for as many years as he could remember.

Poppy laughed. 'One of these Sundays, I'll surprise you, but not today. And yours will be the big breakfast, I presume?'

Cam laughed too. They were comfortable together, two old friends who knew each other inside out. Though she had no idea of the secret desire he harboured to be more than a friend to her.

They were still laughing when the waitress came to take their order. Cam ordered a second coffee for himself and handed back the menus.

'So, how does it feel to have all three married?' he asked.

'A bit odd. It seems like yesterday we were all heading to the beach, the four youngsters arguing about who would build the biggest sandcastle…' Poppy sighed. 'We'll be grandparents before we know it.'

Cam glanced at her in surprise. *Did she know something he didn't?*

Recognising his expression, Poppy laughed again. 'No, Scarlett's not pregnant, or at least if she is, she hasn't told me. But Megan is, and Amber and Chris have been trying for a baby. I'd be willing to bet Scarlett won't let her sisters leave her behind.

'I didn't know about Megan. When…?'

'She's only three months. She told me last week. She didn't want to steal Scarlett's thunder but couldn't keep it to herself any longer. I think she worried about telling Amber too. She's desperate to have a baby, but it doesn't seem to be happening for her.'

'I'm sorry. I hope it will work for them soon.' He and Gail had found no difficulty in getting pregnant, so he had trouble in understanding Amber's pain. 'So, congratulations are in order.'

'I guess. I can't get used to the idea, but it'll be lovely to have a little one in the family again.'

'And with Megan living so close.'

'Yes, I guess I'll be up for babysitting.' She grimaced, but Cam could see she was pleased at the idea.

'How will you manage to fit it in?' He knew how busy she was with the restaurant. It was open seven days a week for lunch and dinner and had a function room which could be booked for special occasions. Cam had been surprised they hadn't used it for the wedding, but the restaurant had been Scarlett and Lachlan's choice. Scarlett said it reminded her of her dad.

'I'm not sure.' Poppy looked pensive. 'Maybe it's time I slowed down, took a step back.'

'Really?'

'It was something Amber said the other day. She reminded me Jack has been gone for five years, and suggested it was time I thought about myself, about what I wanted to do with the rest of my life.'

'And?'

Poppy sighed again. 'She may be right. As you know, after the accident, I threw myself into managing *Crossings*, determined to prove I could make a success of it without Jack.'

'And you have done – the awards, the publicity.'

'Yes, but all the time, it was me trying to prove to a dead man that I could do it. Maybe I was trying too hard, putting the rest of my life on hold, forgetting about Poppy Taylor.' She gazed into space.

Cam was about to reply when their meals arrived, and the moment was lost in the fuss of the plates being placed on the table, and them thanking the waitress who they knew well from their previous visits.

It wasn't till they were finished that Poppy returned to the topic. 'It might be my time now,' she said.

Cam kissed her on the cheek as usual when they parted, promising to meet again the following Sunday, though Cam knew he'd see Poppy again before then – he liked to lunch at *Crossings* at least once each week, and Poppy often called on his help with the accounts. But there was a swing in his step as he made his way along the esplanade past the gate to the marina, stopping to watch a large motor cruiser coming in to moor alongside other similar vessels. Maybe, with Poppy's new outlook on life, there would be a chance for him to become more than her husband's old friend, the person she turned to when she needed someone to sort out her problems. Maybe he could persuade her to see him in a different light.

Three

It was two weeks since the wedding, and the young couple had returned from their honeymoon and were settling into the new home they'd bought together in Canberra. Poppy had enjoyed a long conversation with her daughter who was full of the joys of married life and had spent time with her other two daughters. Maybe she wouldn't be lonely after all. It seemed that both Amber and Megan had decided to make sure she didn't have time to miss Scarlett.

From Amber's upbeat mood when last the three of them had got together, Poppy assumed she still didn't know about Megan's pregnancy. She wished her middle daughter would tell her sister. It made Poppy feel awkward to know about it when Amber didn't.

But today, she had other things on her mind. It was the regular get-together of the group of friends Jack had jokingly called *the gang of four*.

The four women had first met in a mother-baby group when they were all young mothers trying to cope with the challenges of caring for a new baby. They had continued to meet throughout the years, facing the challenges of infancy, through the teenage years, marriage and, for one, the arrival of grandchildren. They still met regularly, now all single for one reason or another. Rachel, like Poppy, was widowed, Liz divorced and Gill, who spent her life arranging the divorces of others, was going through a lengthy divorce herself.

It was Poppy's turn to host the group and she'd spent the morning cooking a spinach and ricotta quiche and a more traditional quiche

Lorraine, plus baking her special apple Bundt cake for dessert which she'd serve with a generous dollop of cream. She was putting together the salad to accompany the quiches when Angus began to bark. His ears were sharper than hers, but it wasn't long before she heard a knock on the door. Soon all four women were seated on Poppy's deck overlooking the ocean with glasses of chilled white wine.

'How are the happy couple?' Rachel asked, as Poppy handed around a platter of cheese, olives and her favourite seaweed crackers.

'Gloriously happy. I spoke with Scarlett last night, and she went into great detail about the honeymoon and how much she loves married life.'

'Has she found a job in Canberra?' Liz asked. 'It must have been a wrench to leave here, and you'll miss her doing all your publicity.'

'She plans to start looking this week, and yes, I need to find a replacement. I've put it off till now.'

'I may know of someone,' Gill said.

'Really?' Poppy never ceased to be amazed at Gill's network of contacts. She supposed it came from being part of the busiest law practice in town, and her membership of various local organisations.

'Give me a minute.' Gill took out her phone and began scrolling. 'Here she is. Bridget Holmes,' she said. 'She's new to town, she and her husband. I met them at a charity do the other week. He's the new resident at the hospital, and she said she used to do PR for a big company in Sydney.'

'Sounds perfect, but won't she be looking for something more upmarket than a local restaurant?'

'It doesn't do any harm to ask.'

'I suppose not.'

'Did you hear about the latest arrival in the marina?' Liz asked, when they were all enjoying their lunch. Liz was always the member of the group to be first with local news... and gossip.

'I guess you're going to tell us,' Gill said, taking a sip of wine.

The others smiled. They were used to Gill's often sarcastic remarks.

'Well,' Liz leant forward and lowered her voice, 'I have it on good authority that Jordan Butler sailed in last night with a group of friends, and...'

Poppy didn't hear any more. Her mind went back to the time before she and Jack married, to the two weeks she'd spent with an aunt in Sydney after a disagreement with Jack. She could no longer remember what they'd argued about, and they'd made up as soon as she returned to Pelican Crossing, but those two weeks were etched in her mind, as was the young stockbroker she'd met. Jordan Butler was unlike anyone she knew. Growing up in the small coastal town of Pelican Crossing, her circle of friends had been made up of young people like herself – Gail, Jack, Cam and a few others, many of whom had now left the town for pastures new. Jordan was like a breath of fresh air, coming from a wealthy family, the product of a private school.

It had been a mad two weeks, something completely divorced from Poppy's real life. They'd met in a hotel in Darling Harbour, the same one in which Mary Donaldson, now Crown Princess Mary of Denmark, met her prince. Jordan Butler might not be a royal prince but to the nineteen-year-old Poppy, straight from the small Queensland coastal town, he seemed like someone from another world.

The two weeks had flown past as Poppy had been wined and dined in Sydney's top restaurants and had even sailed on Sydney harbour in Jordan's parents' catamaran. It was a magical time, but never seemed real, and when she received a frantic call from Jack begging her to return, Poppy didn't need to think twice. She had no regrets as she left Sydney behind, consigning the two weeks to the past. For a time, she'd followed Jordan's exploits in the news, his marriage and subsequent divorce, his many appointments to positions in companies she'd never heard of, but it had been years since she'd thought about him. Her life in Pelican Crossing was so busy, she had enough to do with the day-to-day running of *Crossings* and looking after her family without thinking about someone she'd met fleetingly over thirty years earlier.

'Earth calling Poppy!'

Rachel's words pulled Poppy back to the present. 'Sorry.'

'Liz was just telling us that Jordan Butler – *the* Jordan Butler, the guy who's always in the news when he takes over yet another company or opens a new development – is the latest to sail into town.'

'I heard. I met him once.' As soon as she'd spoken, Poppy regretted it. Her three companions all leant forward.

'You did?' Liz asked. 'When? What's he like? Is he as ruthless as he's painted in the media?'

'He's certainly handsome,' Rachel said.

'Handsome is as handsome does,' Gill said.

'Oh, Gill, we all know how you feel about men at the moment, but they're not all like Max,' Poppy said. 'Jack was a wonderful husband and father.'

'Sorry, Poppy. You were lucky.'

'So? How do you know him?' Liz persisted.

'I don't, not really. It was before Jack and I married. I spent two weeks with an aunt in Sydney. We met there. It was aeons ago. He's probably a completely different person now, and I barely knew him even then.'

'Still...' Liz wasn't going to let it go, '... Mandy says they had dinner at the yacht club last night, ordered the most expensive dishes on the menu and the Moet Chandon.' Liz's daughter worked at the yacht club two evenings a week and was a mine of information for her mother.

'Well, there you go. She probably knows more about him than I do.'

'Hmm. Maybe. Could you get me an introduction?'

'Liz!' It was Rachel who spoke next. 'Someone like that is way out of your league. Are you still planning on looking at online dating?'

Liz blushed. 'I haven't yet. It's all Mandy's idea. She thinks it's time I *moved on*.' She made air quotes with her fingers.

The others laughed.

'Do *you* want to?' Poppy asked. She couldn't imagine moving on from Jack, unless... The image of Cam Mitchell slid into her mind before she firmly dismissed it.

Liz sighed. 'Sometimes I think it would be nice. It's been six years since the divorce, and I can count the number of dates I've had since then on one hand. There's not a lot of choice in Pelican Crossing... apart from the tourists, and they're never a good bet.'

'Neither is online dating,' Poppy said. 'I've heard horror stories from some of my staff. Best to steer clear.'

'I second that,' Gill said. 'You wouldn't believe the tales I've heard from my clients.'

There was silence for several moments, then Liz turned to Poppy. 'You've been on your own almost as long as I have. Don't you miss having someone to talk over your day with, to cuddle up to at night?'

'When I get home, I'm usually too exhausted to think about

anything but falling into bed,' she laughed. But she knew what Liz meant. There was a gap in her life, a Jack-sized gap that nothing could fill. She fingered the necklace Jack had given her. As long as she wore that necklace, it was almost as if Jack was still with her.

'What about Cam Mitchell? You and he are close.'

'He was Jack's best friend. He's been a big help since Jack's been gone.' Poppy felt herself blush and started gathering up the used plates to hide her red cheeks, hoping none of her friends guessed her secret, guessed how she sometimes wished Cam could be more to her than Jack's best friend.

'But…'

'Leave Poppy alone. I know what it's like to lose the person you love. It's not like a divorce, Liz.'

Poppy looked gratefully at Rachel. The loss of her husband hadn't been as sudden as Jack's death had been for Poppy. Kirk had died after a lingering illness which had drained all of Rachel's energy. Poppy had understood and been there for her when he took his last breath.

Liz had the grace to look penitent but, 'I'm only trying to help,' she said. 'We're all in the prime of our lives. Surely we're not going to accept we'll be on our own for however many years we have left?'

'That's enough, Liz. We're not all looking for a man, and I know you weren't either, till Mandy got on your case. How is she, anyway?'

Gill's question changed the focus of the conversation to a discussion of their children, and by the time her friends rose to leave, Poppy had recovered her equilibrium. She was looking forward to sharing Megan's news with her friends but had promised to wait until Megan told her sisters. So far, Rachel was the only one of the group to have grandchildren, and Poppy knew what a comfort they were to her.

Once everyone had gone, Poppy didn't immediately clear up. She poured the remaining wine into her glass and went to stand at the edge of the deck to look out at the view. This was the reason she and Jack had chosen this spot on which to build their dream home, the one they had planned to grow old in together. In one direction was the wide estuary of the Boodalang River, boodalang being the Aboriginal word for pelican. It was probably where the town got its name, the early settlers having anglicised the original place name. In the other direction was the Pelican Crossing main street and the beach where Scarlett's wedding had been held, where they had all swum and partied together when they were young. *Crossings* stood there proudly among several other buildings of similar vintage, now transformed into a newsagency, a craft shop, a hardware store, an ice cream shop and small art gallery. At the far end was the marina, now even busier than ever with the offices of Cam's business, Pelican Marine, with its blue and white signage. She wondered if he was there now, poring over his computer or chatting to a client, his forehead furrowed, his hand pushing through his thatch of prematurely white hair.

She sighed. His face was as familiar to her as her own. She knew every expression, every line, every wrinkle. She couldn't wait to see him again.

Four

Cam stared out at the large, new motor cruiser which had recently arrived in the marina. It was owned by some wealthy Sydney guy who'd booked the berth online and paid in advance for several months. He hadn't met the owner but had seen him and several friends – both men and women – disembark and noisily make their way to the yacht club. He hoped they weren't going to cause any trouble. You could never tell with these city types who didn't understand the unwritten rules of towns like Pelican Crossing. To his relief, this morning all looked calm onboard, only one figure leaning on the rail and gazing towards the town.

It had been ten years since Cam took over the management of the marina. Bored by the accountancy job he'd had since leaving university, worn down by the day-to-day struggle and tired of sitting in an office all day, he had been looking around for something more interesting. When the position at the marina came up, and after sailing for pleasure since he was a teenager, it seemed like a dream come true. Now he knew differently. Some days it was as if he'd only exchanged one office desk for another. But on other days, it was wonderful, days when he could leave the office behind and enjoy his favourite sport out on the ocean.

Today, after catching up on his accounts – his accountancy background did come in handy – he planned to take his yacht out into the bay. It was a glorious day, too nice to spend it inside.

*

Once out in the bay, Cam felt glad to be alive. This is what life was about. Skimming across the ocean which was glistening in the sun, the wind in his hair, breathing in the salt air, he could almost believe he hadn't a care in the world. He looked up to the clifftop where the house Jack and Poppy had built stood proudly facing out to sea. Poppy would be alone there now, apart from the little white dog she doted on. He thought back to their conversation over breakfast a few days earlier. Was it a sign she was ready to move on with her life, the life she seemed to have put on hold ever since Jack died so unexpectedly? He missed his best mate too, but it must be worse for Poppy. They had been close, closer than many married couples he knew, and for him to have been taken so soon, so suddenly… It was no wonder she'd thrown herself into managing the restaurant they'd built together.

When they were growing up, what was now *Crossings*, the popular upmarket restaurant had been a fish shop with a small dining room, providing an outlet for much of the catch from the local fishing boats, and selling fish and chips to residents of the town. Sadly, in recent years competition from commercial fishing and supertrawlers were pushing out the small family-owned vessels. But there were still enough fishermen bringing in their catch to attract the local pelicans, the pelicans from which the town had got its name.

On his way back to his berth, he sailed slowly past the large motor cruiser, noting that no expense had been spared in the construction of this vessel. The man he'd seen earlier had disappeared to be replaced by a couple of women in skimpy bikinis lazing on the deck. Cam averted his eyes and concentrated on letting his boat drift into its mooring.

'Good sail?'

Cam was greeted by Rory, the young man who was his second-in-command. The local lad had come to Cam as soon as he left school, eager to be part of the business and willing to do anything he could. Now, seven years later, Cam couldn't think how he could do without the man who had progressed from following him around the office and marina to becoming his right-hand-man who could be left in charge without fear anything would go wrong.

'Perfect,' he replied. 'Anything happen when I was gone?'

'A few more bookings. Oh, and that guy from the big motor launch – Jordan Butler – he dropped in.'

'What did he want?'

'It was a bit odd. He was asking all sorts of questions about the town, local events, about who ran things and such.'

'What did you tell him?' Cam leant against the doorway, amused.

'I sent him to the library, told him he could look up old issues of the local paper. It was all there.'

'Good man.' Cam clapped Rory on the shoulder. Jordan Butler... the name had rung a bell when he took the booking, then he'd forgotten about it. Now it niggled him again. He'd check the guy out on the internet tonight. He didn't sound like a regular tourist, but what did Cam know? Tourists came in all shapes and sizes with all sorts of agendas. He wasn't sure why he felt suspicious about this one.

He felt a sudden urge to see Poppy. She always managed to help calm him when he was concerned or upset, though that hadn't happened so much recently, not since he'd become more accepting of Gail's choices. She'd have had her coven for lunch today – the name he'd secretly given to the group of single-again women Poppy met with regularly – and, if he knew women, they would probably have some gossip about this Jordan Butler too.

*

By four o'clock, Poppy had loaded the dishwasher, fed Angus, changed into one of the smart black outfits she deemed suitable for the restaurant and was ready to leave.

'Behave yourself while I'm gone,' she said to the dog who by now, was accustomed to being left alone in the evening, and let herself out. As she drove down to the restaurant, she thought again about Liz's question. Coming so soon after Amber's about what she was going to do with her life now Scarlett had left, it had forced Poppy to begin to question the decision she'd made when Jack died, the decision to spend the rest of her life making him proud of what she could achieve with the restaurant they'd built together. Now she wondered if it was what she really wanted, or if she had been doing it as a way of trying to replace Jack in her life. None of the girls were interested in following her into the restaurant trade. *Crossings* would end with her. It was a sobering thought, but one which made her focus on trying to work out what she really wanted out of her life.

As she settled into the evening routine at *Crossings*, there was no time for introspection. It was a typical busy Wednesday evening, with almost every table full. When Cam walked in unexpectedly – he didn't normally appear in the restaurant in the evening – she had to juggle a few bookings to find a spare table for him.

'Do you have time for a break?' he asked, grasping her hand as she walked past him for what must have been the tenth time.

Tempted, Poppy shook her head. She was one staff member down and couldn't afford to take her eye off the ball. 'Later,' she mouthed, as she hurried to respond to a loud-mouthed guest at the other end of the room.

As the restaurant gradually emptied, she noticed Cam was still sitting there with a cup of coffee. Glancing around to ensure all was well with the few remaining guests, she picked up a bottle of wine and two glasses from behind the bar and joined him.

'Wine?' she asked, placing the glasses on the table and holding up the bottle of Prelude Cabernet Sauvignon from the Leeuwin Estate on the Margaret River.

'That would be a treat.' Cam picked up a glass and held it out while Poppy filled it and the other one. 'Busy night.'

'It always is mid-week and continues through the weekend. I don't know where they all come from. Some are locals, of course, but there seem to be more tourists than usual for this time of year.'

'The marina's busy too.' Cam swirled the wine in his glass before taking a sip, enjoying the rich flavour on his tongue. His normal tipple was a much cheaper variety. 'So, what have you been up to? Wasn't today your lunch with your...?'

Poppy laughed. 'I know the names you and Jack called my friends. Yes, it was today and no, we didn't gossip, if that's what you were going to ask. But...' she wrinkled her brow, '... something Liz said made me think.'

Cam raised an eyebrow, but Poppy didn't respond. She was in the habit of sharing all her problems and challenges with him, but she wasn't ready to share this one yet.

'I guess you're caught up on the news about our newest arrival?'

Poppy stiffened, but she managed to keep a smile on her face. 'Liz said something about a Sydney bigshot.' She remembered very well, remembered, too, the memories Jordan Butler's name had evoked. She wondered what had brought him to Pelican Crossing and if their paths would cross. It was a small town and difficult to avoid anyone for long.

She glanced at Cam, wondering what he would think if he knew…

Cam interrupted her musings. 'I thought…' he began, then took another sip of wine. 'I thought, maybe we could have dinner together some time. Not here.' He looked around the now empty restaurant, Poppy's staff silently clearing up for the night and keeping out of their way. 'There's a new restaurant opened in the hinterland. Thought you might like to try it. Check out the competition.'

'*Addison's*? I've heard about it. I'd love to check it out, but it would have to be at the beginning of the week. I can't leave this place on a busy night.' As she spoke, Poppy realised how regulated her life had become. Breakfast with Cam on Sundays, Wednesday lunch with her friends once a month, evenings in the restaurant plus lunchtimes on Fridays and Saturdays, sometimes more often if there were a lot of bookings. It was exactly what Amber and Liz were talking about, the pattern her life had fallen into since Jack died. She wondered again if it was time to make a change.

Her life had already changed with Scarlett leaving. It would no doubt change again when Megan gave birth to her first grandchild. Was she clinging on to a way of life which was changing around her? What would Jack advise her to do?

Five

It was two weeks before Poppy and Cam managed to arrange to have dinner together, the delay a combination of circumstances which could not be avoided, mostly due to a bout of sickness among restaurant staff, plus a rush of new clients at the marina which had kept Cam working late into the night.

But it gave Poppy time to adjust to the idea that Cam had finally invited her out on a date, something different from their usual Sunday morning catchup. It also gave her time – at Amber's insistence – to check out her wardrobe which she hadn't replenished since Jack died.

'Mum!' Amber said, as she pulled one garment after another out of the wardrobe. 'You can't wear any of those. When on earth did you buy this one?' She held up an outfit which had been a favourite of Poppy's but which even she had to admit was woefully out of fashion.

'I know,' Amber said, 'I have a day off on Tuesday. You don't have to be at *Crossings* for lunch, do you?' Without waiting for a reply, she continued, 'There's a lovely little boutique in Bellbird Bay, *Birds of A Feather*. We can drive down and find you something more suitable there.'

When Poppy started to object, saying it was too far, Amber cut through all her objections saying they'd leave early and be back in time for the dinner service at *Crossings*.

Now, Poppy was glad she'd agreed as she slipped into the brightly patterned blue and white dress which suited her perfectly. It was only one of the new outfits she'd bought from the lovely woman who owned the boutique and was an amazing advertisement for her business, wearing a dress covered in tropical birds and flowers. She felt like a young girl preparing for her first date as she applied her makeup and tamed her wild curls into some semblance of a neat style, while telling herself Cam was only being kind. But she couldn't still the butterflies in her stomach at the prospect of a real date with this man who she'd known for what seemed like forever, but until recently had never thought of as anything but a good friend and Jack's best mate.

*

The trip to the restaurant was uneventful, with Cam explaining how one of the fishing charters had become stuck and required to be towed back to the marina and relating how a yachts had been vandalised. It was just like one of their conversations over Sunday breakfast. Why should she have expected anything different? By the time they reached the restaurant, Poppy's butterflies had calmed down, and she had forced herself to accept that nothing had changed. It might be a Monday evening, but Cam was still good old Cam, looking after his best mate's widow.

The restaurant was a surprise. It was one Poppy hadn't visited before and she looked around with interest at the nautical décor despite the fact they were several kilometres from the sea. But once they were seated on the wide, west-facing deck at the rear of the building, she knew the reason. From here, there was a perfect view of the distant ocean and the setting sun.

'Wow!' she said, gazing out as the sky turned through hues of orange and pink, the sun disappearing below the horizon leaving the only light that of the moon and stars. From here, the sky seemed even more vast than it did on the coast, making Poppy feel insignificant.

'I thought you'd like it,' Cam said, handing her the glass of wine which had appeared as if by magic.

'Thanks, and thanks for bringing me here. If the food is as good as the view...'

'I think it is, but I'll be guided by your superior knowledge.'

Poppy picked up a menu, impressed with the range of dishes on offer. She was glad *Addison's* was located here in the hinterland where it didn't present any competition to *Crossings*.

A waiter hovered. 'Might I suggest this evening's special,' he said. 'Tonight, we are offering chateaubriand steak for two. The steak is served with a peppercorn sauce and accompanied by tiny roast potatoes, portobello mushrooms and tender shoots of asparagus.'

He waited.

Poppy and Cam exchanged a glance. 'It sounds delicious,' she said.

Cam smiled. 'We'll order that, thanks. I thought you'd be impressed. I just hope it's up to your exacting standards.'

'Well, everything has been so far. This is lovely, Cam. It's so nice to get away from *Crossings*, from Pelican Crossing. It's been a while since I did.'

'I realise that. I know after Jack's death, you shut yourself off from a lot of things you'd done together. I felt privileged you didn't shut me out too.'

'You were what kept me sane, you and the girls… and *Crossings*.' She put her hand on his on the top of the table. 'I don't know what I would have done without you for the past five years, not only for your help with the accounts, but as a friend.'

'I hope I'll always be that, Poppy.' Cam paused, and Poppy thought he was about to say more. But the waiter appeared to refill their glasses, and the moment was lost. Maybe she'd imagined it.

They chatted comfortably over the meal, about the possibility of Scarlett and Lachlan starting a family, Megan's pregnancy, Poppy's worries about Amber and the challenges Gail was facing with Judy's terminal illness. If Poppy had imagined this evening might mark a turning point in their relationship, she was forced to accept she'd been wrong. She had to be satisfied with Cam as a friend, a very good friend, but a friend nonetheless, no matter how much she might want it to turn into something more. She was lucky, she told herself. Not many women of her age and in her circumstances had such a good male friend, someone with whom she felt comfortable, with whom she could share her ups and downs, and who was always there when she needed him.

But Liz was right when she said they all needed someone to keep them warm at night. It was when she missed Jack most, when she came home from *Crossings* after a busy evening to be greeted only by Angus. The dog was good company, but not the sort of company she longed for. He might listen to her joys and woes but wasn't able to pour her a glass of wine, cuddle up with her on the sofa, massage her aching feet, or take her off to bed. She needed a man to do that, and if Cam didn't see her in that light, then maybe she needed to look elsewhere. But, somehow, the thought of spending time with someone who hadn't known Jack, with a stranger, seemed as if it would be the ultimate betrayal.

'Thanks for a lovely evening, Cam,' Poppy said when they drew up outside her house. 'The view was spectacular, and the food was divine. It compared most favourably with what we offer. I must suggest we try to replicate the dessert. Summer pudding is one we've never had on the menu. I think it would go down well.' The flavour of the fruity bread pudding, this one made with spiced fruit bread which had tantalised her taste buds, still lingered. She turned towards Cam, willing him to kiss her.

'I've enjoyed it too, Poppy. I hope we can do it again.' He gave her his usual kiss on the cheek, this time sending a shiver down her spine.

'I'd love to,' she said, before slipping out of the car and waving him off, then turning back to her empty house.

Six

What was wrong with him?

Cam cursed his cowardice as he drove away. The evening had gone well, just as he'd hoped. It had been a good move to have dinner well away from Pelican Crossing, at a restaurant where they were unlikely to meet anyone they knew. And Poppy had been impressed by both the view and the meal. So why had he been such a fool as to keep the conversation to topics they could have covered over breakfast the day before? Why hadn't he kissed her goodnight properly, the way he wanted to? Was it concern she was still grieving for Jack, or did he feel he'd be betraying his old friend by showing affection for his widow?

Maybe a bit of both, he decided. But he was heartened by her agreeing to go out again. Perhaps if he took things slowly, she'd come to realise he could become more than just Jack's old friend, could become someone worthy of Poppy's affection, maybe even love. His gut twisted at the thought of what that could mean.

Since Gail's defection – as he thought of it – he had steered clear of women. At first, it was due to feelings of inadequacy. If his wife chose another woman over him, what did it say about his masculinity? But afterwards, once he came to accept that Gail's choice of a partner was no reflection on his manhood, he had become accustomed to his own company. It was only since Jack's death that he had come to realise the feelings he had for Poppy were more than those for the widow of an old friend. Even then, it had taken five years for him to act on them and invite her on a date.

He poured himself a glass of the port he'd been saving for a special occasion, savouring the rich full-bodied flavour, and went out onto the deck to gaze at the marina, the sight of which usually calmed him. He was interrupted by his phone ringing. He fished it out of his pocket to see it was Lachlan calling.

'Lachlan, what's up?' he asked.

'Good news, Dad. You're about to become a grandad.'

Cam gulped down the remainder of his port before replying. It was exactly what Poppy had predicted. *Had she already known?* 'Congratulations, son. When is the baby due?'

'Not for a while yet. We've just found out and wanted you and Aunt Poppy to be the first to know. Scarlett's calling her now.'

Cam exhaled. At least the kids were doing the right thing and letting both of them know at the same time. This was too soon to be a honeymoon baby, but they'd been a couple for years, even if it had been an on and off relationship. It would be foolish to have imagined they hadn't been sleeping together. He chuckled to himself, then thought of Poppys oldest daughter. This would be a blow to her. 'Have you told anyone else... Scarlett's sisters?'

'No, you two are the first, as I said. She'll be calling them next.'

'Hmm.' It wasn't his place to warn the young couple about Amber's possible reaction. Probably Poppy would do that. Then Lachlan's news began to sink in. He was about to become a grandfather, to have a tiny boy or girl call him Grandad. While the idea made him feel old, he couldn't hide his delight at the thought of his genes passing down through the generations. And Gail's. 'You'll be calling your mother, too?'

'I guess.'

'You must, Lachlan. I know she's totally focussed on Judy at the moment, but this is a piece of good news. It might give her a lift.'

'I didn't think of that, Dad. Okay, I'll call her.'

'How's everything else? Work still treating you well?'

'As well as ever. And Scarlett's found work with a PR company here. They seem to be pretty flexible, so we're hoping she'll be able to work from home a bit when the baby's born. It all takes a bit of getting used to, but we're excited.'

'Make sure you look after her. Don't let her do too much.'

'Dad! You know Scarlett. As if she'd take advice from me on something like that.' He chuckled. 'We plan to come up to see you and Aunt Poppy soon for a weekend. I know weekends are your busy time, hers too, but it's when we can get away.'

'We'll be delighted to see you both. I'm sure I can speak for Poppy, too. I know it's only been a few weeks, but I can tell she's missing Scarlett.'

When the call ended, Cam poured himself another glass of port to toast the new baby. If it was a boy, it would carry the Mitchell name into the next generation. How he wished his parents were still alive. They'd be thrilled.

He remembered the joy when he and Gail had discovered they were going to have a baby. It had been unexpected and had taken some time to sink in. When it did, they were beset with anxiety. What did they know about looking after a baby? What if they messed things up? It was then that Jack and Poppy reassured them. Already parents to both Amber and Megan, they were happy to share their experience and offer advice. He and Gail would have been lost without them.

Jack! Jack would have been delighted with this news. He'd have come round with a bottle of champagne and a box of cigars – despite the fact neither of them smoked – eager to celebrate the prospect of sharing a grandchild. He stared into his glass thinking of the larger-than-life friend who hadn't lived to see this day.

His phone rang again. This time he didn't have to check the caller ID. He knew it would be Poppy.

'You heard?' she asked as soon as he answered, without giving him time to speak.

'Yes, we're going to be grandparents.'

'Isn't it wonderful… both Scarlett and Megan? Though I feel for Amber. It'll be a double blow to her.' Her voice dropped, and Cam could imagine her biting her lip.

'Amber's tough. She can handle it.'

'Maybe…' Poppy sounded more guarded. 'Scarlett and Lachlan seem delighted. She must have known – or suspected – at the wedding. I wonder why she didn't say.'

'I guess they wanted to wait.'

'I guess so.' She paused. 'I wish Jack was here. He'd have been over the moon. It's not fair he's missing all this. He'd have made a great grandfather.'

'Yes.' *A better one than me,* Cam thought. He could imagine his old friend down on the floor playing games with the grandchildren. Jack had always been like a big kid himself, like Peter Pan, the boy who never grew up. It was what endeared him to people, probably what Poppy had fallen in love with. How could Cam ever hope she would feel the same for him? He was so dull by comparison. He'd been kidding himself to imagine there could be anything more than friendship between them. Poppy might talk about moving on, but she was still grieving for the man she'd lost.

Seven

When Poppy awoke, her mind was a tumult of emotions. Yesterday had been quite a day. First there had been her much anticipated dinner with Cam. The food had been good, the restaurant perfect, but she couldn't suppress her disappointment that it hadn't turned out differently. Then there had been the call from Scarlett, and the wonderful news of her pregnancy. Poppy was thrilled but couldn't help wondering how Amber would react to both her sisters being pregnant when she wasn't, despite her being the oldest and having been the first to marry. She had been so elated she couldn't resist the temptation to call Cam to share her excitement. It had been a good call and she'd been glad they had spoken again. It had put to rest any awkwardness she might have felt after their date. Was it even a date… or had it all been in her imagination?

As she stood on the deck with her first coffee of the morning and stared down at the beach, Poppy tried unsuccessfully to pull her thoughts into order. She knew she'd need an early morning walk with Angus to find some sort of peace.

Calling to Angus, she took his lead and her wide-brimmed hat from their hooks and set off down to the beach. It was deserted at this time of the morning, the waves gently lapping on the shore, the perfect place to calm her thoughts. She released Angus who immediately took off chasing the seagulls he had no hope of catching, and taking off her sandals, walked slowly along in the shallow water, the image of Cam's smiling face in her mind, and her lovely daughters, facing life's trials.

But was getting married and having kids really a trial? Jack and she had never looked at life that way. Jack's smiling face replaced Cam's and Poppy realised that she was blessed. Blessed to have had the love of a wonderful, caring man. And blessed to have such wonderful children, and soon – grandchildren. Cam might not be the love of her life, but she was blessed to have him as a friend.

Angus jumping up at her with his wet paws pulled her from her thoughts.

'I'm blessed to have you, too,' she said, ruffling his shaggy head and clipping his lead back on. 'Ready for some breakfast?'

It was with a clearer head and a lighter heart that she and Angus climbed back up from the beach. She was ready to face the day, whatever it might bring.

Poppy didn't have long to wait. She had barely finished her breakfast of muesli topped with slices of banana and yoghurt, and Angus was finishing his bowl of dried food, when there was a loud knocking at the door, followed by Amber's voice calling, 'Mum!'

Poppy's heart dropped. She'd been afraid of this. Despite her warning, she'd suspected Scarlett would call both her sisters with her news. 'Coming,' she called, hurrying to open the door.

'Mum!' Amber said again as soon as Poppy opened it. 'Scarlett's pregnant!'

'Good morning, darling.' Poppy hugged Amber, feeling some of the tension leave her daughter. 'Come through to the kitchen. I was just finishing breakfast and about to make coffee.'

Amber allowed herself to be led through into the sunlit kitchen where Angus trotted up to her looking for his usual cuddle. But this morning, Amber wasn't in the mood for cuddling the dog. 'It's not fair!' she said, dropping into a chair. 'I suppose she called you too?'

'She did… and it was a surprise, but… we have to be happy for her, for her and Lachlan.'

'I know. It's just…' Amber's eyes moistened. 'Oh, Mum, why was it so easy for Scarlett to become pregnant when it's taking us so long?'

'I don't know, darling. Everyone's different. I'm sure your time will come. You just need to be patient.'

'Patient! Next thing we know, Megan will be pregnant too. What?' She stared at Poppy, her eyes widening.

Poppy realised her expression must have changed.

'She's not, is she? How long have you known?'

Poppy fixed two coffees before replying, 'She told me just before the wedding. She didn't want to steal Scarlett's thunder. I'd hoped she'd have told you by now.'

'You've known all this time... both of you. Who else knew? Am I such a sad case that you've all been keeping it from me? What did you think I'd do when I found out?'

Poppy placed a coffee on the table in front of Amber and took a seat next to her. 'I suppose we all thought we were protecting you,' she said. 'Perhaps we were wrong. I know how much you and Chris want a baby. It would have seemed like rubbing salt into a wound. But I knew you'd have to find out sometime. I just hoped...'

'What? That I'd magically become pregnant too?' Amber burst into tears. 'I did... last year, but I miscarried before I could tell anyone. It...' she looked at Poppy, her eyes filled with despair, '... it seems we may need to try IVF.'

'Oh, honey, surely...'

'It's no use, Mum. We've tried everything, had all the tests. They can't figure out the reason; it's what they call unexplained infertility,' she sobbed.

'If it's a case of money, I can...'

Amber shook her head. 'It's not that. I know people who've been on IVF, have tried several times, spent a lot of money, and still haven't managed to fall pregnant or to carry a baby to full term.' She picked up her coffee, then put if down again without taking a sip. 'Why am I so different from my sisters? Am I destined only to be an aunt?'

Poppy wished she could do something to help, the way she used to kiss a sore knee to make it better when Amber was a child. But there was nothing she could do to help in this instance. 'I'm so sorry, sweetheart. Have you thought...'

'Of adopting? I thought you'd say that. It's what everyone suggests, even saying I might fall pregnant once I have an adopted child. But it's my own baby I want, my own little boy or girl in my arms.' She burst into tears again.

Angus, sensing her distress, chose this moment to nuzzle up to her, his soft nose rubbing on her ankles.

This time, she picked him up. 'Oh, Angus,' she said, cuddling the little white furry creature, 'if only you understood.'

Poppy felt helpless as she watched her daughter cradling the little dog as she would a baby.

'I'm sorry, Mum.' Amber carefully set Angus down and wiped her eyes with a tissue. 'I shouldn't have dumped on you like that, but...'

'I know. It must be hard for you. I wish I could do something to help.'

'You're here now.' She sniffed. 'That helps. But I should go, let you get on with your day. Have you thought about what I said to you... about moving on from Dad? It's time you stopped grieving.'

'I'll never do that, Amber. Your dad was such a big part of my life for so many years. But I do intend to make an attempt to fill my life with things other than *Crossings*. We have a good staff. I don't need to be there every day. I had dinner with your Uncle Cam last night and...'

'Uncle Cam?' Amber stared at her in surprise. 'You don't mean you and he...'

'No, of course not. We went to that new place, *Addison's*, to check it out. The view is superb, and the food was excellent. I got a few good ideas we can try out at *Crossings*.' Poppy knew she was babbling. She didn't want Amber to get the wrong idea about her and Cam.

'You and Uncle Cam... you'll both be grandparents to Scarlett's baby. It's weird.'

'There's nothing weird about it.' Poppy knew her words came out stronger than she intended. 'I mean...' she said in a gentler tone, '... it was always going to happen when Scarlett and Lachlan married. We could see it coming, even when your dad was alive.' *And how he'd have loved it, to share a grandchild with his best mate. They'd have had such fun together, especially if it was a boy they could take sailing and...*

'Mum?'

'Sorry, honey.' Poppy wiped away an incipient tear. 'I was just thinking about your dad.'

'He'd have loved being a grandad,' Amber said sadly.

'He would.'

They sat in silence for a few moments remembering the man who had had such a big heart and who'd have been over the moon to know his girls were going to add to the family, even if they wouldn't carry on the Taylor name.

'Now, I really must go,' Amber said. 'I'm expected at work. I just had to see you first.'

'Thanks for coming. You know I'm always here for you.'

They rose together, and Poppy hugged her daughter tightly.

'Thanks, Mum, for being you. I feel better now I've got it out of my system. Chris doesn't understand. *He* doesn't have any siblings who're pregnant.'

Poppy tried not to smile. Chris was an only child whose parents would no doubt be hoping to hear he and Amber were about to provide them with their first grandchild. It wouldn't help to make this observation right now. 'Try not to worry too much,' she said when they reached the door. 'I'm sure it's not helping.'

'How would you know? You had the three of us without any problems, didn't you?' With that final remark, Amber got into her car and drove off.

Poppy watched her go, before turning back into the house. She sighed, trying to suppress her distress. She knew Amber hadn't meant to upset her, to be so resentful of her sisters' pregnancies. She was hurting, and rightly so. It must be so difficult for her when she was so desperate for a baby and both her sisters – her younger sisters – had fallen pregnant so easily.

It was almost time for Poppy to go to the restaurant if she wanted to be there for lunchtime. She loaded the coffee cups and her breakfast dishes into the dishwasher and wondered if she did need to go to *Crossings*. As she'd told Amber, she had good staff who could manage perfectly well without her. She'd trained them well, and Bridget Holmes, the woman Gill had recommended to take on the restaurant's PR had proved to be very efficient and was working from home. Maybe it was time to make good her decision to take time for herself.

Eight

Cam was still buoyed up with Lachlan and Scarlett's news when he awoke next morning. He hummed to himself all the way to the marina, imagining what it would be like to have a small version of Lachlan or Scarlett tagging along after him. As soon as the pair had started going out together, he and Jack had often talked about what they'd do when they married and had a family, a family which would bring Cam and Jack closer together than they already were. He was devasted his old mate hadn't lived to see it, but it would bring Poppy and him closer too.

They should celebrate. No sooner did the idea occur to him, than he made up his mind to do something about it. A celebration of their joint grandchild would prove the perfect opportunity for him to invite Poppy to dinner again. And this time he'd be sure to act less like her old friend and more like... he scratched his head... what exactly? A potential lover? At the thought, a shaft of desire shot through him.

It was a long time since he'd been with a woman, not since Gail left, and even before that there hadn't been much happening in the bedroom. He should have guessed there was something wrong, someone else. But they say the husband is often the last to know. It certainly hadn't occurred to him Gail would be interested in another woman. After that, he hadn't dared risk forming another relationship.

But now, the thought of becoming closer to Poppy was overriding all his earlier fears. He was about to pick up the phone when the door to his office swung open and a man entered. Cam recognised him right away. It was the guy who owned the large motor launch, the one Rory had said was asking all sorts of questions about Pelican Crossing – Jordan Butler.

Cam had checked the man out on the internet. It appeared Jordan Butler was a well-known Sydney entrepreneur, famous for his habit of setting new trends, taking over and re-energising failing companies and developing old buildings into modern monstrosities. He came from a wealthy family, attended a prestigious private school and started his career as a stockbroker. It seemed everything he touched turned to gold. So, what was he doing here in Pelican Crossing? There was no sign of any of his entourage today.

'Good morning how can I help you?' he asked with a smile.

'Hey, you must be the boss? I spoke with one of your staff the other day. I'm Jordan Butler from *The Odyssey*.' He pointed to the large motor launch.

'Welcome to Pelican Marine. I'm Cam Mitchell. How can I help you?' he repeated.

The other man smiled. He must be around the same age as me, Cam thought, but with his deep tan, sun-bleached hair and trendy outfit of long white shorts and tee-shirt bearing the logo of an expensive brand, he could pass for ten years younger. 'The young man I spoke to was helpful, but I suspect he didn't want to divulge too much. I thought I should speak with you.'

Cam felt his hackles rise. The suspicions he'd had about this guy had been right, there was something fishy about him. 'About?' he asked with a forced smile.

'About Pelican Crossing.' He waved a hand in the direction of the town. 'It's a lovely spot. I've been looking for somewhere to settle down away from the big city. This may be it, and I want to find out all I can before making a final decision. You grew up here?'

'I did. It's a quiet spot. You might miss the buzz of the city if you decided to move here. We get a lot of tourists in the summer but apart from that…' Cam shrugged.

'Hmm. A group of friends came with me, and we had a meal at the yacht club. Not bad for a small place, though a somewhat limited menu. Is there anywhere else you'd recommend?'

Cam flinched. He enjoyed the menu at the yacht club and had never considered it to be limited. In fact, it was where he intended to suggest he and Poppy have dinner to celebrate their forthcoming grandchild. He thought quickly. The man might be a bit over-the-top, and Cam wasn't entirely convinced about his motives, but he could at least send some business in Poppy's direction. 'You could try *Crossings*, on the main street across from the beach,' he said. 'It's won several awards, or *Addison's* in the hinterland. The views from there are stupendous. Now, if that's all...' He gestured to the pile of accounts he had to take care of.

'Thanks. I may pop in again.' Jordan gave a mock salute.

'Always happy to help,' Cam said, but he was glad to see Jordan Butler leave. He was a bit too smooth for Cam's liking, but he'd booked the berth for several months so he wouldn't be leaving anytime soon.

'Did I hear that Butler guy?' Rory came out of the back room.

'You did. He's an odd one. I can't work out what he sees in Pelican Crossing. It doesn't seem to be his sort of place, but he's here for a few more months so we'd better get used to seeing him around.'

'I guess so. Glad you met him too.'

'Hmm.'

When Rory had disappeared again, Cam did what he'd been intending to do before Jordan Butler interrupted him. He picked up his phone.

*

Having decided to spend the day working out how to make changes in her life, Poppy made another cup of coffee and was settling down on the deck, Angus at her feet, when her phone rang.

Seeing Cam's number, a small thrill shot through her before she managed to stifle it, reminding herself he was only a friend; it was all he'd ever be.

'Morning, Cam. Getting used to the idea of becoming a grandfather?' She chuckled. She'd already been thinking about what she wanted the new baby to call her. Before going to bed the previous night, she'd checked on the internet. The options seemed endless. There was Grandma, Nana, Nan, Gran, Granny, Gam Gam, Gigi, Nonna,

Mimsy, Mimi and Bibi to mention only a few. Maybe she'd just settle for Poppy, though perhaps Cam would want to be called that. It had appeared in the list of grandfather names she'd also scanned.

'That's what I'm ringing about. I think the news deserves a celebration, don't you? It's not every day we hear we're going to become grandparents. I thought dinner at the yacht club. What do you say?'

'Oh!' Poppy was too surprised to respond immediately. Coming so soon after their dinner at *Addison's*, if Cam hadn't made it very clear he didn't see her as more than a friend, a good friend, she might have thought... She took a deep breath. 'What a good idea,' she said. 'It's just a pity the prospective parents aren't here to celebrate with us. When did you have in mind?'

'Is tonight too soon? I know you'll be busy at *Crossings* later in the week, and there's no point in delaying.'

Tonight? Poppy thought quickly. There was no reason to refuse. 'That would be lovely,' she said. 'I love the yacht club.' It was where she and Jack had always gone for celebrations, often accompanied by Cam and Gail, then by Cam after Gail left. And while it held memories of her times there with Jack, they were pleasant ones and didn't spoil the club for her now he was gone.

'It's what Jack would have wanted, what he'd have done if...' Cam said awkwardly, as if reading her mind.

'Yes, it was always our place... the four of us.' Poppy smiled at the happy memories it evoked.

'So, pick you up at seven? I'll book a table, though I don't expect they'll be busy on a Tuesday. It's still fairly quiet around town.'

'Perfect. I'll see you then.'

As soon as the call ended, Poppy's mind went to what she'd wear. The yacht club could be dressy or casual and she'd worn a new outfit to *Addison's*. More casual tonight, she decided, going to her wardrobe and pulling out an old favourite, a loose blue dress with three-quarter sleeves. It had also been one of Jack's favourites, and she hadn't worn it since he died. But tonight was a celebration for Jack, too, even if he couldn't be there with them.

'He'd have loved this, wouldn't he?' she asked Angus, despite the fact Angus had never known Jack, and the dog couldn't reply. She often found herself talking to him as if he was human. It was a way of relieving her loneliness, especially now Scarlett was gone too.

Poppy felt restless. It was all very well to decide she needed more time to herself, but what was she to do with it? She experienced a sudden urge to talk with someone, someone who might understand. Out of all her friends, Rachel was the one who came to mind. Rachel had experienced the loss of a husband; she and Poppy had that in common. Also, Rachel was already a grandmother – twice over – so she'd understand Poppy's excitement at Scarlett's news coming so soon after Megan's. And now Amber knew, Poppy was able to share the happy news with her friends. Also, unlike Liz who seemed keen to have a man in her life, and Gill who wanted nothing to do with men, Rachel might also understand Poppy's feelings about Cam.

Ten minutes later, Poppy had arranged with Rachel to meet for lunch in *The Blue Dolphin Café* where she and Cam met for Sunday breakfast. Although it was situated opposite the marina where Cam worked, there was little chance of seeing him there and it was one of her favourite spots in Pelican Crossing. It was close to Pelican Plaza where, each day at two o'clock volunteers fed the pelicans and took the opportunity to educate visitors about the bird colony and keep an eye on the condition of their health.

It all started many years ago when staff at the local fish shop fed scraps to the pelicans every day providing the source of the rumour about the town's name. The spectacle of the gathering pelicans became so popular that eventually the local council arranged the building of a proper feeding platform. A tourist attraction, it became known as Pelican Plaza and in tourist season saw crowds of people gathered there each day to enjoy the spectacle.

The area was deserted as Poppy hurried across the way to the café where Rachel was already seated at a window table.

'Lovely to see you.' Rachel greeted Poppy with a hug. 'You said you needed to talk?'

'Let's order first.'

When the two women had ordered coffees, both choosing cappuccino made with skim milk and adding a slice of carrot cake to share, Rachel asked again, 'What's so urgent?'

'It's not really, but I've decided to take your advice – from our lunch – and make more time for myself. Also, I have news.'

Their orders arrived causing a delay, then Poppy continued, 'I'm about to become a grandmother.'

'Oh, congratulations!' Rachel hugged her again. 'How lovely for you. I know how much my little ones mean to me. Is Amber…?'

Poppy shook her head. 'Sadly not, but both Megan and Scarlett are. I'm excited, of course, but I can't help feeling for Amber. She came round this morning in a terrible state. She'd just heard about Scarlett, and I let the cat out of the bag about Megan.'

'So, two at once. You are going to be busy. You won't have to worry about what to do with your time.' She chuckled.

'Well, Scarlett's in Canberra, but I assume Megan will be happy to have me help out.'

'Just wait. You're going to find yourself spending more time at her house than your own… and with *Crossings* too… Your life won't be your own.'

Poppy grimaced. While she was looking forward to the arrival of her first grandchildren, she didn't know if she liked the idea of them taking over her life.

'Only joking,' Rachel laughed, 'but it will make a difference in your life. Remember what it was like when your first was born, how you depended on your mother for help and advice?'

Poppy thought back. She'd had to work a lot of stuff out for herself. Her mother was busy with the restaurant. Both her parents were tied up from dawn to dusk in their efforts to make a success of their pet project. There hadn't been a lot of time left for babysitting or the offer of advice. But perhaps it could be different for her and Megan; she could be more available.

'I'm sorry about Amber. They intend to keep trying?'

'Yes.' Poppy took a sip of coffee, while Rachel cut the carrot cake in two. 'She's talking about IVF. I don't know.' She shook her head, her mood changing at the thought of her eldest daughter's dilemma.

Rachel patted her hand. 'It may happen naturally. She's still young.'

'Twenty-nine.'

Rachel nodded. 'The same age as Jess.'

Poppy smiled, remembering them both as young mothers together. But now Jess was the mother of twin girls and pregnant again.

'Not everyone falls pregnant easily,' Rachel said, clearly understanding.

'She miscarried a year ago. She didn't tell me.' Poppy felt a tear in the corner of her eye. 'I wish…'

Rachel patted Poppy's hand again. 'We all want our children to be happy, but sometimes there's nothing we can do to help. We just have to be there when they need us.'

'You're right, of course.' Poppy sighed. 'I hate to see her so unhappy, but you're right. It's what Amber said too.'

'She's a wise girl, like her mother, resilient too. I've known her all her life, remember. She'll get through this.'

'I hope so.' Poppy sighed again.

'But that's not all you wanted to tell me.'

'No. I think I've been a bit of a fool, Rach.'

'Never!'

Poppy laughed. 'It was after our last lunch, when Liz asked about Cam… me and Cam. She wasn't so far off the mark. I'd been thinking about him. He was Jack's best mate. We did everything together, the four of us, until Gail left. Then we were three. I thought… imagined… that perhaps… Oh, Rachel, I thought maybe we… Cam and I… could…'

'That was a perfectly natural thing to think. He doesn't…?'

'Since Jack's death, we've remained good friends. He's helped me a lot with the restaurant accounts – I'm hopeless with figures – and sorted out a few small problems for me. We all used to breakfast together on Sundays, and we've kept that up. It's been a comfort to me, knowing the routine I had with Jack could go on.'

'So what's changed?'

'I guess I have. I've started to think about what I'm missing, to want a man in my life again. Is that wrong of me? I'm not desperate like Liz seems to be, but I'm not anti-men like Gill. You seem to get along okay without one in your life, but I… sometimes it's lonely, especially now Scarlett's married, not that she was much company even before then. She was often out or away, but I always knew she'd be back.'

Rachel didn't answer immediately, taking a sip of coffee and a bite of carrot cake first. Then she said, 'I do have some idea of what you mean, how sometimes the bed seems too big for one person, how you long to feel a pair of arms around you, to have someone to unburden yourself to after a long day, when you're worried about something, or when your children annoy you. But I've managed to concentrate instead on my blessings, on my healthy children and grandchildren, on my own good health, on this beautiful town I live in. It's not a complete solution, but it helps, it helps a lot. But... you and Cam...'

'He invited me out to dinner, to *Addison's*, and I thought... I thought maybe he wanted to be more than good friends.'

Rachel raised one eyebrow. 'And he didn't?'

Poppy shook her head. 'It was no different from when we have breakfast together.'

'Oh! Well, maybe he felt awkward, didn't want to scare you off. Men have feelings too, you know.'

'I know all that, and Cam's very different from Jack – quieter, more thoughtful. I don't know what I expected, maybe some sign that... Oh, I'm being foolish, but thanks for listening to me. I would hate for the others to know.' She looked worriedly at Rachel.

'My lips are sealed. But you believe there's no hope... that he won't invite you out again?'

'Oh, he has done. We're having dinner at the yacht club tonight to celebrate Scarlett and Lachlan's pregnancy. We'll both be the baby's grandparents.'

'Well, that's bound to bring you closer together. Maybe you just need to be patient.'

'You think?' It was what she'd advised Amber to do earlier that day, Poppy realised. It wasn't so easy when the boot was on the other foot.

Nine

Patient! It's what Rachel recommended and what Poppy would be. But it wasn't going to be easy, she thought as she dressed to go out. Patience had never been her strong suit. 'But I can do it, Angus,' she said to the small dog who had his head to one side as if listening intently. She checked her hair and makeup, pleased with the result. She looked smart but casual, suitable for having dinner with an old friend to celebrate the news of a new grandchild on the way.

At seven o'clock precisely, she heard Cam's car stop outside, followed by his knock on the door. Angus gave a small bark, then settled down in his basket. He'd never make a guard dog.

'You're looking lovely as usual.' Cam greeted her with his usual peck on the cheek, and she inhaled the scent of his aftershave, different from the Old Spice Jack had always worn.

'Thanks, Cam.' He was looking pretty good himself, she thought, in a blue and white striped shirt and a pair of neatly pressed jeans. She was glad she'd chosen a casual outfit too.

As Cam had predicted, the yacht club wasn't busy. They were shown to a table overlooking the marina and offered menus.

'Champagne?' Cam asked.

'That would be nice.' Poppy hadn't had the sparkling wine since Scarlett's wedding, and it was an appropriate drink to celebrate the new addition to the family. Hopefully they weren't tempting fate by celebrating before he or she was born.

'To our joint grandchild,' Cam said, raising his glass when the sparkling liquid had been poured.

They drank the toast, then focussed on the menu, each choosing a smoked salmon starter followed by filet mignon, a 240gram hickory smoked eye filet wrapped in prosciutto served with garlic mash and pan-fried greens.

'That was delicious,' Poppy said when they had finished. 'As good if not better than our chef can provide.'

'Praise, indeed.' Cam chuckled. 'Dessert?'

Poppy wasn't sure if she could eat anything else, but the sight of a waiter carrying a chocolate mousse to a nearby table tempted her taste buds. 'Maybe…' she said, gesturing towards it. Cam ordered two servings of the milk and dark chocolate mousse served with a raspberry gel.

'Now,' he said, 'what's bothering you?'

During the meal their conversation had been all about the new addition to the family, what the baby might be called, who it might resemble and what they as grandparents should call themselves. Poppy had shared the variety of names she'd found on the internet, and they'd laughed at some of them, remaining undecided. Now, Poppy gazed out at the dark outlines of the various vessels in the marina, wishing Cam wasn't so perceptive. 'It's Amber,' she said, '… and me.'

'Can you tell me about it?' Cam reached across the table to take her hand in what Poppy knew was only a friendly gesture. They knew each other so well.

'I think I may have told you how Amber and Chris are desperate for a child. I'm afraid hearing about Scarlett and Megan has emphasised their failure. She's extremely upset, and I feel so helpless. If there was something I could do…'

'You know there isn't, and I'm sure Amber knows that too. You're a good mother but you can't work miracles.' His thumb moved across the palm of her hand sending ripples of pleasure through her. Poppy swallowed hard, trying not to let him see how his touch affected her.

'Is that all?'

'Not exactly. Amber and several of my friends have been urging me to make more time for myself, to move on with my life. I still grieve for Jack, for the time we could… should… have had together, but I've come to the conclusion they're right. It's time I stopped burying myself in work and started to live a little.' As she spoke, Poppy felt a lightening of her mood. She hadn't actually put it in these words before, but it was exactly what she had decided to do.

*

At Poppy's words, Cam's heart lifted. It had been five long years since Jack's death, and he knew how Poppy had grieved for him – he had too. But she was still young, had her whole life ahead of her. They weren't living in the dark ages when a widow was expected to wear black and grieve for ever.

'I think that's a wise decision,' he said, not wishing to sound too enthusiastic, although inside he was rejoicing.

'You do?' she said, seemingly unsure.

'It's what Jack would have wanted. Remember how he was always so full of life. He wouldn't have expected – or wanted – you to lose yourself in *Crossings*. You've done amazingly well. Jack would be proud of what you've managed to achieve. But you're right to want to step back.'

'Thanks, Cam. Your opinion means a lot to me. You and Jack were so close. You knew him better than anyone. Sometimes I think you even knew him better than me.' She chuckled.

'We go back a long time, met in primary school. He was a livewire even then. I could tell you a few tales…'

'I think Jack may have told me them all – several times over.' She laughed. 'But I never tired of hearing them.'

Cam shifted uncomfortably in his seat. Reminiscences about Jack were all very well, but it didn't help advance his relationship with Poppy. 'More champagne?' he asked, holding up the almost empty bottle.

'Thanks.' Poppy held out her glass.

'And have you decided what you're going to do in your attempt to live a little?' He held his breath.

'Not yet.' Poppy twisted the stem of her glass. 'I had lunch with Rachel earlier today and she was full of suggestions. But I'm not sure I'm cut out for volunteering at the library or the retirement village, and the childcare centre's out as I'll soon have grandchildren of my own. She also mentioned the local choir, amateur dramatic society and the gardening club.' She grimaced.

'I don't see you in any of those either. I wonder…'

'What?'

'Have you considered taking up a new sport? You know Rory who works with me at the marina? His brother, Gary, is a qualified divemaster and is planning to set up a dive school. He's going to run it out of the same office as their dad's fishing charter business.'

'Diving? I've never…' But her eyes lit up. 'Do you dive?'

'Not recently, but I've offered to help him out. It's a very satisfying leisure pursuit. Under the ocean, there's so much to see. It's like being in another world.'

'Mmm.'

Cam could see she was interested.

'You say he's planning to set this up? It's not available yet?'

'Not yet. He's working on being ready to open in time for the tourist season. That's a few months away.'

'Well, it's definitely worth considering.'

Cam thought quickly. 'In the meantime, how about picking up sailing again? Remember…?' When they were all teenagers, the four musketeers as they called themselves spent almost every weekend out on the two-man sailboats, sometimes Gail and Poppy together on one with the men on the other, sometimes Jack and Poppy paired up, and Cam and Gail. They had been good times which had fallen off after Poppy and Jack married and Poppy became pregnant.

'Oh,' Poppy beamed, 'I'd love to get out on the water again. I do remember. I wonder why we let it drop.'

'I think you and Jack got busy having babies, and Gail and I… We never seemed to get around to going on our own.'

'But you do now? I've seen you heading out of the bay.'

So, she'd been watching him. It was a good sign. 'I like to get out of the office from time to time, feel the wind in my hair, forget about everything and just enjoy the freedom.'

'I'd love to join you sometime.'

'Really?'

'Really. I often want to get away from everything too.' She frowned as if it was something that hadn't occurred to her before.

'What about next Monday, weather permitting? We can leave early morning, make a day of it, take a picnic, perhaps moor up the coast a bit?'

'Lovely. Thanks, Cam. I'll look forward to it.' She smiled.

Cam thought how pretty Poppy looked when she smiled. She hadn't had a lot to smile about after Jack died, but the awards *Crossings* had won, coupled with Scarlett's wedding and now the news of grandchildren were bringing back the old Poppy, the Poppy he knew so well. He had almost told her how he felt when she said she'd decided to live a little but something, some innate sense of preservation had held him back. He was terrified of speaking too soon and spoiling the friendship they had.

Ten

The rest of the week flew past. The restaurant was busier than usual giving Poppy little time to think about the proposed sailing outing with Cam. But when she did think about it, she felt a shiver of excitement, not only at the prospect of spending more time with him, but also in anticipation of being out on the water again.

She had always loved sailing, not sure why she'd stopped. Jack hadn't, and it had led to his death. For a time afterwards, the idea of trusting her life to a small boat had been anathema to her, but now she discovered she couldn't wait to experience again the heady pleasure and the sense of freedom she remembered.

Pulling on a pair of shorts she hadn't worn for some time, a blue and white striped tee-shirt – very nautical, she thought – and her blue hoodie, Poppy popped on one of Jack's old caps, packed water, sandwiches, sunscreen and her phone into a small backpack and was ready to leave. 'Be good, Angus,' she told her pet, after ensuring he had plenty of food and water and was able to go in and out of the house as he pleased. Typically, Angus gave her a look of disgust at being left alone again.

'All set?' Cam greeted her at the marina. He was wearing his usual shorts, a tee-shirt bearing the Pelican Marine logo and a cap similar to the one she had donned. With the tan he managed to maintain all year due to spending a lot of time outdoors, he looked like one of his own adverts – he used male models to advertise the marina interstate.

Poppy stifled the urge to throw her arms around him. 'All set,' she said tremulously, her confidence beginning to desert her at the thought of being out on the ocean in a small boat again.

The boat he led her to was larger than she expected, a thirty-four-foot monohull beauty sitting side-by-side with several others of similar size. It must be the one she'd seen him on from her deck but appeared larger close to. She was relieved it wasn't like the small skiff which had been Jack's downfall, smiling to see the name *Classy Lady* painted on the side in large blue lettering.

Cam leapt onto the deck and held out his hand to help her. 'Welcome aboard,' he said with a grin. 'You'll be quite safe,' he added, seeming to sense her uncertainty.

'I know, Cam. I trust you,' she said, her confidence returning. Cam was an experienced sailor, and it was a calm day, not like the one on which Jack had met his death. Also, Cam was a more competent and cautious sailor than Jack had ever been. Jack had always loved to take risks and live on the edge; it had been what led to his demise. He'd been a fool to go out on that day and it had cost him dearly.

Cam cast off, and in no time they were sailing out of the bay. Poppy discovered she hadn't forgotten the skills she'd learned as a teenager and enjoyed working with Cam; they made a good team.

As the sun beat down on them, Poppy became warmer and was able to remove her hoodie and enjoy the sun on her arms. It would soon be summer and even warmer than today, and summer would bring the tourists making both their lives busier. There might not be time for adventures like this. She should make the most of it and enjoy it while she could.

As they sailed along, they were joined by a pod of dolphins, and Poppy laughed at their antics as they swam parallel to the yacht for some distance before disappearing off into the distance.

Just as Poppy was beginning to feel hungry, Cam said, 'May be time for a bite of lunch. We can anchor in the next bay.' He gestured towards the coast.

'I brought some sandwiches,' Poppy said.

'Good of you, but I arranged a picnic hamper from *The Blue Dolphin*. I loaded it earlier. Rory said they do a good spread. He does this sort of thing more than I do.'

Poppy wondered what he meant. Go sailing or take a woman

sailing? Probably the latter as she knew Cam went out on his boat regularly.

It was glorious out here, the water glistening in the sunlight, so clear she could see shoals of tiny fish under the surface and the odd small shark, which make her shiver. She was never comfortable around those creatures, originally called the dogs of the sea. There were so many reports of surfers and swimmers being mauled and sometimes killed by them. Fortunately, she had never come into close contact with one herself, but always avoided swimming in the ocean at dawn or dusk.

They dropped anchor in a bay Poppy hadn't visited for years, not since she and Jack had sailed with Cam and Gail. Happy memories flooded back. It was as if Jack was with them.

'You too?' Cam asked, handing her a glass of white wine from the open picnic basket he'd brought up from the cabin. 'I always feel Jack's presence out here.'

'Mmm.' Poppy nodded taking a sip of wine. But strangely, the memories didn't evoke the tumult of grief she normally felt when she thought of Jack. It was as if he was giving her permission to move on. She prodded the memory again, as she would a sore tooth, but all she felt was a sense of calm, as if Jack was giving his approval.

The picnic hamper more than met her expectations. It was filled with tiny quiches and sausage rolls, spears of asparagus wrapped in prosciutto, several different cheeses, a selection of crackers and small containers of fruit salad. It put her tomato and cheese sandwiches to shame, but they managed to polish off the lot, sandwiches included.

When they had finished, and Cam had tipped the final drops of wine from the bottle, Poppy dropped her head back and looked up into the clear, blue sky, listening to the sound of the waves lapping against the side of the yacht and the cries of the seagulls circling overhead. 'I wish I could stay here for ever,' she said dreamily. She closed her eyes and almost fell asleep, lulled by the gentle movement of the vessel.

Her dreams were interrupted by Cam's voice.

'We should get back. I don't like the look of the sky. It's beginning to cloud over.'

Immediately, Poppy's eyes flew open. 'A storm?' The memory of the day of Jack's death came back in a rush.

'Probably not. The forecast was clear, no storm warning. But I don't want to take any chances. Even if the weather does turn, we'll be back in the marina before the worst of it.'

They quickly tidied away the remains of their picnic and set sail for home, but the mood had been lost, and Poppy didn't enjoy the return trip as much as the outbound one. She kept looking worriedly at the sky which had, as Cam said, clouded over, though there was no sign of the storm she feared. This was why she had avoided anything to do with boats, she remembered. The weather could be unpredictable. One minute the sky was clear, the sun beaming down, the next, the sun had disappeared, and a stiff breeze could blow up heralding a storm.

But that didn't happen. They made it back to the marina in record time with no sign of rain or storm.

'Thanks, Cam,' Poppy said when they were safely moored again. 'I had a lovely time. It was kind of you to suggest it. I'm sorry I started to panic.'

'You did? I didn't notice,' he grinned.

'It's been too long since I did any sailing.'

'We could do it again? Perhaps an evening sail? It's pretty spectacular to watch the sun go down from the middle of the ocean.'

'Perhaps.' While Poppy believed him, she wasn't ready to risk being out on the ocean in the darkness, not yet anyway. 'I know you're an experienced sailor and I trust your confidence but...'

'Okay, we can take it easy. I'm happy with that.'

Something in Cam's tone made Poppy glance at him quickly, but he seemed impervious to her scrutiny. Perhaps she'd imagined it, imagined that when he spoke of taking it easy, he wasn't only referring to going sailing.

Eleven

Poppy and Cam fell into the habit of spending more time together. They went sailing when they were both able to free up some time and had dinner at the yacht club on several occasions. But he never made any overture to suggest he wanted more than the friendship they'd enjoyed for so long. Poppy knew she should accept this was it, and if she wanted to find another partner, she'd have to look elsewhere. But she still continued to hope.

The previous evening, after she returned from *Crossings*, Scarlett had called, and Poppy had enjoyed a long chat with her daughter who, now she was pregnant, wanted to share all her symptoms and worries with her mother. How Poppy wished she lived closer, that they could meet regularly, and she could offer the support her over-anxious daughter craved.

Megan was the opposite. Although she lived in Pelican Crossing, she rarely called on Poppy's advice, seeming to sail through her pregnancy without any effort. Although not much of a knitter, Poppy was attempting a simple pattern for a cot blanket which she hoped would be finished in time. She intended to knit one for Scarlett too, if time permitted.

Then her mind went to Amber, and she frowned. Her oldest daughter had confided in her that she and Chris were about to try a procedure called IUI – Intra-Uterine Insemination – in the hope that it might work. Poppy had never heard of it, but it sounded less invasive than IVF, and Amber said it was less costly. She hoped it would be successful.

Today was the regular lunch with her friends, and it was Liz's turn to host the group. It was a cloudy morning with a slight breeze, and Angus was restless, so Poppy decided a walk on the beach before she left for lunch might tire him out. Pulling a jacket over the tee-shirt she'd donned when she got up, she grabbed his lead. The little dog leapt up in an attempt to grab it as soon as they reached the door. She attached it to his collar and set off down the path to the beach.

They had the wide stretch of sand almost to themselves, only two others were braving the elements, both with dogs like Poppy. Poppy nodded a greeting to the women when they passed but didn't stop to chat. As soon as they reached the edge of the ocean, she released Angus who immediately ran off chasing seagulls, his favourite pastime, though he never managed to catch them.

The beach was Poppy's happy place, the place she'd always gone to when she wanted to think or had a problem she needed to solve. Today, as she walked briskly along, Poppy thought back to the last time she and Cam had gone sailing. It had been a fine day, warmer than usual for the time of year, and when they'd anchored off the bay, they'd leapt into the water for a swim. It was when they climbed back onto the yacht that Poppy realised all her attempts to put the idea of a relationship with Cam out of her mind had been useless. The sight of him standing on the deck in his board shorts, the water streaming from his tanned body, a body too toned for a man of his age, had sent a wave of lust through her. It had been too long since she'd seen a man's naked chest, she told herself, taking a few deep breaths as she attempted to hide her blushes by rubbing her face as she towelled herself dry. Luckily Cam didn't appear to have noticed. He merely pulled out a couple of cans of beer, and they sat companionably together drinking them, towels around their shoulders, until they were dry enough to get dressed.

But the experience had served as a warning to Poppy, a warning to avoid repeating any chance of seeing Cam undressed. With the advent of summer, it wouldn't be easy. Maybe she'd need to curtail their outings, find some other way of spending her time.

Realising how much time had passed as she thought about Cam, Poppy called to Angus, and they returned home where she had a quick shower before dressing in a pair of loose striped pants topped with a sky-blue sweater which she'd purchased on her trip to Bellbird Bay. She wished there was a shop similar to *Birds of a Feather* in Pelican Crossing; the local dress shops were a sad disappointment.

Poppy was last to arrive at Liz's. The others were already started on the wine when she walked into the apartment her friend had purchased after her divorce. It was situated on the opposite side of the bay from Poppy's home, but the view was equally good. Today, the group were seated in a sheltered spot on the wide balcony which Liz had almost covered with pots of vegetables and herbs. She'd been impressed by a book by Indira Naidoo and had followed the author's example of establishing what she called her edible balcony.

'What kept you?' Liz asked as Poppy walked in. 'You've a bit of catching up to do.' She handed Poppy a glass of wine.

Poppy gratefully dropped into the one empty chair. 'Thanks, Liz. I'm afraid time got away from me. I took Angus for a walk on the beach and...' She shrugged.

'No worries,' Rachel said. 'You're here now. We were just discussing the spring fair.'

Poppy tried to summon up some interest, but the spring fair wasn't on her radar. For Rachel with her grandchildren, it was one of the highlights of the year. Maybe it would be for Poppy too in a year or two, but right now, she had other things on her mind.

Poppy gazed out at the view. Liz's home was closer to the marina than Poppy's, and from here she had a clear view of the lines of vessels of all shapes and sizes. She could see the large motor launch belonging to Jordan Butler. So, he was still here. So far, their paths hadn't crossed, but it was too much to hope that would continue. Of more immediate concern was how she could change things with Cam.

'Mandy tells me you and Cam have been at the yacht club a few times recently,' Liz said to Poppy when they were all enjoying the delicious avocado and chickpea salad she had served with thick slices of ham. 'Anything we should know?'

'Nothing at all.' Poppy felt rather than saw Rachel's sympathetic expression. She'd known when Mandy saw them at the club, she'd report to her mother. 'We've always been friends. You know that.' She forked up some of the salad. 'This is delicious, Liz. You must give me the recipe.'

'Don't change the subject. It has come to my ears you've also been seen out sailing.'

Poppy felt herself blush. 'My, the grapevine has been busy.' She took a sip of wine. 'I've been brushing up my skills. Jack and I used to go sailing with Cam and Gail, but we… I… let it drop when Amber was born and never got back to it. Then, after Jack… I… Anyway, I thought it was time. Cam kindly offered to take me out on the water. If I remember correctly, it was you who told me it was time I moved on. I plan on learning to dive too, as soon as Gary Whittaker's dive school opens.'

To Poppy's relief, her reference to the dive school started a conversation about how it might bring a different sort of tourist to the town, then to the need for more space in the marina which led to questions about the forthcoming council election. Poppy was able to sit back and listen, only agreeing when Gill said how Jack would have made an excellent local councillor, and what a pity he wasn't around to "keep them all on their toes".

As they were all about to leave, Rachel drew Poppy aside. 'Don't mind Liz,' she said. 'She can't help herself. She assumes everyone is like her. Between you and me, I don't think she's having much success with this online dating thing Mandy has set her up on. Maybe she just hopes you're having more luck than she is.'

Fat chance. 'Thanks, Rach. I'll remember that next time she tries to stick her oar in. Thanks for a lovely lunch,' she said turning to Liz.

'Sorry if I got things wrong,' Liz said. 'It was only that Mandy…'

'No worries.' Poppy smiled and touched her arm gently. 'It was a natural mistake.'

As she drove home, Poppy wondered how many others had seen her and Cam together and drawn the same conclusion. Pelican Crossing was a small town, and it didn't take much for tongues to start wagging. Maybe she and Cam should be more careful.

Twelve

Cam worried that Poppy was still grieving for Jack and continued to regard him as Jack's friend. Despite the fact she had said she wanted a life of her own, he saw no real evidence that anything had changed. They dined together, went sailing, but apart from a peck on the cheek, the odd clasping of hands, there was no sign she had any warmer feelings for him.

He sat at his desk in the building at the edge of the marina, watching a pelican land on one of the bollards and wishing his life was as simple as that of the large bird. These graceful creatures were monogamous in each breeding season, the male attracting the female with a courtship dance. Would that it was that simple for him. He sighed and continued to watch the bird as it glided off to land in a typically ungainly fashion on the surface of the water, where it was joined by several others flapping their wings. Although elegant in repose, the large birds always seemed to land awkwardly, like a plane touching down on a slippery runway.

His phone rang.

'Dad?'

'Lachlan, is everything okay?' It was unusual for his son to call him at work.

'Very okay,' Lachlan laughed. 'How would you like some visitors this weekend?'

'You're planning to come to Pelican Crossing?'

'Both Scarlett and I are able to take a long weekend. She's keen to see her mum, and I thought you and I could maybe do a bit of fishing.'

'Sounds good. Has Scarlett called her mum?'

'She was planning to call today to check if it would work for her, too. All going well, we plan to fly up on Friday, returning Monday. Scarlett wants us to stay with Aunt Poppy, but we aim to spend time with both of you. Scarlett wants to catch up with her sisters too. She hasn't said as much, but I think she misses them.'

'You'll be most welcome. I'm sure Poppy will agree. I know she misses Scarlett. Can't wait to hear all your news.'

Cam had a smile on his face when the call ended. It was always good to talk to Lachlan, even though his son was a man of few words. The prospect of his and Scarlett's visit was good news. It gave him an excuse to contact Poppy again, if he needed one. He'd drop into *Crossings* for lunch in the hope she'd be there today.

'You're looking pleased with yourself.' Rory appeared in the doorway.

'Had a call from Lachlan. They're coming to visit on the weekend.'

'About time he remembered his old friends.'

'Did you want something?'

'Yeah, it's the guy from *The Odyssey*.'

'Jordan Butler?'

'Mmm. Seems he and his mates have been causing a bit of a rumpus. We've had a few complaints about noise – music going on all hours. There's no actual law against it, but...'

'I'll have a word.' Cam sighed. He hated any sort of disagreement, especially with someone like Butler who he already disliked. But he couldn't ignore complaints from other boat owners. He checked the time. He'd have lunch first, then confront Butler about being more considerate of other residents on the marina, several of whom lived on their boats all year round.

*

Cam was pleased to see Poppy at the rear of the restaurant when he entered and was shown to a table close to the entrance. *Crossings* was busy, and she appeared to be sorting out some issue with a group of customers. She gave him a distracted smile and a wave indicating she'd catch up with him later.

It wasn't till he was drinking coffee after a very enjoyable lunch of calamari served with chips and salad, that she joined him, slipping into the seat opposite with her own cup of coffee.

'Wow!' she said, taking a gulp of the coffee.

'Trouble?'

'Not really. Just a few tourists wanting to make a point. We get them from time to time, though most people are pretty good. These ones were satisfied with a complimentary bottle of wine.'

'I wasn't sure you'd be here today. I thought you were taking more time to yourself.'

'I was… I am, but Michelle called in sick today, so…'

Michelle was the new member of staff who was handling front of house.

'And you'll be here until she's well again?'

'Probably. It's not a chore, Cam. I do enjoy it.' She paused. 'But sometimes… Oh, I don't know…' She pushed a stray lock of hair out of her eyes. 'It would have been different if Jack had lived.'

'You are taking time for yourself?'

'I am. I've even been persuaded by Gill to join the mad group of women who swim across the bay in the early morning. It's invigorating. I don't know why I haven't done it before now.'

'How is Gill?' Cam knew the divorce lawyer who'd helped Gail and him come to an amicable settlement when their marriage ended.

'She's good, considering. You do know she's having challenges with her own divorce. The bastard she married is making it difficult for her.'

'Sorry to hear that. On a happier note, I'm assuming Scarlett called you.'

'About the weekend. Yes, she did.' Her face softened. 'It'll be lovely to see her, Lachlan too. He's told you they'll be staying with me? I hope you don't mind.'

'Not at all. It was Scarlett's home. I moved into the apartment after Lachlan moved away. It doesn't hold any memories for him. I thought we could do a few things together.'

'What a good idea. I know Scarlett wants to catch up with Amber and Megan. Maybe we could arrange a family lunch or dinner – if I can organise *Crossings* to manage without me?'

'Great plan. Lachlan mentioned getting in some fishing, too. I'm guessing Scarlett may not be too keen on that. It would give you women time together.'

'Michelle should be back at work by then, and I have a few others I can call on.'

'No one's indispensable, Poppy. What about your decision to take time for yourself?'

'You're right,' she nodded. 'It's been a while…'

Cam covered Poppy's hand with his. 'Jack would be proud of what you've accomplished,' he said, 'but sometimes you have to know when to let go.'

'How did you know I was thinking of Jack?' Poppy raised her eyes to meet his. 'He should be here, too,' she said, a note in her voice Cam hadn't heard before. 'This was to have been *our* time, once *Crossings* was established, when the girls were all settled. We had plans… Sorry, Cam.' She wiped her eyes. 'It just hit me again. He's not coming back. You're right.' She straightened her back.

'Here.' Cam handed her a handkerchief. He was old-fashioned enough to always keep one in his pocket, but rarely used it.

'Thanks. You must think me a fool. It's the thought of us all being together, everyone except him… and Gail. Still no word about Judy?'

'No, but I expect to hear soon. Last time we spoke, Gail said she didn't have long. It's taken a toll on her. I'm not sure what she'll do when Judy goes.'

'They have friends?'

'Yes, there's a group of women they seem to spend a lot of time with, but…' He shook his head. He worried about Gail, knowing how fragile she was.

'She has the new baby to look forward to, but… It's a long time since we spoke. We were such good friends, then…'

'What happened?' Cam had never been clear as to how Poppy and Gail's friendship had fallen apart.

'I don't know. I think maybe Judy saw me as some sort of threat, especially after Jack died. Silly, really. We all need friends. Maybe when…'

'Maybe. I think Gail will need all the friends she can get.'

'Mmm.'

'Now, about the weekend…'

Poppy smiled, and they started to make plans for Lachlan and Scarlett's visit.

Thirteen

Everything was ready. As Poppy had predicted, Michelle was back on board, and she had engaged two of her casual staff for the weekend to be ready for an influx of visitors now the weather was warming up. She'd noticed a growing number of cars with interstate numberplates, a sure sign the tourist season was on its way. It would be the first weekend she hadn't spent at the restaurant and despite a niggle of worry, she was looking forward to it.

Angus, too, seemed to sense her excitement as she made up the bed in Scarlett's old room and set vases of flowers around the house, filling it with a wonderful fragrance. After his morning walk on the beach, taken after Poppy's early morning swim, followed by breakfast, he refused to settle in his usual spot. Instead, he followed Poppy around the house, demanding her attention.

Poppy was checking the time – Scarlett had said they'd be arriving for lunch, and she had prepared a salad – when there was a loud knock at the door, followed by the sound of it opening.

'Mum, we're here!' Scarlett's voice was almost drowned out by the sound of Angus's barking as he raced to greet her. 'Angus!' Scarlett picked him up and gave him a hug. 'Have you missed me?'

'Scarlett!' Lachlan put a restraining hand on her shoulder. 'Should you be…'

'I'm fine,' she said, but let Angus slip to the floor, turning to hug Poppy.

'My darling, it's so good to see you.' Poppy returned the hug then held her daughter at arm's length. 'You're looking so well.'

'I'm feeling wonderful. No more morning sickness, thank goodness. I can't wait to see Megan, to share...'

'Be careful when Amber's here,' Poppy said. 'She and Chris have been trying to get pregnant. I'm afraid she feels a bit resentful that you and Megan are pregnant and she's not.'

'Oh, I didn't know. She seemed all right when we spoke on the phone. But that's my big sister for you,' she said to Lachlan. 'She has been the first to do everything else. I can see how she must hate that Megan and I have beaten her to it. But she won't be far behind us.'

'I hope not.' If Amber hadn't shared her worries with her sister, Poppy didn't intend to.

'It's going to be so lovely,' Scarlett enthused. 'Our baby will have a cousin almost the same age, and if Amber...' She glanced at her mother. 'Is there something you're not telling me?'

'Nothing. Sorry.' Poppy turned to hug Lachlan. 'It's good to see you too. Your dad's busy till later, but we thought we could all eat at *Crossings* tonight. I think he has plans for the two of you tomorrow, and we girls can get together. How was your trip?' she asked belatedly. 'You must be hungry.'

After a leisurely lunch on the deck, during which Angus lay in his usual spot under the table, Scarlett decided to take a nap, while Lachlan headed down to the marina to catch up with his dad. Left alone, Poppy tried to relax, but found she was too excited about having her daughter under her own roof again to settle.

Angus, sensing her restlessness, went to the door and started to whine.

'Okay,' she said, 'I guess I need another walk, too.'

*

Cam was frowning and staring at his computer screen when Lachlan's tall figure walked into the marina office. 'Hey,' he said, his face clearing. He stood up and pulled his son into a hug. 'You made it. Scarlett not with you?'

'She's having a rest, but I wanted to catch up with you, see how the world's treating you.'

'Not much changes here, as you see.' Cam gestured around the office.

'Hmm.' Lachlan's eyes followed his. 'You were frowning when I walked in. Problems?'

Cam shrugged. He didn't want to spoil Lachan's visit with the issues that were troubling him, but he could see his son wanted an answer. 'The usual – complaints about noise on the marina and…' he rubbed his chin, '… a few other things.'

'Want to talk about it, Dad?'

'Not now. I don't want to spoil our reunion. Maybe later.'

'I'll hold you to that. Now, do you have time for a beer? Does *The Grand* still serve the local craft beer?'

'Does it ever.' *The Grand Hotel* was an institution in Pelican Crossing, having existed close to the marina for as long as Cam could remember. There was nothing grand about it, the hotel having retained its original frontage and décor which the locals all accepted and loved. In recent years, it had graduated from serving the more familiar brews to experimenting with craft beers from a local brewery set up by two enterprising young men who had been at school with Lachlan, resulting in it attracting a younger crowd and becoming trendy. When it had changed hands a few years earlier, there had been a move to change the name, but the locals had rebelled, so it had remained as *The Grand*, and probably always would.

Cam glanced at his watch then at the computer screen, where he'd been listing the yachts for sale and composing emails to the owners of those which had been vandalised. 'Why not?' he said, closing his computer. 'It's not every day I get the chance to have a beer with my son.' He grinned. 'Rory,' he called through to the back room, 'I'm off over to *The Grand* for a beer with Lachlan. Give me a call if you need me.'

In the pub, Lachlan ordered one of the new craft beer varieties, while Cam chose the James Squire 150 Lashes which he preferred. 'So,' Cam said, when they were settled in one of the small booths, 'how are you finding married life?'

Lachlan reddened. 'It's pretty good, Dad. Scarlett…' He spread his hands. 'She's amazing.'

Cam chuckled. 'She's like her dad, always on the go.'

'She sure is.'

'And you're about to become a dad.'

'Yeah.' Lachlan pulled on one ear. 'It was a bit of a shock.'

Cam chuckled again. 'You missed out on the sex education talks at school?' He raised an eyebrow.

'Ha ha. We were taking precautions, but I guess...' He scratched his head. 'But it's all good. We can't wait to be parents. If it's a boy, we plan to call him Taylor... after Uncle Jack.'

Cam felt his eyes moisten. 'He'd have liked that.' Although Jack had loved his daughters to bits, often jokingly complaining he was surrounded by a bevy of women, he'd have loved to have had a son to carry on the family name. He'd sometimes told Cam how he envied him having Lachlan. 'It's a big responsibility, you know, having a child. It's a lifetime commitment. You'll never stop worrying about them, even when they have children of their own.'

'Dad!' Lachlan seemed embarrassed. He took a gulp of beer then held his glass up to the light. 'Not a bad drop,' he said. 'You should try it.'

'Thanks, but I'll stick to what I know.' Cam took a sip from his glass. 'And how's work?'

'Good.' Seemingly relieved to be now on a less emotional topic, Lachlan broke into a long diatribe about the pitfalls and politics of working in the capital, finishing with, '... and it looks like I may be up for a promotion. It should help when Scarlett has to take maternity leave... though she says she intends to keep on working from home.'

'She may change her mind when the baby's here.'

'You know Scarlett. She's pretty determined.'

Like her dad, Cam thought again. *How could he even contemplate having a chance with Poppy, after her having been married to a man like Jack, a man who was his complete opposite?*

'How's Aunt Poppy?' Lachlan asked as if reading his mind. 'She seemed a bit strange at lunch.'

'Strange? In what way?'

'Dunno, distracted or something.'

'She was probably just excited at seeing you and Scarlett again, and the prospect of becoming a grandmother. You do know Megan's pregnant, too?'

'Scarlett said. We're seeing her and Gav tonight, Amber and Chris too. She's not…?'

'No. She'd like to be. So, try not to rub it in over dinner. It's hard for her with both Scarlett and Megan…'

'Okay. Now, what's worrying you? You had a frown on your face when I walked in.'

'Yeah.' Cam sighed. There was no point in trying to keep it from Lachlan. He'd find out soon enough. 'It's the marina. We're experiencing a bout of vandalism. At first it looked as if it was just a few kids letting off steam, but it's become more targeted – several of the yachts we have for sale have been splashed with paint and a few windows in the office were smashed. It looks like a planned campaign of attack.'

'You've called the police?'

'Not yet. I was contacting the yacht owners when you arrived. The police will be next. I've delayed calling them till I was sure.'

'You have CCTV, don't you?'

'Yeah.' Cam rubbed his chin. 'All we can see is several figures in hoodies. They've been careful not to show their faces.'

'How long has it been going on?'

'Oh, about…' he thought back, '… six weeks.' Around the same time Jordan Butler and his crowd arrived in the marina. But there couldn't be any connection, could there? What would someone like him have to gain from vandalising other vessels and the marina office?

'What?'

Cam realised his expression must have changed. 'Nothing, something just occurred to me. Now, I should get back, finish what I was doing when you interrupted me – an interruption I must admit I was glad of.' He grinned. He still had trouble accepting that the little boy he and Gail had given birth to, had turned into this tall, handsome young man, who was now about to have a child of his own. 'Have you spoken to your mum lately?' he asked as they were leaving the pub.

'Before we left Canberra. We're stopping off to see her and Judy again on our way back. She sounded exhausted, Dad. I wish there was something I could do to help. I wish I had been more understanding when…'

'You were young. All you could see was that the mother you loved was leaving, had found she loved someone other than me. You were full of teenage angst and didn't understand that she hadn't stopped loving *you*. She understood. She worked with teenagers every day. I know it was hard for you.' He patted Lachlan on the shoulder. 'The main thing is you got over it, you're there for her now when she needs you. And...' he exhaled, '... when it's Judy's time, she'll need us both.'

'Right, Dad. Thanks.' Lachlan pulled Cam into a hug. 'Thanks for everything. I only hope I can be as good a dad to our child as you've been to me.'

Cam's eyes moistened again. He'd never heard Lachlan speak like this before. His son had turned out well. He was proud of the man he'd become.

Fourteen

Crossings was busy, as was usual on a Friday night. Poppy greeted her staff as she made her way to the table she'd reserved, as far away from the door as possible. It felt strange to be there as a guest, dressed in a smart three-quarter sleeved, knee-length dress in bright orange and pink, instead of welcoming the diners wearing her usual black tunic and pants.

'Mum!' Megan rose to greet her, her face glowing. 'I can't wait to see Scarlett and compare notes.' She patted her stomach. 'Where are they? I thought they were staying with you.'

'They are, but they wanted to drive themselves, in case they needed to leave early. I think Scarlett's a bit tired from the flight.'

'It was only from Canberra.' Megan sounded disappointed. 'Oh, here they are now,' she added, as Scarlett and Lachlan made their way through the restaurant. 'Look at you, little sister,' she said, hugging Scarlett, then holding her at arm's length. 'Sorry I couldn't make this afternoon. Work!'

While Poppy had been disappointed not to have spent the afternoon with all three of her daughters, it had probably been good for Scarlett to meet Amber on her own. After an initial mention of the younger sister's pregnancy, the conversation had moved on.

'Now, both of you, remember to be sensitive to Amber's feelings. Keep talk of babies to a minimum. You can catch up tomorrow.'

'Okay, Mum,' they said in unison, reminding Poppy of when they were little, and she had chastised them over some misdemeanour or other.

There was no time for more as Amber and Chris arrived, followed by Cam, and there was the usual fuss as they all got seated, Poppy ending up sitting next to Cam.

To Poppy's relief, the conversation at dinner centred on how Scarlett was settling into married life and to living in Canberra, and with Amber and Megan relating local happenings in Pelican Crossing. It wasn't till they were eating dessert – a decadent tiramisu – that Lachlan said, 'I hear you may beat us to become parents, Megan.'

There was a deathly hush, before Gavin replied, 'January. You?'

'Around March, we think.' Lachlan glanced at Scarlett, who shifted uncomfortably in her seat.

Before anyone else could speak, Amber rose from the table. 'I just need to...' she said and rushed out.

Poppy heard Scarlett say, 'Lachlan!' in a strained voice as she left to follow Amber out of the restaurant.

She found her daughter on the other side of the road, leaning against the wall bordering the walkway to the beach.

As soon as Poppy reached her, Amber said, 'Sorry, Mum. I shouldn't have left. It was just... I couldn't bear it.' She burst into tears. 'I know it's not Scarlett and Megan's fault they're pregnant, and I'm not,' she sobbed. 'It's just so hard.'

'I know, my darling.' Poppy hugged her daughter.

'Are you okay, Amber?' Chris came rushing up to them. 'Megan and Scarlett wanted to come, but I persuaded them not to. Is there anything...?'

'I just want to go home,' Amber said.

'We can do that. What about...?' He looked helplessly at Poppy.

'I'll call you in the morning and we can work out a plan for the rest of the weekend,' she said. There already was a plan in place. The women were to spend Saturday together, while the men went fishing with Cam, then there was to be dinner at Poppy's. Nothing special had been planned for Sunday apart from breakfast at *The Blue Dolphin Café*, but there was the possibility of going out on Cam's yacht if the weather stayed fine.

'Thanks, Mum.' Amber hugged her mother before Chris led her off to their car.

When she returned to the restaurant, Poppy discovered they had all ordered coffee, and hers was waiting for her. 'Thanks,' she said, taking a welcome gulp.

'I'm sorry if I spoke out of turn,' Lachlan said, with a guilty glance at his wife. 'I didn't realise…'

'It's not your fault,' Poppy said.

'How's Amber?' Megan asked. 'I can't pretend not to be pregnant.' She dropped her eyes to her stomach where her pregnancy was beginning to show.

'She'll be fine,' Poppy said. 'Now, what have I missed?' She took another sip of coffee, the caffeine going some way to settling her anxiety about Amber.

'Cam was telling us about some problems he's having at the marina,' Gavin said. 'Sounds like something we should be looking into.' Gavin was a member of the local police force, currently monitoring a rise in youth crime.

'Not sure it's kids,' Cam said, looking serious.

'What sort of problem?' Poppy stared at Cam. It was news to her.

'I didn't want to bother you with it. It started with some graffiti, paint being thrown at several of the yachts. But it's become more seriously targeted.'

'And you can't link it to anything, any changes in the marina, any reason for it to be targeted?' Gavin asked.

'Not really. It started about the same time as a big motor launch berthed, but so far, it hasn't been hit. It may be a coincidence.'

'Jordan Butler's boat?' Poppy stared at Cam in surprise.

'Yeah. A bigwig from Sydney,' Cam explained to the others who appeared puzzled. 'You'd heard about him, Poppy?'

'I heard he was in town. I met him.'

'Here, in Pelican Crossing?' Megan asked.

'No,' Poppy shook her head. 'In Sydney. It was a long time ago, before you were born, before I married your dad.'

She thought Cam gave her a strange look. 'Remember when Jack and I had that big argument, and I went to stay with my aunt for a couple of weeks?' she said.

'Vaguely. Was that the time he got drunk and bent my ear till I told him to call you?'

'Probably.' Poppy smiled, her eyes prickling with tears as she remembered their passionate reunion when she returned from Sydney, how Jack vowed never to let her go again. 'I came back as soon as he did, never saw or heard of Jordan Butler again – till now.' It was a small lie, but she could feel her face going red. She took another drink of coffee then drained the last of the wine in her glass.

'All set for tomorrow, guys?' Cam asked Lachlan and Gavin as they all rose to leave.

'Sure. What about Chris?' Lachlan asked.

'I'll check with Amber,' Poppy said. She needed to make sure her daughter was okay.

'Thanks,' Cam said.

Back at the house, Scarlett said, 'About Amber, Mum. She's taking it hard. Is there anything we can do?'

'She'll be fine.' Poppy hoped she would.

Fifteen

By the time Scarlett and Lachlan emerged next morning, Poppy had fed Angus and was making bacon and eggs for breakfast. She'd decided to dispense with her early morning swim while Scarlett and Lachlan were there.

'Hey,' Scarlett said walking into the kitchen and stretching her arms above her head, before giving her mum a hug. 'I slept like a log, and just look at the day.' She went over to the window and gazed out at the ocean. 'I miss the beach,' she said with a grimace. 'I'll need to keep coming back to get my ocean fix.'

'Sounds good to me.' Lachlan appeared and wrapped his arms around Scarlett's waist. 'Mmm, breakfast smells good, Aunt Poppy.'

'Morning, Lachlan. I checked with Amber last night. Chris will be joining you today.'

'Good.'

'How was she, Mum?'

'Embarrassed. She'll be here after breakfast, along with Megan. I'm not sure what you girls want to do today.'

'I'd be happy to chill out. Maybe go for a swim or a walk along the beach.'

'Angus would like that too.' The little dog looked up and gave a short bark at the mention of his name and a walk.

'I miss Angus, too. Maybe we should get a dog, Lachlan.'

'You'll be busy enough with a baby, darling,' Poppy said.

'I suppose.'

Once breakfast was over, Lachlan disappeared to meet up with his dad and the other men, and Scarlett joined Poppy on the deck with coffee.

'I'm sure we're going to have a boy,' Scarlett said, patting her still flat stomach, 'and we plan to call him Taylor, for Dad.'

'Oh, Scarlett!' Poppy's eyes misted. 'But what if it's a girl?'

'I don't know, maybe Tayla? What do you think?'

'That's a lovely name, too.' Poppy imagined a tiny version of Jack running around, playing on the beach and getting into mischief just as Scarlett had.

There was a loud knock on the door, and Angus began to bark. Then Megan's voice called, 'Mum?' and she appeared on the deck, the little dog dancing around her ankles.

'Hey, you two. Oh,' she said,' seeing their mugs, 'coffee looks good. I brought some pastries. She held up a bag with the logo of the local patisserie.

'We've just finished breakfast,' Poppy began.

But Scarlett, said, 'Yum, I'll get some plates,' and joined Megan in going into the kitchen.

Poppy smiled. It was good to have her girls home again, even if only for a short time. Amber would be here soon too.

Just then, there was another knock on the door and the sound of her oldest daughter's voice. Going into the kitchen, Poppy saw Amber opening her arms to enfold both Megan and Scarlett.

'I'm so sorry for my behaviour last night,' she said. 'I was tired and sometimes… Anyway, I'm glad we're all together this weekend, and I promise not to do anything else to spoil it.'

Poppy gave a sigh of relief. 'We're having coffee with some pastries Megan brought. Will you have some?'

'Oh, yes please, Mum. I suppose you two are always hungry.'

Poppy smiled to herself. It was going to be okay. Amber seemed to have recovered from her upset of the previous evening. 'I'll leave you three with the pastries,' she said, smiling. 'I have a few things to take care of in the office, while you decide how you want to spend the day.'

'Okay, Mum,' Scarlett said, but Poppy could see they had already almost forgotten she was there. It had always been like that when the three of them were together. She was lucky they were such good friends, not all sisters were as close.

Once in her office, Poppy opened her computer. She had been so busy preparing for Scarlett's visit, she hadn't checked her emails for a couple of days and wanted to make sure there was nothing urgent she needed to take care of. She was able to quickly delete the usual collection of junk mail and was about to delete one from an unknown source when she stopped. It looked official. She opened it and stared at the contents. It was from a Sydney realtor with an offer to purchase *Crossings*.

*

Cam and the other men had boarded the flat-hulled boat he'd borrowed from Rory. It was more suited to the day's fishing he had in mind, and Rory was happy to let him use it. Like Poppy, Cam had taken the weekend off work to enable him to spend time with his son and the others. Although both Chris and Gavin were a few years older than Lachlan, they had all known each other growing up in Pelican Crossing, and now they were related, Cam was pleased to see them forming a close bond.

There was a fair amount of joking as they made their way out to sea, the two who had remained in their hometown teasing Lachlan that he had become a city dweller and forgotten his roots.

'Is that…?' Lachlan asked as they glided past the large motor cruiser at the far end of the marina. Several scantily clad women were sunning themselves on the deck, a group of men were drinking beer, and Jordan Butler was leaning on the rail. He waved at Cam as they passed on their way out to sea.

'Jordan Butler, yes.' Cam's lips tightened but he returned the man's wave.

'Sounds as if you don't like him, Dad.'

'I don't know the man well enough to form an opinion, but there's something about him I don't trust. It's not clear why he's here in Pelican Crossing, why he's staying so long. He says he's looking to move here, but it doesn't seem like his sort of place.'

'He doesn't fit in here,' Gavin said, screwing up his eyes as if to get a better look at the cruiser and its occupants. 'But we can't pin anything on him. He may just be what he says, Cam – a wealthy guy tired of city life, looking for somewhere quieter to settle down.'

'Hmm, maybe.' But Cam wasn't convinced. There was something about the man... and the news Poppy knew him... or had met him... didn't sit well with him. Now he'd had time to think, he did remember that two weeks when she'd gone to Sydney. Jack had been like a bear with a sore head, insufferable till Cam had finally told him to call Poppy if he was so unhappy without her. They'd become engaged as soon as she returned, and Cam had forgotten all about it till Poppy mentioned it. He wondered exactly how Poppy had met Butler and how well she'd known him.

Sixteen

Poppy and Cam stood together waving the young couple off. The remainder of the weekend had gone smoothly, and they were both sad to see Scarlett and Lachlan go, despite the couple promising to come back again soon.

'They look so happy.' Poppy turned to Cam and wiped away a tear. It had been such a wonderful weekend, so good to have all her chickens together again. Now she'd feel the emptiness of her house more than ever.

'Coffee?' Cam asked. 'I don't have to be back at the marina for a bit. You look as if you need it. In fact, you've seemed a bit distracted all weekend. I noticed it when we got back from fishing on Saturday.'

'It's… an email I received. I opened it when the girls were here on Saturday but didn't want to say anything.'

They walked inside, and Cam started up the coffee machine. He'd spent so much time there over the years, it must seem like a second home to him. Angus loved him and was nosing around his ankles in the hope of something to eat.

'Now,' Cam said, when they were seated on the deck with mugs of steaming coffee, 'what's this about an email?'

'It's a bit odd. It's from a real estate firm in Sydney with an offer to buy *Crossings*.'

'To buy…?' Cam raised one eyebrow. 'I didn't know you planned to sell.'

'I don't. This came completely out of the blue.' Poppy picked up her coffee. The offer had kept her awake for the past two nights. She'd refuse it, of course, but who wanted to buy her restaurant?

'Did they give you the name of their client?'

'No, that's what's puzzling me. They were very guarded about it, only mentioning they had received instructions to contact me, and the amount. Look.' She opened her phone and scrolled down to the email, then turned it towards Cam.

'Wow!' he said when he saw the figure, 'They're not joking. This would set you up for the rest of your life. You were talking about making more time for yourself...'

'But not like this.'

'You replied?'

'Not yet, but I'll refuse, of course. *Crossings* is part of me, a part of Jack still remaining. I'd never sell it. I live in hope that one of the girls might decide to become involved – or the grandchildren.' She smiled faintly. So far, none of her children had shown any interest in being involved in the restaurant, even when Scarlett had been doing the PR, *Crossings* was only one of her clients.

Cam looked at the email again. 'I recognise the name. It's a firm specialising in commercial properties, usually land and development.'

'That's odd. There's no land involved. The building which is now *Crossings* has been here all of my lifetime, and my parents'. Even before that. I remember Dad telling me one time. I think there are old documents in the attic, detailing the history of the place. We used to live above the restaurant.'

'I remember.'

'Of course you do.' Poppy could recall times when she and Gail, Cam and Jack, had snuck up to their apartment when both her parents had been busy in the restaurant. It had been fun to gather up there, the aroma of cooking filtering up from below, along with the sound of voices.

'Well, it's best to put it out of your mind.'

'I suppose.' But Poppy couldn't dismiss the feeling it wasn't over. The tone of the email and the amount offered was an indication that whoever wanted to buy the restaurant was serious about it. They might not take no for an answer.

'I'm glad Lachlan and Scarlett are dropping in on Gail on their way back. She needs all the support she can get.'

'Yes, I wish I could get away.' As she spoke, an idea began to take shape. Maybe she could. She'd been able to leave the restaurant to her staff all weekend, and it was never as busy on weekdays.

They spoke at the same time.

'Maybe...'

'Why not?'

They laughed.

'You were about to say?' Cam asked.

'Maybe I can get away. I tend to think I'm indispensable, but I may not be. I have a good crew in the restaurant. I'll need to go in today and check how it went over the weekend, but all being well, I might take a quick trip down to see Gail and Judy.'

'I'm sure she'd like that. Everything appeared to be running smoothly on Friday evening.'

'Mmm,' Poppy agreed, although it wasn't always easy to know what was going on behind the scenes. But now the idea of a trip to Sydney had been mooted, she was beginning to look forward to it. Maybe she could even combine it with a trip to Canberra to visit Scarlett.

As soon as Cam had left, Poppy took Angus for a walk along the beach. He was missing Scarlett, too. Her daughter spoiled the little dog, cuddling him and feeding him treats when she thought Poppy wasn't looking.

It was quiet on the beach. The summer tourists had only just begun to stream into town, and this was a little way from the main beach where they were able to swim safely between the flags. Poppy and Angus only met one other person, an elderly woman who was also walking her dog.

'Good morning, Agnes.' Poppy greeted the aging hippie, her long, white hair flowing in the breeze, unheeding of her long multi-coloured skirt trailing in the sea as she meandered slowly along in the shallow water at the edge of the ocean, her old spaniel padding along beside her. Agnes was an institution in Pelican Crossing. She owned a piece of land by the river where she cared for rescued and injured pelicans and other seabirds, dependent on donations and a grant from Parks and Wildlife to supplement her pension. She was also known for her friendly advice, knowledge accumulated through years of dealing with both the wild creatures and members of the local community. She had never married, often been known to claim she preferred to live alone with her winged friends, and she was surprisingly agile for someone who must be in her eighties.

'Good morning, Poppy, and a glorious morning it is. Did I hear you were going to become a grandmother? Which of your girls is pregnant? Let me see, there's Amber, Megan and Scarlett. Have I got that right?'

'You have, Agnes. Both Megan and Scarlett are pregnant. This time next year, I'll have two grandchildren.'

'Congratulations,' Agnes said, 'Is that why you're looking so... worried?'

Poppy wondered if she could read her mind. 'Not so much worried,' she said, 'more...'

Agnes nodded. 'It's a major thing, isn't it, a new life to help care for. Or in your case, two new lives.'

'Daunting,' Poppy said with a sigh.

'Don't dwell on it,' the old woman said. 'Someone with your constitution will sail through it.'

'I hope so,' Poppy said, wondering exactly what her constitution was. 'How are things with you?' she asked, changing the topic.

'The same as ever. The injured birds are an ongoing occurrence. It keeps me busy. And happy,' she added with a smile.

'Yes, I imagine it's very rewarding.'

'Keep smiling!' Agnes said and called for her dog.

Poppy sighed as the older woman continued on her way, the dog splashing along with her. Her life seemed so simple in comparison to Poppy's. She had her dog, her pelicans, and always appeared to be happy and contented. Maybe Poppy could learn a few things from Agnes on how to simplify her life.

Seventeen

'Thanks for the use of the boat, Rory,' Cam said to his assistant as soon as he walked into the office.

'No worries. Anytime. You only have to ask. Catch much?'

'Lachlan managed to catch a couple of snapper, proving he hasn't lost his touch. Chris and Gavin weren't so lucky, only a few flathead, too small to keep. But we had a good day. Saw that Butler chap on our way out into the bay. He doesn't seem to be in a hurry to leave.'

'He was in again on the weekend. Wanted to know how long we'd been here and had a few more questions about the town. He's a weird one. Not many visitors are interested in the history of the place.'

'Hmm.' Cam's suspicions were aroused again, but he couldn't put his finger on the reason. On the face of it, there was nothing wrong with someone asking about the town… or the marina.

'Glad you had a good day out. I guess you managed to catch enough for dinner.'

'We did.' Cam thought back to the barbecue they'd all enjoyed. On their return to the wharf, Lachlan and Chris had cleaned the fish, watched by a group of pelicans perched on the wooden posts, ready to swoop on any scraps which fell to the ground.

Then, after showering and changing, they'd joined the women at one of the council-owned barbecues on the grassy area above the beach, where he and Lachlan had cooked their catch. It had been a cheerful evening, without the emotions of the previous one.

'How's your dad?' Cam asked. He felt guilty he hadn't seen Rory's dad for some time. He and Jamie went back a long way. They'd been at school together, then Jamie had followed his father into the fishing industry, while Cam had chosen to study accountancy. He'd often envied his old schoolmate who had opted for an outdoor life, despite the hardship he often suffered. These days, Jamie had graduated from owning a fishing boat, to a larger vessel which offered fishing charters to the wealthy city-dwellers who visited Pelican Crossing. He also owned several smaller flat-hulled boats, similar to the one Cam had borrowed on the weekend, which he rented out.

'He's good,' Rory replied. 'Funny thing, though,' he rubbed his chin, 'he recently received an offer for the business. It gave him a shock. He hadn't considered selling up, not yet anyway. But it's made him think about the future. He wanted to know my opinion. He's spoken to Gary, too.'

'And?' Cam felt a twinge of concern. This, on the back of the offer made to Poppy... it was an odd coincidence though of course, there might be no connection.

'I'd never considered what I might do if... when... Dad decided to retire. I'm happy here, but I guess Gary and I could take it on between us, if his diving school gets underway.'

'I'd have thought Jamie's a long way off retirement. We're the same age.' Cam chuckled. It must have been a generous offer for his old mate to even consider it.

'Yeah.' Rory didn't elaborate.

No more was said as the pair went about their business. Cam was kept busy by a stream of enquiries about a new yacht for sale. In addition to managing the marina, he acted as a broker for individuals who wanted to sell their boats. They ranged from small tinnies to large ocean-going yachts and motor cruisers. Only last year he'd sold a whale-watching boat to a guy from Bellbird Bay who was interested in expanding his business.

After arranging for several viewings in the next few days, he headed over to *The Blue Dolphin Café* for a much-needed caffeine hit. While he'd often considered buying a coffee maker for the office, he found it was good to get away from the place from time to time.

He took his first sip of coffee and began to relax, his mind going over his conversation with Poppy. He hoped she'd take his advice to visit Gail. They had been such good friends, but Cam sensed they had grown apart over the years. He blamed himself. When he and Gail split up, he had expected his friends to take sides, and of course Jack took his... as did Poppy. She had always followed Jack's lead. Now, he regretted the impulse which had forced them apart.

His mind wandered to the offer for the restaurant. He supposed it wasn't so strange. It had received a lot of publicity recently, especially since it was featured on Channel Seven's *Weekender*. That feature had resulted in an increase in demand, of which he was aware from his management of the accounts. The resulting success had been bound to attract the interest of an interstate buyer. He wondered who it was, and if they would accept Poppy's refusal to sell. From his experience in business, he knew how persistent some business types could be.

'Hey, Cam. How're you going?'

Cam looked up to see his old mate, Jamie. The other man was carrying a takeaway coffee.

'I'm good. Was just talking about you with Rory. Join me?'

Jamie only hesitated for a moment before taking a seat opposite and placing his coffee on the table. 'Can't stop for long. I'm taking a group out after lunch. The guy from that big motor launch on the marina and his mates.'

'Jordan Butler?'

'That's the one. I thought they'd prefer to do their own thing, but I'm not about to turn away business.' He shrugged.

'How is business?' Cam felt guilty he hadn't spoken to Jamie for some time. He'd allowed himself to become sidetracked by the marina and Poppy. 'Rory told me you'd had an offer to buy it.'

'Yeah.' Jamie took a sip of coffee and turned the cup around a few times. 'Some Sydney hotshot probably thinks he can make a killing. But it's damned hard work. Not like the fishing boat where you can rely on your skill and your crew. I have to be polite to groups of well-heeled guys who haven't a clue what they're doing and only want to post photos of themselves on the internet with the big fish they've caught.'

'But you love it. Admit it.'

'Well...' Jamie looked sheepish, '... I don't need to get up at the crack of dawn to catch the tide or come home stinking of fish. It was what...' He paused.

Cam knew what he meant. Jamie's lifestyle had resulted in the end of his marriage. It was a sad state of affairs that shortly afterwards, he'd sold the fishing boat and started his charter business. But perhaps Jamie's lifestyle hadn't been the only reason for the marriage failing. His ex, Rory's mother, hadn't stayed around. She'd been off to the bright lights of Melbourne before the local gossips knew what was happening.

'So, this offer to buy,' Cam said, 'it came out of the blue?'

'Yeah,' Jamie said again. 'If it had been a year ago, I might have been interested, but business has picked up recently, and there's this new venture of Gary's. I'd like to have something to pass on to him and Rory when I'm done.'

'Mmm.' Jamie was lucky his sons had stayed in Pelican Crossing and, given Rory's earlier comments, could well be interested in taking over their dad's business. Although Cam was proud of what Lachlan had achieved, he regretted it had taken him all the way to the nation's capital. And now he was going to become grandfather to a child he'd rarely see. But that was life. He sighed.

'What about you? Rory tells me the marina is busy, and now you're brokering boat sales…'

'Keeps me out of mischief.' Cam drained his cup. 'Like you, I've no one waiting for me at home.'

Jamie nodded. 'We should catch up for a beer. It's been too long.'

'You're right. I'll give you a call. Now, I should be getting back.'

'Me too,' Jamie said, with a glance at his watch. 'Don't forget about that beer.'

'I won't.' Cam clapped his friend on the shoulder, then they went their separate ways, Cam pondering on how easy it was to lose touch, and the importance of old friends, as he made his way back to the marina.

Eighteen

Everything was going well at *Crossings* when Poppy arrived that evening. Pleased to see all the procedures she'd put in place were being followed, she made up her mind. First thing tomorrow, she'd call Gail and check flights to Sydney. It would be good to have a few days away, help her put things in perspective and forget the disturbing offer for the restaurant.

The restaurant was busy for a Monday evening, and she had little time to think of anything other than making sure the staff got the meals out in time, and the customers were all satisfied. It was a relief to lock the door behind her and drive home to where Angus was waiting for her, ready for a cuddle.

'Oh, Angus, what would I do without you,' she said to the little dog, as she swept him up into her arms. She missed Scarlett's company even more after the young couple had been with her for the weekend. Maybe she should take Amber's advice and look for somewhere smaller. Then her mind went back to the offer for the restaurant. Was it time to make a complete change? But she couldn't bear to think of selling what had been Jack's pride and joy – her parents' too. It would be like betraying all of them... and sullying Jack's memory. And what about all the effort she'd put into *Crossings* over the past five years? It had been what kept her alive, her reason to live, to get out of bed each morning, even when she felt all she wanted to do was curl up and die.

Too tired to do anything else, Poppy made herself a mug of hot chocolate and took it to bed with her, Angus padding behind her.

For once, she didn't force him back to his basket, glad to have some company, even if it was a small dog who couldn't talk to her.

*

Next morning, Poppy wakened to the sound of Angus barking at a couple of noisy myna birds outside her window. The sun was shining brightly.

Breakfast over, Poppy changed into a dress, determined to face whatever the day had to offer looking her best. Then she picked up the phone and entered Gail's number.

But the call with Gail didn't go the way she'd expected.

'Gail,' Poppy bit her lip. It was too long since she'd been in touch. 'I'm sorry I haven't called before now. It's been…' But she had no excuse. She had called after the wedding, but not since then. 'Cam told me Judy's failing. How are you coping? I thought I might come down to see you both.'

There was no response. She waited.

Then, 'Now's not a good time. Jude could go any day. I only leave her side to fetch food or water. I want to spend as much time with her as I can. While it was good of Lachlan and Scarlett to stop in, and it was nice to see them, I resented my time away from Jude. I'm sorry, Poppy. Maybe later, after…'

'Oh Gail. I hadn't realised.' Poppy's throat tightened. 'It must be so difficult for you…' Her voice trailed off. What could she say? She understood grief, but not grief of this sort. Jack had gone so suddenly. She remembered the time after his death, how she'd felt.

The days and weeks passed in a blur. Poppy was vaguely aware of her three girls moving around her darkened bedroom, of their softened voices murmuring to each other, of them bringing in dishes of food which she returned uneaten. Until finally one day when she opened her eyes, she noticed the curtains which had been closed were open and the sunlight was shining in. She blinked. Beside her bed was a plate of toast, thinly spread with vegemite and a soft boiled egg. It was nursery food, invalid food, and suddenly Poppy felt hungry. Nothing had really changed. Jack would never come back. But she had a restaurant to run. It was what Jack would expect her to do and she couldn't let him down.

She didn't make an immediate recovery, but from that day she slowly regained strength, her energy, her will to live, and the determination to do whatever it took to make *Crossings* a restaurant Jack would be proud of.

And she had. The restaurant had given her a reason to live. But what would be left for Gail when Judy was gone? Rachel would understand. She too had cared for a partner through his terminal illness. But she'd had her children to support her, whereas Gail had no one.

'Are you sure, Gail? Surely it would help to have someone to support you when…?' She couldn't say the word, mention what they both knew was about to happen. Strange how one felt awkward mentioning death, when it was inevitable, when it happened to everyone eventually. But it was as if by mentioning it, one brought it closer.

'I'm sure. Thanks for calling, for thinking of us, but… I need to get back to Jude.'

'I understand. Let me know if there's anything…' But Poppy was talking to an empty space. Gail had hung up.

'Oh, Angus,' Poppy said. 'Poor Gail. I wish I could do something to help.' Angus gave a small whine, as if he understood, and nuzzled closer to her. 'At least I have you,' she said, reaching down to fondle his ears, 'and the girls… and Cam.' Thinking of Cam, she had a sudden urge to talk to him. She picked up her phone, then put it down again. A phone call wouldn't do. She needed to speak to him face-to-face.

*

Cam was feeling frazzled. There had been another incidence of vandalism overnight. This time the target had been the motor cruiser belonging to Jordan Butler, and he was not amused. He'd stormed into the office as soon as it opened, demanding Cam do something about it. Cam had called the police, who had responded around an hour later, dismissing it as just another sign of bored teenagers. Butler had not been pleased, threatening to take the matter further and declaring he had friends in high places.

Cam wasn't sure what these supposed friends could do, but it did weaken his suspicions Butler might have something to do with the other acts of vandalism. He still wasn't sure why he mistrusted the man. There was no reason to do so. It was just a gut feeling, and Cam always trusted his gut feelings. They'd never let him down yet.

But despite his dislike of the man, he'd promised to arrange for the splashes of paint to be removed and for a cleanup of the rubbish which had been thrown onto the deck, presumably when all the occupants were asleep. He hoped that would be an end to it but decided to have a quiet word with the local police about keeping a closer eye on the marina overnight. Maybe Poppy's son-in-law, Gavin, would help. It was a pity he hadn't been the one to respond to his call that morning.

He was about to take a break, and was thinking about his last conversation with Poppy, wondering if she had contacted Gail, if she was going to take a trip to Sydney, when she pushed open the door.

'Poppy! This is a surprise. Don't usually see you down this way. Is there a problem?' He rose to greet her with a peck on the cheek, wishing he dared show more affection.

'I needed to see you. I spoke with Gail. It sounds as if Jude's in a bad way. I…'

'Come here.' He pulled her into a warm hug, loving the feel of her body against his. Sensing her tense, he released her. 'Sorry, you sounded as if you needed a hug.'

'I did. Thanks. Can we talk?' She looked around the office.

'I was about to have a coffee. Why don't we go across to the café? We can talk more privately there. Rory,' he called through to the back office, 'I'm just off for a coffee with Poppy. Call me if you need me.'

'Righto,' Rory's voice came back.

'Thanks,' Poppy said as they made their way to the café. 'I didn't mean to take you away from work.'

'I was in need of a break anyway. It's been quite a morning. Another attack of vandalism, a visit from the police…' He shook his head. 'It seems never-ending.'

'They haven't found the culprits?'

'Not yet, and last night they targeted Butler's motor cruiser. He's not happy and blames the marina for not taking due care. We'll arrange the cleanup, of course, but it's all cutting into our profit.'

'I'm sorry.'

By this time, they'd reached the café and were seated at their usual table from where Cam could keep an eye on the comings and goings at the marina.

'Skinny cappuccino?'

'You know me so well.'

Cam ordered the coffees and two slices of carrot cake. It seemed to have been a long time since breakfast which had only consisted of a couple of slices of toast with vegemite. Poppy looked as if she could do with something to eat too.

'Thanks,' she said, when their order arrived.

'Now, what's bothering you? Are you off to Sydney?'

'No. As I said, I called Gail, but… She sounded very down, Cam. She says she doesn't want anyone there. She wants to spend all her time with Judy, but… I wish…' She played around with her spoon, avoiding his eyes. 'Do you think I should go anyway?'

Cam thought for a moment. He could understand Poppy's feelings. 'No,' he said, 'we have to respect Gail's wishes. I think I can understand her desire to spend as much time as she can with Judy before it's too late. Having someone else there would mean she'd have to try to be polite when all she wants to do is take care of the woman she loves. It sounds as if they may not have much longer together.'

'You may be right.' Poppy sighed. 'You usually are. I remember how, when Jack died, you understood exactly how I felt. You knew when I wanted to be alone and when I was ready to pick up the reins at *Crossings* again. You're a good man, Cameron Mitchell.' She smiled.

Cam's heart leapt at the unexpected compliment, just as Poppy's phone pinged. 'Do you want to get that?'

'It's just an email,' Poppy said, checking her phone. 'Oh!'

'What?'

'It's from Hammond and Erskine – the people who sent me the offer for *Crossings*. They're probably only acknowledging my reply.'

'Why don't you check?'

Poppy opened her phone and scanned the screen. 'How odd,' she said, raising her eyes to meet his. 'They've upped the offer. They're now offering…' Her eyes widened as she looked down again at the screen. She turned the phone to show Cam.

He read the figure and whistled. 'They're not messing around, are they? This is serious money.'

'The last one was too.' Poppy bit her lip. 'This morning, before I rang Gail, I was wondering if it was time for a change, to stop rattling around in that big house with only Angus for company, but this…'

'Makes you want to sell up?'

'Quite the opposite. If someone thinks *Crossings* is worth that much, then I must be doing something right. The house is one thing, but the restaurant is something else, and I have no intention of selling it, no matter how much this client of theirs wants to offer.'

Nineteen

Poppy dressed in her best jeans and a pink and white striped top. She pulled her hair into a low ponytail, dabbed on some lipstick and fixed a pair of gold hoops in her ears. Gazing at herself in the mirror, she grimaced. She found it difficult to believe she was soon to become a grandmother. Picking up her bag and slinging it over her shoulder, she told Angus to behave before heading out to the car.

Poppy was thrilled Megan had asked her to go baby shopping with her. She was still feeling helpless after her call to Gail, when Megan rang to suggest it, since Gavin was going down to Bellbird Bay with a few mates to take part in the triathlon on the October long weekend. Poppy had been surprised her daughter wasn't going too. In previous years, Megan had gone with her husband to cheer him on, but she said she didn't have the energy this year; her feet were beginning to swell and her back ached. She couldn't face standing in the crowd to watch the event. But she could manage a day of shopping where she'd be able to stop and sit down if she became tired.

Megan was still getting ready when Poppy arrived at the small house the young couple had purchased a year earlier and were justifiably proud of. When they bought it, it had been owned by the same family for several generations, and like many such homes in Pelican Crossing, was in need of renovation. It soon became apparent to Poppy that Gavin had a number of unexpected skills. Before joining the police force, he'd often helped his father out in his building yard, so he'd been able to do much of the work himself, with Megan helping out where she could.

'I won't be a minute,' she said to Poppy when she opened the door, 'and there's something I want to show you before we go.'

'Okay.' Curious, Poppy followed her into the kitchen, Megan leaving her there to finish dressing. While she was waiting, Poppy, seeing the dirty breakfast dishes in the sink, and knowing the young couple hadn't yet installed a dishwasher, filled the sink and washed up, setting them to dry on the wooden rack on the draining board.

'Oh, Mum, you didn't need to do that. I was going to... But thanks.'

'It was no trouble. Did Gavin leave early?'

'He went last night. He's staying down there with a mate and will drive back tomorrow. I expect they'll put away a few beers after the race. It'll do him good to let off a bit of steam. He's had a busy time recently with the spate of vandalism.'

'Mmm. Cam told me about that... at the marina. Is it still going on?'

'Not only the marina. Some of the businesses in Main Street have been hit, too. Gav's boss thinks it's teenagers, but Gav's not so sure. He thinks it's too targeted to be youngsters out for a bit of fun.'

'Oh!' Poppy remembered Cam saying something similar.

'Anyway, let's not bother about that now. Come and see my latest project.' She led Poppy into the small back bedroom. Last time Poppy had been here, the room had been filled with boxes. When she walked in, her eyes widened. The walls had been painted a pale green, and a frieze of nursery creatures had been added at eye-height. The only furniture was a low white cane chair. 'Wow!' she said. 'You did this?'

'You like it?' Megan grinned. 'All it needs is a cot and change table and we'll be ready for the sinker.'

'Don't call the baby that!' But Poppy couldn't help smiling. 'It's amazing. You've done a wonderful job, darling.' She gave her daughter a hug.

'Gav's done so much of the rest of the house, I wanted to do this room myself. I hope Baby likes it.' She gazed around as if picturing her baby there.

'I'm sure he or she will. You still don't want to find out?'

Megan shook her head. 'No, we want it to be a surprise. We don't care whether it's a boy or a girl, as long as it's healthy. I know Scarlett feels differently.'

'That's no surprise. You two have always seen things differently.'

Megan's expression suddenly became more serious. 'How's Amber taking it all? Last time we spoke, I could tell she was trying hard to be happy for me, but I was sure she was hurting inside.'

'It's difficult for her, but her turn will come.' Poppy hoped fervently she was right. 'There's no way of rushing these things and…'

'She said she was trying some new thing, not IVF, but something similar.'

'Yes. Let's hope for her sake that it works, and she gets pregnant, too.'

'Then you'll have three grandchildren to fuss over.'

'Don't! You're all making me feel old. Imagine… me, a grandmother!' It was Poppy's turn to become serious. 'Your dad would have been so thrilled. He'd have loved to be a grandad.'

'Yeah.' Megan clasped Poppy's hand so tightly, her rings cut into the skin.

'Now, we should go.' Poppy released her hand and patted her daughter's. 'I think you said you wanted to visit Purdies?' The large store which aimed to rival IKEA had recently opened just outside town and was a popular addition to the local retail outlets.

'Yes, I've checked out their catalogue online and love the simple lines of their cots and change tables. Gav has promised to put them together in plenty of time for the baby.'

'Okay, let's go.'

*

'Wow!' Poppy said, when she pulled into the large carpark. 'I didn't think it would be so big.'

'Not as big as IKEA,' Megan laughed. 'Last time we drove down to Brisbane, we stopped at the one in North Lakes, and we got lost when we tried to leave. This one is small in comparison.'

'If you say so, honey.' It looked big to Poppy.

Once inside, Megan picked up a store guide, and they set off to find the section they were looking for, pausing several times on the way to admire the various displays.

'What do you think, Mum?' Megan asked when they came to the section containing baby furniture. She pointed to a white cot with a drawer underneath and a matching baby table. 'See, the baby table can be turned into a chest of drawers and a wall shelf when the sinker gets bigger.'

'I wish you wouldn't call your baby that. The name might stick.'

'Of course it won't. It's just like the picture in the catalogue,' Megan said, running her hand over the white surface of the change table, her eyes glazing over as if imagining her baby lying on it. 'We'll need a cot mattress too, and…'

'Oh, look at this,' Poppy picked up a soft green caterpillar which turned out to be a musical toy, 'and this.' She put down the caterpillar to pick up a mobile with soft figures inspired by nature. 'I must get these.'

By the time they reached the bistro, where they intended to have lunch, they had quite a collection of soft toys which Poppy insisted would be her gift for the new baby, and Megan had taken note of the reference numbers for the larger items she intended to purchase.

'I think we can count this as a successful trip,' Poppy said, as they enjoyed the coffee and salmon filled bagels they'd chosen from the menu.

'I noticed you picked up two of everything.' Megan chuckled. 'I'm guessing you're shopping for Scarlett's baby, too.'

'It's too good an opportunity to miss. I just wish…' Poppy bit her lip. She hadn't meant to spoil their shopping expedition by mentioning Amber.

'I know.' Megan sighed. 'I wish there was something I could do to help Amber. She's always been there to help us, to show us the way. Now it will be Scarlett and me who become parents first. It doesn't seem fair.'

'Life's not always fair, darling.' Poppy was thinking of her own loss, Rachel's, and Gail's approaching loss of Judy.

'But you've got over the loss of Dad.'

'Oh, sweetheart, I'll never get over it, not completely. I'll always love your dad, but life goes on, and soon there will be your baby and Scarlett's to love too.'

'I know. It's strange to think he'll never know them, and my baby won't know him either.' She seemed to think for a moment, then said, 'Would you ever... I don't know... think of getting married again?'

Poppy was too stunned to reply immediately, then she said slowly, 'I don't know. Perhaps. If the right person came along. But... he'd have to be pretty special.' Cam's image flitted through her head, before she dismissed it. He was special, but not for her.

'I guess.' She gave Poppy a sideways glance. 'Uncle Cam's pretty special.'

A wave of heat threatened to overpower Poppy. 'Yes, he is, Megan, but we're just good mates. He was your dad's best friend.'

'Maybe it's what Dad would want. He's been gone for five years now, and Uncle Cam's on his own, too. Amber and I were talking...'

'That's enough!' Poppy couldn't believe this conversation. Her daughters had been talking about her and Cam, making up all sorts of unrealistic scenarios. 'There's no way we could ever be more than friends.' Even if she wished there was. 'Now, if we're done here, we should head to the checkout and get our purchases organised. It may take us a bit of time to work out how to fit everything into the car.'

'Okay.' But Megan gave her a strange look, as if she could read her mind and didn't believe her when she denied being anything other than friends with Cam.

Twenty

Two weeks had passed since Poppy had told Cam about her call to Gail, and there had been no news. He texted Gail regularly, but the reply was always *no change*. She had promised to let him know when it happened, so it was only a matter of time before he received the grim news that the silent killer had taken one more victim.

Meantime, for Cam, life went on as usual in Pelican Crossing. He met Poppy for breakfast on Sundays and lunched at *Crossings* a couple of times each week. In addition, the pair met for dinner at various spots along the coast, had the occasional coffee together and had gone sailing a few times. Cam's hope of a closer relationship was no nearer to coming to fruition, but he was grateful for their good friendship.

He was relieved there had been no further acts of vandalism. It might be that the regular police presence had frightened off the culprits, or they may have decided to find their enjoyment elsewhere. Whatever the reason, the marina was now free from their mischief-making.

The one thing that did bother Cam, was the continued presence of Jordan Butler and his vessel in the marina. Each morning he looked out, hoping to see a space where the motor cruiser had been berthed, but it was still there, although the bevy of skimpily clad women seemed to have disappeared.

It was no surprise one morning to be awakened by the call from Gail to tell him of Judy's passing. Cam was still half asleep when his phone rang, in that strange zone between asleep and awake, not quite one or the other, where he might have thought he was dreaming, if he hadn't been expecting the call.

'Cam, Jude's gone!' Gail's voice broke and she began to sob. 'She passed away in my arms an hour ago. She was sleeping peacefully, and her breathing just stopped. What am I going to do?'

Cam's heart sank. No matter how anticipated a death might be, it was still a shock when it happened. 'Oh, Gail, I'm so sorry. Do you have anyone with you? You shouldn't be alone at a time like this.'

'We have friends I can call on, but none of us would have any idea of what to do next. We've never been in this position before. And I don't think I can... Could you... I'm sorry. It's a lot to ask, but...'

Cam didn't have to think twice. 'Of course I can come and help. I know the procedures. I went through it all when Mum passed... and Jack. I just have to put a few things in place here.'

'Oh, would you? I wouldn't ask, but...'

'Of course I'll help, Gail. You have called a doctor... to get the death certificate?' He felt awkward stating it so plainly, but it had to be done.

'Not yet, but I will. When...?'

'I'll text you when I have a flight booked, and I'll hire a car at the airport. Hopefully, I can be there by tomorrow at the latest.'

'Thanks,' Gail said through her tears.

When the call ended, Cam stared into space, the rows of boats in the marina only a blur. He had been expecting this news for so long, it was almost a relief. But it wouldn't be for Gail. For her it was a disaster, the end of the loving relationship for which she'd thrown away her marriage to Cam and, for a time, the love of her son. He wondered if Lachlan knew. He should call. He picked up his phone again.

'Hey, Dad,' Lachlan's cheerful voice answered. 'What's up?'

'It's sad news, Lachlan.'

'What's...? Oh, is it Judy? Mum said she didn't have long when we were there, and it's been a few weeks.'

'Yes,' Cam sighed, 'your mum just called to let me know. I'm heading down to Sydney as soon as I can book a flight.'

'You are? Why are *you* going?'

'Your mum's in no state to take care of the arrangements, and it sounds as if none of their friends have a clue what to do.'

'But Dad...'

'It's the least I can do, son. Your mum loved Judy. She needs help, my help. It's not an easy time for her.'

'I realise that, Dad, but *you?*'

'I've known your mum for most of my life. Who else would she ask? If she hadn't asked, I'd have offered.'

'Trust you. What does Poppy think?'

'Poppy? What does she have to do with it?'

There was a pause, then, 'Scarlett and I thought… when we were up there… that there might be something between you two. We'd be happy for you if there was.'

'No, nothing like that,' Cam said, reddening, and glad Lachlan couldn't see his face. 'We're good friends. We always have been. You know that. Jack and I…'

'I know, you and Jack, Mum and Poppy. We've heard about it often enough. But now you and Mum are divorced, and Uncle Jack's been gone for five years, we thought, maybe…'

'Scarlett hasn't mentioned this to Poppy?' Cam's heart plummeted at the thought.

'I doubt it. You can rest easy. But how do you know it's not what Aunt Poppy wants?'

'Believe me, son. If she did, I'd know.' But would he? Although he and Poppy had been to seeing more of each other, there had been no hint of anything other than friendship from her, and he'd been very circumspect with holding his own feelings in check. What if…? 'Has Scarlett said anything about her mum to make you think otherwise?'

'Not really,' Lachlan hedged. 'We just thought it would be ace if you did get together. You'd make a great couple.'

'Hmm.'

'Well, let me know how Mum is, and if you want any moral support, I can maybe…' But Lachlan sounded doubtful.

'Thanks, son, but I think I can manage, though you might want to come for the funeral. Your mum has a group of women friends who'll no doubt rally round to support her. I'll just make the necessary arrangements, then I'll be coming back home.' *To Poppy*, he thought, Lachlan's words affecting him more than liked. Maybe it was time to make an attempt to take things further with her, to become more that just Jack's old mate. He thought of something he'd read somewhere

– *faint heart never won fair lady.* 'I'll call you from Sydney,' he said, mindful Lachlan was still on the phone.

*

Poppy had just returned from walking Angus along the beach and was settling down in her office to check her emails, when Angus started barking and running to the door. With a sigh, Poppy got up and went to see who was there.

'Cam,' she said, her face widening into a smile of delight, when she opened it to see him standing there. 'What brings you here at this time?' She saw his expression. 'Is it…?'

'Sad news, I'm afraid.'

'Judy?'

'Yes.'

'Oh, I'm sorry. We knew it was coming but one's never prepared. How's Gail?'

By this time, he had followed her into the house. They were standing in the kitchen, Angus running between them.

Cam took a seat. 'In pieces, as you might expect. I've promised to go down and offer what help I can.'

'Of course. Would you like me to…' In her head, Poppy started to list all the things she'd have to cancel if she was to accompany him to Sydney, starting with lunch which was to be held at Gill's today.

'Not this time, Poppy, though it's good of you to offer. Gail and Judy have a group of women friends who'll rally round. I'm only going to make the funeral arrangements and such. I don't intend to be gone for long. Maybe, after it's all over…'

'Right.' That was what Gail had suggested. "After" she'd said. 'When will you go?'

'As soon as I can. I'm booked on a flight this afternoon. Rory can take care of things at the marina. There's nothing else to keep me back.'

Poppy's heart dropped. But of course, he was right. Why should she expect him to consider her, that she'd miss him? 'Sounds good,' she said. 'But you've time for a cup of tea?' If he was going to be gone for several days, she wanted to spend some time with him before he left.

'A quick one.'

Poppy put on the kettle and took a couple of mugs and two peppermint teabags out of the cupboard. She knew he wasn't a big fan of herbal teas but did like peppermint.

They took their tea out on to the deck, a subdued Angus following as if he knew this was not a time for his customary exuberance.

'Poor Gail,' Poppy said. 'She and Judy seemed to be so happy together. Life deals some dreadful blows.' She thought about Jack, how his life had been cut short in an instant. At least Gail and Judy had had time to prepare, though did that make it any easier?

'Yeah.' Cam dropped both hands, clutching his mug, between his knees and stared at the wooden deck.

'Do you… do you know when you'll be back?' Poppy was aware how funeral arrangements could take time and, while she was sympathetic towards Gail, and understood Cam's desire to be there to help and support her, she *had* left him. His life was here.

'I don't know.' He shook his head and looked up to meet her eyes.

Her heart leapt. Did she imagine what she saw there?

'I guess I'll be there for as long as it takes, but all going well, I should be back by next Tuesday.'

'I'm counting on it. Melbourne Cup Day wouldn't be the same without you. Since Jack…'

'I know. I promise to be there if I possibly can.'

That was enough for Poppy. Like Jack, Cam was a man who kept his promises.

They sat in silence for a time, then he rose to go.

'Give Gail my love. I'll call her,' Poppy said as they stood at the door.

'I'm sure she'd like that.' Cam looked at her again with the same expression as before, then he pulled her into a warm hug, sending a thrill right down to her toes. When they parted, he looked at her again. 'Poppy, when I get back… we need to talk. I… Now's not the time, but… You'll be here?'

'Always.' Did Cam mean what she thought he did? Were all her dreams going to come true?

He stroked a strand of hair out of her eyes and tucked it behind her ear. Their eyes met, his face so close to hers, she could see the flecks of colour in his eyes. Her breath caught. Was he about to kiss her, kiss her properly, on the lips? Her heart thudded so loudly she thought Cam must be able to hear it. But he pulled away and gave her his usual peck on the cheek. 'When I get back,' he said again, touching her cheek gently, his smile so warm it sent warmth flooding through her. Then, before she could reply, he was gone, striding off to his car.

Poppy stood in the doorway watching Cam drive away, a finger on the spot on her cheek Cam had touched. Could Cam have been trying to say that when he returned, he... they...? She hugged herself with excitement.

Twenty-one

Poppy was still encased in the bubble of happiness Cam's words had created, but she couldn't stop thinking about Gail as she got ready to go to lunch. She was still thinking about her friend as she drove across town to the townhouse Gill and Max had purchased before they separated and which Gill was determined to hang on to. It was in a new development on the outskirts of town, still close enough to walk to the main street and the marina but away from the tourist trail.

Poor Gail, Poppy thought. Now she had joined the rank of single women. Poppy hadn't known Judy well, but she did know how much Gail loved her. It must have taken a lot to have thrown away her marriage and risked losing her son. Poppy had been shocked when it happened. She and Gail had been friends since primary school; she thought she knew her. But how well do we ever know anyone?

As she drew into the parking lot outside Gill's home, Rachel's car stopped next to hers.

'You're looking very solemn today,' Rachel said. 'Who's died?'

'My old friend Gail's partner.'

'Oh, I'm sorry. I didn't mean... I've heard you talk about Gail. Wasn't her partner the one who had breast cancer?'

'That's right. We've been expecting it, but...' She shook her head.

'It's always a shock. I can sympathise with her. When Kirk went...' She put a hand on Poppy's arm. 'Your friend was married to Cam, wasn't she?'

'Yes. He's going down to Sydney to help with the arrangements.'

And he's going to be gone for some time. Although she hadn't been in the habit of seeing, or even talking to Cam every day, she'd always known he was there, just across the bay at the marina. She'd been able to sit on her deck and imagine him sitting in his office, peering at his computer – he'd always refused to wear glasses – and dragging a hand through his thick white hair. She'd never been to Gail's Sydney home. She couldn't imagine him there, and even if she could, he'd be too far away for her to join him.

'That's mighty noble of him… after she left him.'

'Cam's like that.' Jack wouldn't have been so magnanimous if she'd been in Gail's position. It was another difference between the two men.

'Will you be going down for the funeral?'

'I don't think so. I didn't really know Judy, and Gail and she have a circle of friends there. I'd feel out of place. I may go down later.'

'Good idea. Your friend is probably feeling out of it right now. I remember after Kirk died, I went around in a daze for ages. You know what it's like, too.'

'Mmm.' She gazed into space, remembering…

'Are you all right?' Rachel's voice brought Poppy back to the present.

'Sorry, I was remembering. You're right. For a while, I didn't know which end was up.'

'But you recovered and look at you now. You should be proud of what you've achieved.'

Poppy sighed. She'd had *Crossings*, Jack's legacy. Gail didn't have that.

'We should go in. Gill will be wondering where we are.'

'Okay.'

The two women made their way into the two-storey building which was located on the edge of the development, in a prime position facing the river. There were several people walking along the pathway and a mother supervising two small children who were feeding ducks, despite notices instructing people not to do so. Poppy could remember bringing Amber, Megan and Scarlett down here, long before the development was ever thought of.

When Poppy pushed open the door, she could hear Liz's voice. She grimaced at Rachel, who grinned back. Liz was always the loudest member of the group.

When they walked into the living area, Liz was still talking.

'I couldn't believe it,' she said. 'You read about these things, but when it actually happens…' Liz turned to greet them. 'Hi, you two. I was just telling Gill about the text this guy sent me, with an image of…'

'I don't think they want to hear about that,' Gill interrupted. 'Liz's finally taken the plunge and joined Happy Hearts,' she said, laughing. 'I think she may be regretting it.'

'I'll certainly have something to say to Mandy next time I see her,' Liz said. 'She told me Happy Hearts was one of the most reputable dating sites. If it's one of the best, I dread to think what the others are like.'

'I told you,' Gill said, while Poppy and Rachel grinned.

'I know, I know. You warned me, too, Poppy. But Mandy was so insistent. I only did it to please her.'

'Did you actually go on a date with one of them?' Poppy asked. 'Thanks, Gill,' she said, accepting a glass of wine.

'Two of them. They were such creeps. I had no intention of seeing either of them again, then…'

'They can imagine,' Gill said quickly, to stem further revelations.

Poppy could. She'd heard stories of such things from her staff. Even Michelle had been caught out by unscrupulous men who imagined women were titillated by images of their private parts. She shuddered at the thought. 'Well, I guess you won't be continuing your search.'

'I've already cancelled my membership,' Liz said. 'I should have listened to you guys. I'd rather stay single.'

'What's been happening with you two?' Gill asked.

'Poppy's friend's partner has passed away,' Rachel said. 'We were talking about it on the way in, about how the death of a loved one can knock you for six.'

'Sorry, Poppy,' Liz said. 'You didn't need to hear about my dating disasters.'

'Actually, it's cheered me up,' Poppy said, realising that it had. For a few moments she'd been able to forget about Gail, about Cam going to Sydney, even the memory of Jack had faded as they'd laughed about Liz's disastrous experience with the dating site. 'Cam's gone down to Sydney to help with the arrangements,' she said, repeating what she'd already told Rachel. She loved having an excuse to say his name.

'Of course,' Gill nodded. 'He was married to Gail. I...'

'You handled their divorce.' Poppy remembered.

'It was an easy one. All very amicable. But I could see how upset he was. It must have been a shock.'

'To all of us. We grew up together. There was never any sign that...'

'When you've seen as many marriages break up as I have, nothing would surprise you,' Gill said, a note of bitterness in her voice.

'I'm sorry, Gill. Is Max still being difficult?'

'Difficult doesn't begin to describe it. But let's talk about something more cheerful. What's everyone wearing to the Melbourne Cup lunch at *Crossings?*'

Poppy was glad to take part in the conversation about the event to be held the following week, which lasted through the meal of quiche and salad served on Gill's elegant glass-topped dining table. Unlike Poppy's home, which was still furnished as it had been when she and Jack first moved in and had survived three growing children, Gill and Max had moved here after their daughter left home and chosen an austere Scandinavian style. It suited them, but always made Poppy feel as if she had wandered into a furniture store.

They had just finished coffee and the delicious slices of orange coated in chocolate which Gill served with it, when Rachel checked her watch. 'I'm afraid I have to leave,' she said. 'I have new guests arriving this evening and I still have their room to prepare.' After her husband died, Rachel had started taking guests for bed and breakfast, explaining to anyone who asked, that the house was too big for her on her own, and the company stopped her grieving. Now, two years later, she had developed a successful business which kept her busy when she wasn't helping look after her grandchildren.

Everyone dealt with loss in different ways, Poppy thought as she, Liz and Rachel prepared to leave. For her and Rachel, it had been work that got them through and continued to do so. It wasn't the same for Liz and Gill. Their husbands were still alive, choosing to live with other partners; their grief was different but no less painful, maybe even more so. Poppy had seen Cam's distress when Gail left.

Poppy wondered how Gail would deal with it, when the initial tsunami of grief began to lessen, when she came to accept Judy was gone. She knew nothing about their life in Sydney, apart from the fact she and Judy had both found teaching positions there. She presumed there would be a period of compassionate leave, then what? As she'd promised Cam, she'd make time to go down to visit. Maybe it would help Gail to see an old friend, one who wasn't part of her life with Judy, her new life, as Poppy thought of it.

'Still thinking about your friend?' Rachel asked, when they reached their cars. 'She'll be fine. We women always are... eventually. It's why women have babies. We're resilient. We know that life goes on, regardless of what it throws at us.'

'You may be right.'

'I am. Trust me. We survived, didn't we?' Rachel got into her car and gave Poppy a wave a she drove off.

But, as she pressed the ignition, Poppy wasn't so sure. Gail had always been more emotional than her, more liable to be crushed when things went wrong. What if she couldn't pick herself up again after this? What could Poppy, who'd always been the stronger of the two, do to help?

Twenty-two

It didn't take Cam long to pack, throwing a couple of shirts and some clean underwear into a bag, along with a pair of jeans and his toiletries. He'd travel in the suit he'd need for the funeral but wanted something more casual to change into. He'd been lucky to find a place on the afternoon flight which would get him into Sydney early evening. Rory had been happy to take on the extra responsibility for however long it took, but Cam didn't expect to be away for more than a few days, just long enough to make the necessary arrangements and attend Judy's funeral.

The flight was comfortable, but Cam found it difficult to relax, his last moments with Poppy going around and around in his head. Had he said too much... too little? Should he have kissed her? He had been so close, breathing in her familiar fragrance, her lips so tempting. But he had pulled back, realising he had to leave. Now he was cursing himself for being a fool.

His mind went to what was ahead of him. Gail had sounded dreadful, and he wasn't looking forward to being in a house of mourning. He'd never visited her and Judy there, never had any reason to. Initially, when she left, he'd been filled with bitterness, then as he came to accept her decision, to realise it wasn't about him, their lives had been so different, there had been no reason to make the trip to Sydney.

He knew the city, of course. He had spent three years at university there, before returning to Queensland to work. He hadn't been back and expected it had changed a lot since then.

As the red rooftops of Sydney appeared beneath him, Cam thought back to his time there as a student. They had been heady days, experiencing the freedom of being away from home, the opportunity to do whatever he wanted with no risk of his parents finding out. But, even then, he had been more moderate in his behaviour than many of the other students, than Jack would have been in the same position. He had never attended any of the wild parties his friends had boasted about or experimented with the drugs that seemed to be all too available. And he had rarely ventured beyond the confines of the university campus or the surrounding suburb.

He checked the address Gail had given him all that time ago, when she and Judy had set up home together. It was situated close to the university in Redfern, an area which had now become trendy having once been a working-class suburb with a large Aboriginal community. Gail had suggested he stay with her, saying she'd like the company, and he'd agreed, though he was uncomfortable with the idea. It was a long time since he and Gail had shared a home. But at least he was familiar with this part of Sydney – or had been thirty years ago.

As the pilot announced they were about to land, Cam took a deep breath and prepared himself to meet his ex-wife and to comfort her for the loss of her partner.

*

Cam's head almost touched the roof of the little Honda Civic he'd rented at the airport, as he drove through the heavy Sydney traffic, then searched for somewhere to park close to Gail's home. At this time of the evening, it seemed that most of the occupants of the houses on the street had already taken their usual spots, and he considered himself lucky when he found one. Taking his bag from the back seat he headed to number thirty-two.

'Cam! You came!' Gail greeted him, a very different version of Gail from the one he remembered. Her hair was unkempt, her face streaked with tears, the bags under her eyes evidence of broken sleep, if she'd had any at all since Judy's passing.

Cam dropped his bag and pulled her into a warm hug, noticing how frail she felt, as if she would break if he hugged her too tightly. It felt strange to have her in his arms again after so long. 'I told you I would,' he said. 'Didn't you believe me?'

'I did, but…' She shook her head. 'Everything has been such a blur. I wondered if I'd imagined it.' She led him through the hallway into a large room which had clearly once been divided into two. A group of women were sitting there. They stared at him. 'These are our friends,' she said to Cam, then, 'This is Cam. I told you about him. He and I were once married – a long time ago.'

Cam felt uncomfortable, being the focus of attention of the group of women, all of whom had known Gail and Judy as a couple. 'Hello,' he said awkwardly, as Gail introduced each of them, knowing he'd have trouble remembering their names.

'We were just leaving,' one of them said. 'We'll see you tomorrow, Gail.' They all hugged Gail who went with them to the door.

'They've kept me sane,' Gail said when she returned. 'I couldn't have survived without them. But none of us have a clue how to go about arranging the funeral.' She broke down.

'Hey, it's okay. That's what I'm here for. How about a cup of tea?' Cam knew it was a good idea to give Gail something to do. It was a tip he'd learned from his mother.

'Tea,' Gail said as if it was a strange request, but she headed into the kitchen, and there was the sound of a kettle being filled, then cups being taken from a cupboard.

Cam took a seat in a comfortable looking armchair, and dropped his head back against it, wondering why he was here, if this had been such a good idea. Surely Gail could have found someone else to help, rather than reaching out to her ex-husband?

'Here you are. Hope you don't mind herbal.' Gail handed Cam a cup of tea with an unfamiliar aroma, before taking a seat in the other armchair. A cat Cam hadn't noticed before, leapt on to her lap and started to purr when Gail stroked it.

'It's fine.' Cam said, taking a sip and trying not to grimace at the flavour. It wasn't one he recognised, not the peppermint Poppy had served him. Was it only this morning? Thinking of Poppy made him wonder what she was doing now. Would she be at the restaurant, or at home with Angus, reading or watching television? He wished he was with her, instead of sitting in this strange room with Gail who was grieving for the woman she'd left him for. He wondered again what he was doing here, why he'd agreed to come all this way to arrange the funeral of a woman he didn't even know.

*

The funeral was a solemn affair as such events always were. The crematorium was filled to capacity. There were teachers from the school where Gail and Judy taught, members of the various social groups they belonged to, and Judy's parents, shedding copious tears. Apart from Cam, Lachlan and Scarlett, there was no one representing Gail's family. Her parents hadn't approved of her relationship with Judy, or her divorce from Cam who they'd loved like a son. They'd never felt comfortable in Pelican Crossing after Gail left and when they retired had moved to Brisbane. Cam didn't know if they'd kept in touch with their daughter at all.

Cam sat on one side of Gail, Lachlan and Scarlett on the other. Although Lachlan hadn't been close to Judy and had never entirely understood why Gail had left him and Cam, he'd come to accept her as part of his mother's life.

Cam was glad he was there to share the burden of Gail's grief as, despite the room being filled with her friends, she clung to Cam's hand. They sat together, alongside Judy's parents in the front row, the polished wooden coffin covered with wreaths sitting there in front of them – a stark reminder of the woman who was no longer with them.

Gail gasped and clutched Cam's hand tighter, tears streaming down her face, as Judy's choice of Stevie Wonder singing *You Are the Sunshine of My Life*, rang out across the room. 'She was mine,' Gail sobbed, 'my sunshine. It was our song.' Even in her anguish, Gail had a glow about her, as she remembered. *Had she ever felt as much for him?* 'Jude!' She reached out as if she could halt the proceedings, bring her loved one back to life. But the curtains had closed. Judy was gone.

It was only a group of close friends who returned to the house with Cam and Gail, Lachlan and Scarlett. Judy's parents had travelled up from the country and were eager to get back. There was nothing for them here in the city now their daughter had been laid to rest. They promised to visit the memorial garden later, when Judy's ashes had been scattered and a rose bush planted in her memory.

Lachlan and Scarlett had arrived a few days earlier. The young man had been a tower of strength but had little idea of how to handle his grief-stricken mother. Scarlett, on the other hand, had managed to comfort her mother-in-law and had spent what seemed like hours looking through books of photographs and listening to Gail's memories of her and Judy's time together. While Cam had come to accept the two women's relationship, this was one task he was happy to leave to Scarlett.

'You'll stay?' Gail clutched his hand.

All the other mourners had left, the crowd of women with whom Gail and Judy had developed friendships over the years they'd been together. They were like a flock of twittering birds with their continual chatter. Cam wasn't surprised if Gail was pleased to see them leave. But they were her friends now. He was only the discarded husband.

'You and Lachlan, you'll stay?' Gail asked again. 'Scarlett too. Just for a few days, until…' She shook her head. 'I need to get used to the fact Jude's gone. And there's all her stuff.' She looked around the room which was filled with Judy's artwork. An art teacher when they'd met, she'd gone on to develop a reputation for painting city landscapes, many of which graced the walls of their home, and Cam knew one of the rooms in the house had been turned into a studio.

'The studio,' Gail said as if reading his mind. 'I don't think I can bear to go in. It's as if she's still there, painting, waiting for me to call to tell her dinner's ready.' She burst into tears.

'Of course we will,' Scarlett said, putting her arms around her and looking up at Cam and Lachlan. 'I can help you with Judy's things and Lachlan and Uncle Cam can take care of everything else that needs doing. How about a cup of tea?' She looked up at the men again.

Cam felt he'd been drowning in tea ever since he arrived, but he went to put on the kettle. Lachlan followed him into the kitchen where Gail's cat had taken up residence in a corner, spooked by all the visitors.

'Scarlett and I can only stay till Monday, Dad. We'll need to get back to work. What about you?'

'I'll stick around as long as your mum needs me. It's the least I can do.' Cam sighed. He had an urge to call Poppy, to speak to someone who wasn't mired in grief, who might be able to lift the mood of desolation that had fallen on him in this house of mourning. He was looking forward to returning home, to seeing her again, and to making good his promise.

Twenty-three

It was one of the most important days in the Australian calendar year, and everyone at *Crossings* was prepared for the big day. The Melbourne Cup, *the race which stopped the nation*, was an important racing event, even taking precedence over Christmas in the eyes of many Australians, and, like most other restaurants in the country, *Crossings* was hosting a Melbourne Cup lunch.

Cam had been in Sydney for almost a week now, and there was no sign of him returning. Poppy had hoped he'd be back in time for what was one of the highlights of the year, but his call yesterday had put paid to that. It seemed Gail still needed his help, and while Poppy admired him for his sense of duty, she couldn't stem the disappointment that had flooded her when he told her he had to stay in Sydney for a little longer. He normally acted as master of ceremonies on this occasion and, although Amber's husband, Chris, had agreed to step into the breach, it wouldn't be the same without him. There was also the matter of what he'd meant about their needing to talk.

Poppy tried to put on a brave face as she dressed in the calf-length turquoise and white dress she'd bought specially for the occasion on another trip to *Birds of a Feather* in Bellbird Bay and fixed the arrangement of feathers and flowers that passed for a hat on her upswept hair. She was conscious she looked her best, smart enough for the owner of *Crossings*, but no competition for the local ladies competing for *Fashions on the Field* which was always part of the event – even though they were a long way from the Flemington Racecourse.

The restaurant was a hive of activity when she arrived. There were technicians installing the large wall screen on which the race would be transmitted, a jazz trio organising themselves in one corner, and the staff busily setting tables. In the kitchen, everything was being prepared for the meal itself, a three-course luncheon with a complimentary glass of champagne. As well as being a popular event, the lunch was a great money-spinner for the restaurant, always fully booked months in advance.

Satisfied all was going well, Poppy began to relax and accepted a glass of white wine from Michelle who was dressed in a smart black sheath dress and wearing a tiny black and white fascinator on her cropped black hair.

'Might as well get in the mood, boss,' she said with a grin. 'Once everyone arrives, it'll be like a madhouse.'

Poppy agreed, her eyes darting around to ensure everything was in place, before taking a sip of wine. She checked her watch. It would soon be time for the door to open, then they wouldn't have time to breathe till it was all over.

Michelle unlocked the door, and the diners streamed in, a collection of glamour and fragrances more suited to an upmarket city venue or the racecourse itself than a humble restaurant in a small coastal town. It was an occasion for which many had prepared for weeks, choosing outfits and designing hats, each hoping to outsmart the others in their desire to be noticed and take the prize. It wasn't surprising there was a preponderance of women among the diners who took their places at the long tables chattering like a group of brightly coloured birds.

Poppy moved around the room, greeting those she knew and welcoming strangers, before taking her place at one end of a table close to the kitchen, from where she had a good view of the room and could easily move if required.

'A bigger crowd than usual this year,' Rachel said, when Poppy joined her and the other two members of their lunch group. 'You must be pleased.'

'Yes.' Poppy glanced around the room. By rearranging the tables, the staff had managed to accommodate a larger crowd than in previous years.

'No Cam?' Liz asked. 'Is he still in Sydney?'

'Yes.' Poppy didn't expand. She had spoken to Cam several times since he left but he hadn't said a lot about his plans, only that Gail still needed him. Surely he couldn't be away from the marina for much longer?

When lunch was over, it was time for the fashions to be judged, and Chris called upon a visitor to the town to act as judge. Greta Carlson was the owner of the boutique in Bellbird Bay where Poppy had bought several outfits and, as a stranger to the town and the owner of a boutique, was deemed an appropriate person to take on the role.

Poppy watched with interest as the entrants paraded between the tables and applauded with everyone else when the winner was announced – a young woman wearing a short red dress and a matching hat with a wide brim.

Then it was time for the race to begin, and like everyone else Poppy focussed on the wide screen. While she enjoyed watching the race, she always felt sorry for the poor horses and hoped none of them would be injured this year. She wasn't a gambler, so had never placed a bet, not even on this special day, but she knew many people there had, and those who had secured a horse in one of the sweeps would be watching with bated breath.

At last it was all over. Poppy breathed a sigh of relief, though as her eyes took in the devastation left by the attendees, she was glad she'd decided not to open for dinner that evening. It would take some time to set the restaurant straight again. But it was worth it. Not only did the event bring in a good return, it cemented *Crossings'* reputation in the town as *the* place to dine.

'Another successful event,' Michelle said, her fascinator now somewhat askew.

'Thanks to you and the rest of the crew.' Poppy headed into the kitchen to thank everyone there. 'You did well today,' she said. 'There'll be a bonus in your wages this week. I couldn't have done it without you. The lunch was superb, and everything went off without a hitch.'

The staff smiled their thanks.

Although it was only mid-afternoon, Poppy was exhausted. She had been on edge all through the lunch, worried something might go wrong. Now it was all over, all she wanted to do was go home and lie down. But, despite everything, the success of the event reinforced her determination not to sell the restaurant. To her relief, there had been no further emails from the realtor, so it seemed they had accepted her rejection of their second offer.

*

As soon as she got home, Poppy kicked off her shoes. The heels, higher than she was accustomed to wearing, had made her feet ache. In her bare feet, she padded through to the bedroom followed by Angus. Taking off her dress, she stepped into the shower, feeling her energy return as the cool water flowed over her. It had been a good lunch, but she'd missed Cam, missed Jack too, as she always did on this day. Jack had loved Melbourne Cup Day, always choosing a horse to bet on, rarely a winner, but he didn't care. It was the thrill of the race he enjoyed, shouting and cheering with everyone as they raced towards the finishing line. Cam was so different from him, quieter, more measured, more cautious. Perhaps that was what attracted Poppy to him, that difference.

Twenty-four

Lachlan and Scarlett had left. It was Tuesday, Melbourne Cup Day, and Cam was still in Sydney. He'd intended to be back in Pelican Crossing by now, promised Poppy he would be there to perform his role as master of ceremonies, but he'd found himself unable to leave.

After Lachlan and Scarlett had driven off the day before, Gail had started going through her and Judy's joint accounts, intending to change the name. But it had proved too much for her. She had broken down, collapsed and taken to her bed. She was still there, refusing food and only accepting the occasional glass of water. Cam had tried everything – calling her friends, threatening to call a doctor, even to ring her parents – all to no avail. She wouldn't budge. He knew she couldn't survive like this for ever. She'd eventually regain enough energy to make some sort of effort to go on living. But in the meantime, all he could do was be there to make sure she didn't decide to harm herself.

Cam had hoped one or more of the friends who'd come back after the funeral would be able to help, maybe even be willing to stay with her to allow him to go back home. But Gail refused to speak to them, insisting she didn't need anyone. He was in a dilemma. He'd loved this woman. They had a son together. He couldn't leave her alone in this state. So, he stayed.

It had been difficult when he called Poppy to tell her he wasn't going to be back for the Cup Day lunch, to try to make her understand his predicament. She'd been good about it. Although he sensed her disappointment, she'd reminded him how, when Jack died, it had taken her weeks to make any kind of sense. Weeks! He didn't have weeks. He couldn't stay here for that long.

For want of anything better to do, he'd turned on the television, keeping the sound on low, to watch the race, imagining the lunch at *Crossings*, picturing Poppy dressed to kill, the cheerful atmosphere, the food. It was all so different from the house of mourning in which every tiny sound seemed to be magnified. He wasn't really listening to the commentary, but suddenly the words of the announcer caught his attention.

'Butler's Leap is in third place, and it looks like...'

Cam stopped listening. The name of the horse reminded him of his suspicions about Jordan Butler. He might not be able to do anything about the man in Pelican Crossing, but now he was in Sydney, he could make some enquiries about him. He'd start with a more in-depth search on the internet than he'd done earlier. He opened his laptop.

*

An hour later, Cam rubbed his eyes and stretched his arms above his head. Jordan Butler came from one of Sydney's moneyed families. His father had been the owner of a large construction company. He had political ambitions, but there had been some scandal and he'd never been selected, though their wealth hadn't suffered.

Jordan himself was a product of an elite private school, had studied business at Sydney University where he'd been a popular member of SUDS – Sydney University Dramatic Society – and a renowned sportsman. After graduation, Butler had joined his father's company, but had soon branched out on his own.

That's when things started becoming hazy. He'd started off as a stockbroker, then there were a few years unaccounted for before he appeared again, heading up a development in western Sydney. He had been involved with a group which aimed to redevelop a Heritage listed row of homes fuelling the anger of several factions of protesters. The protestors had won, but Butler had become the darling of the media, appeared on breakfast shows, and secured a spot on *The Project*. He'd been married twice, divorced twice. There was no mention of children.

In recent years, his name had been linked with one photographic model after another, none lasting more than a few months. He lived the high life. The motor cruiser currently berthed in the Pelican Crossing marina was his latest expensive toy.

Cam closed his laptop, satisfied for now. But he wasn't done. He intended to discover more about Jordan Butler. None of what he'd uncovered explained why he was in Pelican Crossing, why he was still there. The successful businessman Cam had just read about wasn't one who'd decide to retire to a small town on the Queensland coast. He had to have an ulterior motive, and Cam intended to discover what it was.

Twenty-five

Poppy drew in her breath. This was the third time Jordan Butler had dined in *Crossings*. Tonight, he was alone. There was no sign of any of the women who'd accompanied him on the two previous occasions.

They hadn't spoken on either occasion. There had been no need as Poppy stayed in her usual position at the rear of the restaurant, out of sight of the customers, but able to keep an eye on everything that was happening, ready to intercede if a problem arose, which it rarely did. Over the years, she had become adept at hiring staff who were skilled at their jobs, whether it be in the kitchen or front of house.

When she'd seen Jordan, it was as if she had travelled back in time and was nineteen again, her stomach lurching as it had back then at the sight of the tall, darkhaired man who belonged in a different world from her. She was no longer nineteen, and not so easily impressed by good looks, but even from her vantage point, she could see Jordan Butler was still an attractive man, the silver threads in his hair only adding to his appeal.

Tonight, for some reason, she decided to behave differently. Moving from her place, she took the plate containing the bill from the surprised waitress and carried it to the table where Jordan Butler was finishing his coffee. He looked up as she placed it on the table, but there was no sign of recognition in his eyes. Why should there be? It had been a long time ago, and they had only known each other for two weeks.

'I hope you enjoyed your meal.'

He gave her a closer look, an expression she couldn't identify flitting across his face. 'Do I know you?' he asked.

'You don't remember me.' It wasn't a question. He clearly didn't. For a moment, Poppy felt foolish. Then her customary self-confidence reasserted itself. This was *her* restaurant, *her* hometown. He was the stranger, a visitor, a guest.

Puzzled, he shook his head.

'It was a long time ago... in Sydney.' She waited. If he didn't remember, she didn't intend to remind him.

He stared at her for several moments without speaking, then he snapped his fingers. 'Pretty Polly Perkins of Paddington Green!' He laughed.

Poppy laughed with him, remembering now what she'd forgotten, how he had always got her name wrong, jokingly confusing her with the old song he said he'd learnt as a child from his English nanny.

'What are you doing here? You work here?' He glanced around the restaurant which was now beginning to empty.

'We... I own it.'

'You and...' He looked around again as if expecting someone else to appear. It was as if they were waiting for Jack's ghost to emerge from the woodwork.

'It belonged to my parents. My husband and I renovated it, made it into what it is today.'

'You've done well,' he said, and she detected a note of admiration in his voice along with something else she couldn't quite identify. 'Who'd have thought it? Little Polly...'

'Poppy. It's Poppy.'

'Of course it is.' He grinned, and suddenly it was as if the years fell away and she was once again the young girl in the hotel in Darling Harbour, impressed by the handsome young man who was way out of her league.

Then she came to her senses. She was no longer that young girl. She was a fifty-one-year-old widow, mother to three grown-up daughters, about to become a grandmother, and owner of one of the best restaurants on the coast.

'Will you have a drink with me... for old times?' Jordan glanced at her quizzically and Poppy felt herself fall under his spell, just as she had done all those years ago.

Telling herself there was no harm in having a drink with a customer, with a man she knew from the past, she glanced around the restaurant. Seeing everything was going smoothly, and aware it was almost closing time, she nodded. 'I'll fetch a bottle of wine.'

Jordan put up a hand to stop her. 'Let me.' He called over the waitress who appeared surprised to see the boss liaising with a customer but took his order, returning almost immediately with a bottle of champagne and two glasses.

As if in a dream, Poppy took the seat opposite him, reminding herself he was a customer and he was only in town for a short time. But with Cam down in Sydney and no indication of when he'd return, she'd been feeling lonely. What harm was there in having a drink with an old friend? Though she hadn't expected champagne.

'It's been a long time,' Jordan said. 'To old friends, and renewal of friendship.' He raised his glass in a toast.

Flustered, Poppy raised hers in return, almost choking on her first sip of the expensive beverage. 'What brings you to Pelican Crossing?' she asked. It was something not even Liz had been able to discover, despite all her sources of local gossip.

'Why not?' Jordan drained his glass and refilled it, clearly accustomed to drinking the French champagne which was the most expensive item on the *Crossings* wine list. 'I noticed you on my previous visits to the restaurant, but I didn't realise you were the owner. How long…?'

'My husband and I took over *Crossings* over twenty years ago, when my parents decided to retire.'

'Your husband?' Jordan peered around.

'He passed away five years ago.'

'Oh, I'm sorry. And since then, you've managed this on your own?'

Was he surprised or…? Poppy couldn't identify the expression that flitted across his face, to be quickly suppressed.

'I have,' she said, proud of what she'd achieved.

'I saw the episode on *Weekender*, the one featuring coastal food. *Crossings* was mentioned.'

'Yes.' It had been one of Poppy's proudest moments, to have the popular television show visit her restaurant. It had brought many new customers, people who chose to visit Pelican Crossing to eat here. Was Jordan one of those? Stealing a glance at him out of the corner of her eye, she doubted it.

To Poppy's surprise and delight, Jordan continued to draw her out about the history of the restaurant and of Pelican Crossing. By the time they'd finished the wine, the restaurant was empty. At Poppy's request, the waitress brought them cups of coffee. She knew it might keep her awake, but she needed something to mitigate the effect of the champagne.

'I've really enjoyed this evening,' Jordan said, when it was clear they would have to leave to allow the staff to finish up. 'Can we meet again… for lunch or dinner? I've eaten at the yacht club a few times. They have a good menu, almost as good as here.' He chuckled.

As Poppy agreed, she felt a tinge of guilt as she wondered what Cam would think. Then she dismissed it. It was none of Cam's business who she had dinner with. Although he kept in touch while he was in Sydney, nothing had changed. The bubble of happiness she'd experienced at their last meeting had long since disappeared. Even though they'd fallen into the habit of spending more time together than before, apart from that one occasion, those few words, the touch on her cheek, there had been no hint from Cam that he regarded her as anything other than his best friend's widow. Poppy had come to the conclusion that was what she'd always be to him, and that if she wanted a man in her life, she'd need to look elsewhere.

While she doubted Jordan Butler was the answer, it felt good to be invited out by someone whose company she'd enjoyed in the past, would be something to share with her friends when they next met for lunch and she couldn't suppress the trace of excitement that he wanted to see her again.

Twenty-six

Although Cam had called again last night, he still hadn't said when he was intending to come home, and while Poppy felt a tinge of guilt about accepting Jordan's invitation to dinner, she had no reason to do so. There had been nothing in Cam's call, either last night nor any other time to make her believe he had any feelings for her other than those he'd always had for her when Jack was alive, nothing to stop her going for dinner with Jordan Butler.

Angus fussed around her feet as she dressed in the same outfit she'd worn for dinner with Cam, as if even her pet could sense her ambivalence. What would Jack think, she wondered, if he'd known about her and Jordan all those years ago. Not that there was anything to know, not really. But for those two weeks, she'd been living in a dream world from which she'd come down to earth when Jack called. When she boarded the plane for home, she'd closed the door on everything that had happened in the harbour city. What Jack didn't know couldn't hurt him, and she'd loved him too much to cause him pain. As soon as they reunited, he'd proposed, and she'd become caught up in wedding preparations. Amber's birth had followed a year later, and her life had become too busy to worry about a two-week friendship with a dreamlike quality that hadn't really amounted to anything.

She'd arranged to meet Jordan at the yacht club, somehow unwilling to have him come to the house, so, telling Angus to be a good boy, she picked up her bag and went out to her car.

As soon as she was in sight of the yacht club, Poppy saw Jordan's tall figure. He was pacing up and down outside the building. He was taller than she remembered, as tall as Cam. Jack hadn't been much taller than she was, but she had to stand on tiptoe to kiss Cam on the cheek. Cam! What was she doing here, about to have dinner with another man when she had feelings for Cam? But Cam didn't appear to want her in the same way, she remined herself. And this was Jordan Butler, the man she'd once considered to be a godlike creature who was way out of her league.

Taking a deep breath and pasting a smile on her face while trying to subdue the butterflies doing cartwheels in her stomach, Poppy got out of the car and made her way across the road.

Jordan's eyes lit up when she joined him, taking both her hands in his and giving her a peck on the cheek. He smelled of expensive cologne, different from Jack's Old Spice and the fresh tang of Cam's aftershave. It made her feel as if she was about to venture into unknown territory. She gave a shiver of what might have been excitement.

'You're looking even lovelier than I remember, Po… Poppy,' Jordan said with a grin.

Poppy felt herself redden. She was sure he'd been about to call her Polly. Did he remember her at all, remember the unsophisticated young girl she'd been back then, impressed by the ways of the handsome boy from the city? Or did he only have a vague memory of meeting a girl he regarded as a joke and who he'd confused with a nursery rhyme?

What did it matter? She was only having dinner with him, a way to spend an evening away from the restaurant, a way of filling time to stop her overthinking Cam's absence. But could it be something more?

The yacht club was busy, as was to be expected on a Friday evening. Poppy felt another flicker of guilt. She was normally in *Crossings* on Fridays. But she had every faith in her staff, and she'd be back on duty the following evening.

A waitress led them to a table in a prime position by the window overlooking the marina, from where Poppy couldn't help but see Jordan's motor cruiser. It was lit up, giving her a clear view of the magnificent vessel. It must be worth a packet. Whatever Jordan was involved with these days, it must pay well.

Poppy was amused when her companion insisted on ordering the most expensive items on the menu, along with a bottle of Moet

Chandon. It reminded her how he had managed to impress her all those years ago by what seemed to her his sophisticated taste. She wasn't so easily impressed these days, having long ago come to the conclusion that expensive didn't equal better, but it was nice to be treated, and to feel flattered by the attention of a good-looking man. And Jordan Butler was still as handsome as he had been when they first met. His face might have more lines, his hair some silver streaks, but these only served to emphasise his attractiveness. She guessed he was what some people would call a silver fox. She tried to remember what Liz had said about him.

They chatted amicably over a glass of champagne while they waited for their meals. Jordan had a raft of stories about places he'd travelled to over the years and celebrities he claimed to count as friends. While Poppy took much of it with a grain of salt, it was fun to listen as he chatted on, relieving her of any effort to make conversation. He hadn't lost the charm she remembered, the ability to make her feel at ease in his company.

'Tell me about yourself,' Jordan said, when they had progressed to coffee, after sharing a delicious seafood platter, followed by a decadent dessert of Turkish delight pavlova. 'Apart from your restaurant, how do you spend your time?'

Poppy took a sip of coffee before replying. Her life must seem very humdrum to him. 'Well,' she said, 'I have a small dog who I take for walks, and three daughters, two of whom are pregnant. I'm about to become a grandmother.' She smiled.

'That I find difficult to believe,' he said with a grin. 'You're far too young to be a grandmother.'

'No, really.' She shook her head. 'Both Megan and Scarlett will be giving birth early next year, and Amber – my oldest – is hoping for a baby too. It happens to all of us sooner or later. Do you have any children?' She was curious to know more about what made this man tick.

'No, never stuck with one woman or stayed in one place long enough.' He chuckled. 'Don't you get bored living here? Don't you ever want to spread your wings, travel?'

'Where would I go?' Poppy laughed. 'I love it here. I've lived in Pelican Crossing all my life. Just look at it.' She pointed out the window. 'It's such a lovely spot. Many people would give their eye teeth to live here.'

'Hmm. All those old buildings.'

Poppy's sense of pride in Pelican Crossing came to the fore. 'That's one of the things I love about it, the sense of history. Some things haven't changed in my lifetime. Take the building *Crossings* is in, for example. It's been there for the past hundred years, like most of the buildings on Main Street.'

'Are they classified buildings?'

'No, we've never bothered to go down that route, and I doubt *Crossings* would fit into the category anyway. It wouldn't make any difference to how I feel about it.'

Did she imagine he exhaled?

'What is it you do these days, anyway?' She didn't want to reveal that she knew about his reputation as an astute businessman, known for his takeovers of smaller companies. She only had Liz's word for it.

'Oh, this and that. I worked for my dad for a few years before branching out on my own. It enables me to take more risks. The old man can be a tad conservative.' He chuckled. It seemed he'd done well over the years, though he was somewhat vague about specifics, only saying it made him enough to live the way he wanted and to travel when the notion took him.

The waitress appeared with their bill, and without looking at it, Jordan dropped his credit card on the plate, the sign of someone who didn't have to worry about money. But she already knew that. He reeked of money, always had done. But whereas, all those years ago it had been his parents' wealth, now it was his own.

'Shall we go?' Jordan rose and held out his hand.

Poppy rose too but avoided taking his hand, leading the way to the door and catching sight of Liz's daughter, Mandy, on the way. She winced, knowing news of her dinner with Jordan would soon reach her friend's ears.

Outside the club, they stood awkwardly together. 'Thanks for a lovely evening,' Poppy said.

'Good to see you again, Poppy. See, I got it right this time.' Jordan moved closer and put an arm around Poppy's shoulders. 'Can we do it again? I'd love to show you *The Odyssey*, and I can barbecue a mean steak.' He tipped up her chin with one finger and gazed into her eyes.

For a moment, Poppy was mesmerised, taken back over thirty years to when they'd first met, to when he had seemed to her to be the epitome of sophistication. Then she returned to the present. The thought of spending another evening in his company was tempting, and even though there could be no future in it – their lives were still so far apart – she had a sneaking desire to see his motor cruiser for herself. Cam was still in Sydney, and it would give her something to tell her friends, would really put Liz's nose out of joint. 'That sounds lovely,' she said, but she moved her head, so his kiss fell on her cheek, not her lips.

Twenty-seven

Poppy wandered along the wide stretch of beach, watching Angus running ahead of her and thinking about the previous evening. She had to admit it had been pleasant to be wined and dined, and Jordan had been good company. In some ways, he reminded her of Jack. Both were larger than life. But Jack had always been the champion of the little man... and he had loved Pelican Crossing just the way it was with all the old buildings, some a little quirky, but all with a sense of history. She wasn't sure Jordan felt the same way. It was nothing he'd said, just an impression.

She couldn't help comparing him to Cam, who was the kindest and most honest man she knew... so kind he was still in Sydney with his ex-wife, she reminded herself with a grimace. With Cam gone, it would be easy to fall under Jordan's spell again.

At that moment, Angus chose to find the carcass of a dead seabird and began to drag it along the sand, managing to become entangled in its wings. 'Angus,' Poppy said in despair, 'what am I going to do with you?' She hurried to free the bird, but the little dog was having so much fun with the dead creature, it took her some time to release it. By that time, Angus was smelling pretty bad. 'Angus!' Poppy said again, attaching the dog's lead for the walk home. She wasn't going to risk him finding some other dead creature to play with.

Once they were home, Poppy headed for the shower situated off the laundry. She took Angus into it and turned on the water, taking care to stay out of the spray while she washed away the odour of the dead bird. Then she let the dog outside to dry in the sun and went to the ensuite to have her own shower.

Dressed in a pair of white three-quarter length pants and a pale blue linen shirt, she began to feel better, and started to prepare lunch. She was looking forward to seeing her three friends again. It seemed ages since their last lunch together, and she hadn't spoken to any of them since. They'd all been too busy to catch up for the coffee they often did between lunches. Even Rachel, who Poppy tended to see more often than the others, had been caught up with her B&B guests and grandchildren.

Today, as the weather had warmed up, she planned to serve a cold lunch, so she only needed to make a few salads to complement the sliced ham and turkey she'd bought at the delicatessen. She cut up the sweet potato and sliced the red onion for her favourite sweet potato salad, before sprinkling them with oil and sliding them into the oven. Then she sliced the mango and red capsicum for the mango salad and took the bag of spinach and the feta cheese out of the fridge. That done, she went out to the deck to set the table. It would be lovely to eat out there again. She couldn't believe it was three months since they'd last met here, just after Scarlett's wedding, and her turn to host the lunch had come around again. They shared it between the three of them as Rachel was often busy with her B&B guests.

Angus came trotting round the corner of the house when he heard the two cars draw up, as Rachel and Liz both arrived together. Rachel bent down to make a fuss of him.

'Who's a good boy?' she asked, ruffling his head.

'Not such a good boy today, Rachel. He managed to get himself entangled with a dead bird on the beach and stank to high heaven. I had to stick him in the shower when we got back.'

'Well, he smells okay now.' Rachel sniffed the dog, then stood up. 'It's what dogs do. My Molly is just the same.'

'It's one of the reasons I prefer cats,' Liz said. 'They look after themselves.'

'Hmm.' Poppy didn't intend to get into a cat versus dog argument. They'd been through this on several occasions in the past. 'Come in. You both look in need of a drink.'

'I wouldn't say no,' Liz said, as they made their way through the house to the deck, and by the time Gill arrived, they all had glasses of wine and the conversation was well underway.

'Mandy tells me she saw you at the yacht club with someone,' Liz said, when Poppy had placed the platter of cold meat and the bowls of salad on the table.

'I expect she also told you who the someone was,' Poppy said.

Liz gave a sly grin. 'Jordan Butler!'

The other two stared at Poppy in surprise.

'I thought you said you barely knew him?' Rachel said.

'I said we'd met a long time ago. I barely knew him then,' she lied. 'But he's been coming into the restaurant, and on one of these occasions we spoke. He invited me to dinner.'

'How could you refuse?' Liz asked. 'I'd have accepted too. What's he like?'

'He was an interesting dinner companion, but I'm not sure why he's here, to be honest.' Poppy decided not to reveal how she'd felt history repeating itself, reminding herself they lived in different worlds, just as they had back then.

'Mandy says…' Liz began.

'We all know about your Mandy,' Gill said. 'Biggest gossip in town… after her mother.'

They all laughed, except Liz who grinned again. The others often teased her about being a gossip, and she was always good-natured about it.

'Are you seeing him again?' Rachel asked.

'Well…' Poppy reddened. 'He's offered to show me around his motor cruiser – *The Odyssey*.'

'I hope you accepted. I'd love to know what it's like,' Liz said.

'Oh, Liz!' Rachel said, frowning. 'Not everyone's like you. Perhaps Poppy…'

'I did. Liz's right. It was too good an opportunity to miss.'

'Enough about Jordan Butler. How are your girls, Poppy? Megan must be what… around six months now, and Scarlett?'

Liz and Gill turned to look at Poppy, too.

'That's right, and Scarlett's only several weeks behind her. It's going to be a pretty uncomfortable summer for them both. I'm hoping Scarlett will make it up here for Christmas, that we'll all be together. How are your two, Rach?' Poppy knew that while Rachel's oldest daughter who was the same age as Amber, still lived in Pelican Crossing with her two daughters, her son was working in England. 'Any sign of Alexander returning home?'

'Not yet, but I live in hope,' Rachel said. 'I know he'll be back when he's ready.'

The conversation turned to Christmas in Pelican Crossing, and the plans each had for the celebration. While both Poppy and Rachel planned family get-togethers, Liz and her younger daughter, Mandy, were going to spend the day with her elder daughter, Tara and her husband. Gill, whose daughter, Freya, was overseas, didn't have any plans.

'I'll be happy to have the day to myself,' she said, when both Poppy and Rachel offered to have her join them. 'Maybe, by that time, everything will be settled, and I'll be able to relax.'

'And what about Cam?' Liz asked, turning to Poppy.

Poppy squirmed. She'd been hoping to avoid this question. 'He's still in Sydney. Gail has taken Judy's death hard, and he's providing what support he can.'

'A bit unusual for an ex-husband,' Liz said.

'Cam's an unusual person,' Poppy said, coming to his defence. 'He's a good man, one of the few.' She glared at Liz who had opened her mouth to respond.

'And you're not...' Liz's words trailed off.

'What?' Poppy felt a spurt of anger. Was Liz going to repeat her hints about Poppy and Cam?

'I think you've said enough, Liz,' Rachel said. 'We all know how close the four of them were – Jack, Poppy, Cam and Gail. It's only natural Cam would want to support Gail now. It's nothing to do with Poppy.'

Poppy exhaled, glad Rachel had stepped in.

'I think it's lovely the way they've remained friends,' Gill said. 'Not many couples manage that. And it makes it difficult for the children if they are expected to take sides. I suspect that's why Freya's staying away. She was always close to her dad and now...'

'Still difficult?' Rachel asked what they all wanted to know.

Gill sighed. 'I'm beginning to realise how my clients feel. I don't want to talk about it.'

The remainder of the lunch passed amicably without any reference to Cam, or to Gill's divorce, but as she was preparing to leave, Rachel pulled Poppy aside. 'If you want to chat, I can always find a window of time. I'm relatively free of guests until after Christmas, then the holiday rush starts in earnest.'

'Thanks, Rach. I may take you up on that.'

'My place, next month,' Liz said as they were all making their way to their cars. 'It'll be close to Christmas, and I know you'll all be busy, but let's do Secret Santa. It'll be a lot of fun.'

They all groaned but agreed. It was always difficult to argue with Liz.

Poppy waved them off. All the talk about Christmas had disturbed her. In previous years, Cam had joined them in their celebrations. It was still weeks away. Surely he'd be back from Sydney by then.

Twenty-eight

It was over a week since Melbourne Cup Day, and Cam was beginning to champ at the bit, tired of the inactivity, but still feeling unable to leave Gail alone. He was eager to get back to the marina, despite frequent calls and texts to Rory who assured him he was happy to continue to hold the fort a bit longer. And he was missing Poppy. The news that Butler was still in town disturbed him too.

That morning, when Cam went in to check on Gail, she waved him away as usual, but she did seem a little brighter.

'Do you mind if I go out for a bit?' he asked.

Gail shook her head and burrowed under the bedclothes, but he sensed she'd be fine for a couple of hours at least. He took her up a cup of tea and placed it on her bedside table; in the past couple of days, she'd managed to eat and drink a little. Then he slipped his phone into his pocket, checked he had his credit card, and set off.

Cam's first port of call was the head office of Jordan Butler's father's construction business. It was situated in Double Bay, and he enjoyed the drive across Sydney to the Eastern suburbs. Once there, he sat in the car for some time, looking at the tall office building, trying to work out his approach. He checked his phone again, and noted the company's most recent development was an apartment block in the neighbouring Rose Bay. Perfect! He'd pretend to be a potential investor and see what information he could pick up. He wasn't confident he'd discover anything about Jordan, but he had to start somewhere.

Once inside, he managed to charm the receptionist into making an appointment for him with Butler senior later in the morning, then, with time to kill, he found a café and ordered coffee and an almond croissant.

It was pleasant, watching the passing parade of fashionable women and smartly dressed men, greeting friends or doing business. This was Jordan Butler's natural environment, where he lived and worked – his office was in the same block as his dad's, and he owned a penthouse apartment a stone's throw away. Cam became even more convinced there was something odd about his visit to Pelican Crossing and his claim he intended to move there.

He checked his watch. Time to go.

This time, when he entered the office building, he was shown into a large office where a silver-haired man was seated behind an ornate wooden desk which looked to be antique. Behind him was a floor-to-ceiling window overlooking the street where Cam had enjoyed coffee only a short time earlier. On one side of the room was a long table on which stood several models of apartment buildings. Cam was glad he'd thought to wear the suit he'd brought for the funeral. This wasn't an occasion for jeans.

'Mr Butler.'

The older man rose and held out his hand. 'I understand you're interested in investing in one of our projects, Mr...'

'Taylor, Jack Taylor.' Cam was wary of giving his own name and was sure Jack wouldn't mind him using his; he might even be amused. He shook the outstretched hand.

'Mr Taylor. Take a seat.'

When Cam had sat down, Butler leant his elbows on the desk and steepled his hands. 'What brings you to Butler Associates? Where did you hear about us?'

Cam thought quickly. 'I'm looking for an investment which will give me a good return, and a friend suggested I contact you. I admit I checked out your website and I see you're about to commence developing a block of retail spaces and residential apartments in Rose Bay. It may be a good fit for me.'

'Hmm. Come over here.' Butler stood up and headed over to the table. Cam rose to follow and, as he did, he caught sight of a photo on the older man's desk. It was of the man himself, standing on the deck of his motor cruiser, leaning on the rail, a wide grin on his face, looking as if he hadn't a care in the world.

Butler senior must have caught his glance. 'My son,' he said proudly. Then he peered at Cam, who realised his expression must have given him away. 'You know Jordan? Was it he who recommended me?'

'Yes and no. He didn't recommend you, but I do recognise him. I think we may have been at university together. Sydney?'

'That's right. A lot of water's flowed under the bridge since then. He was with me for a while but has his own business now. Doing very well, too. Jordan's more of a risk taker than his old man. If you're looking for something more out of the ordinary, with the potential for huge returns and are willing to take a risk, you could do worse than talk to him.'

'How so?' Cam felt his temperature rise. Was this what he was looking for?

'He has an idea for a development in a small Queensland coastal town, thinks he can turn it into a tourist mecca if he can buy up enough of the existing property and some fishing charter or other, maybe the marina. You wouldn't get me throwing money into it, but a younger man like yourself... it may be what you're looking for.'

Cam felt his heart racing. He could barely contain his excitement. 'Sounds interesting,' he said, trying to sound cautious. 'Do you have more information?'

By the time Cam left, his head was in a whirl. He knew now what Jordan Butler was up to, why he had come to Pelican Crossing and why he was still there. It was obvious he was behind the offers for *Crossings*, no doubt the one for Jamie's business too, and who knew how many other shop owners in Pelican Crossing had been approached, who might already have agreed to the sale? The mention of the marina was another shock. How and when did Jordan intend to approach him about that?

He couldn't wait to return home, to report on his discovery and to unmask Jordan Butler for the charlatan he was.

Twenty-nine

Gail seemed to be finally making an effort to get back to some semblance of normality. This morning she'd announced that she'd arranged for Carrie and Debra – two of the friends who'd come back after the funeral – to come round and help sort out some of Judy's clothes and her studio. 'I can't face doing it by myself,' she said, 'and I know these two will treat everything sensitively. They're good friends. The four of us did a lot together.' She gave a small sob, and Cam was heartened to see that sob turn into a smile and not the torrent of tears he'd become used to.

It had taken longer than Cam anticipated to reach this point, but he'd used his time profitably in finding out more about Jordan Butler. Everything he heard and read pointed to the fact that he was a ruthless businessman who'd stop at nothing to get his way. The puzzle was why he wanted a stake in a small town like Pelican Crossing. According to Butler senior, Jordan had some idea of turning it into another version of the Gold Coast Glitter Strip complete with music festivals and maybe even movie sets. Cam couldn't see it happening, and he certainly wouldn't want it to.

Now Gail had reached out to her friends, he was free to leave.

Cam opened his laptop and booked a flight for next morning, then sent a text to both Rory and Poppy to let them know his plans. He couldn't wait to get back to Pelican Crossing. He'd been gone too long. What he had meant to take only a few days had stretched out into three weeks.

Rory's reply came immediately.

Great news, boss. Missed you.

But an hour later there was nothing from Poppy. He supposed she was busy. She had a restaurant to run. But he'd expected an immediate reply. He was impatient to see her again, to have the talk he'd promised, and take their friendship to the next level.

Now Cam had discovered the truth about Jordan Butler, he was anxious to get back to Pelican Crossing to confront him. He was tempted to tell Poppy his news but thought it best to wait till he returned to tell her face-to-face. He remembered her saying she'd met the guy, but she hadn't elaborated. What if she'd done more than just meet him, what if…? His skin crawled at the thought.

Although he called her regularly, it wasn't the same as seeing her. He missed their Sunday breakfasts, her ready ear listening to the challenges of managing the marina, the smile that lit up her whole face. She said she missed him, too, but for her life was going on, while he felt himself to be in limbo.

Poppy had made no mention of any further communication from the realtor who made the offer to purchase *Crossings*, but from what Butler senior had said, Jordan Butler would stop at nothing to get what he wanted – and he wanted a foot in Pelican Crossing. Cam wondered exactly what lengths he'd go to in order to get his way.

*

Poppy was having lunch with Jordan on *The Odyssey*, glad he'd suggested lunch rather than dinner. It was a less intimate meal, but even so, she felt a tremor of uncertainty when he helped her step onto the deck of the large vessel. Reminding herself she was no longer the innocent nineteen-year-old who had been easily impressed by Jordan, but a fifty-one-year-old widow with grown up children. She was about to become a grandmother, for goodness' sake. What made her think he might try to ravish her? She smiled at the thought, even as she trembled with nerves.

'Something amusing you?' Jordan was looking even more attractive than usual today, dressed in a pair of white knee-length shorts and short-sleeved shirt, which emphasised his tanned legs and arms.

Poppy's stomach lurched. If he did attempt to ravish her, would she be able to resist?

'No, I'm just admiring the boat... or should I call it a cruiser? I'm more familiar with yachts or small motorboats. This is enormous. Do you manage it all by yourself?'

'No, I have a couple of crew. They're not on board today,' he said, adding to her discomfort. 'Let me show you around.' Jordan held out his hand forcing Poppy to take it, lest she appear impolite. She was his guest, after all.

After a tour of the vessel, which included a luxurious cabin containing a large round bed, as well as several others clearly intended for guests and a well-appointed living area which wouldn't have looked out of place in an expensive city apartment, Poppy was glad to return to the fresh air and the deck where a barbecue was set up.

Jordan poured them both glasses of white wine, then set about cooking the steaks, which he served with a salad Poppy suspected he'd purchased readymade. It was all very pleasant, the conversation focussing on various aspects of *The Odyssey* and the places to which they'd sailed.

This time, when she rose to leave, Jordan pulled her into an embrace. 'I'm so glad we've found each other again,' he said, stroking her hair and turning her face up to his. As their lips met, there were no bells and whistles, instead Poppy was disappointed to experience only a slight frisson. It had been so long since she'd been kissed, she reminded herself. But surely she should have felt something more than a vaguely pleasant sensation?

Jordan didn't appear to notice her lack of response, pulling her into a closer embrace and sighing. As he did, she was aware of the buzz of a text arriving on the phone which was in the pocket of the pants she was wearing.

'Can I see you again?' Jordan asked, gazing into her eyes.

'I'd like that,' she said, deciding the only way to discover if there could be any future in this relationship was to see him again, despite her sense that there was something unreal about their apparent reunion after all this time. Perhaps she was being unfair. She was sure most women would jump at the chance to spend time with him, but he just seemed to be a bit too... practiced.

'I'll call you,' he said, seeming reluctant to let her go.

*

It wasn't until Poppy was home, had taken an irate Angus for a walk, and filled his food and water bowls, that she remembered about the text. Taking out her phone, she saw Cam's name, and her heart did a double flip – a more instinctive reflex than her response to Jordan's kiss. But Jordan was here and keen to spend time with her. Cam was still in Sydney.

She opened her phone.

Gail getting back to normal. Booked a flight home on Saturday. Dinner? Cam

Poppy's heart leapt again. She remembered Cam's words to her before he left, the words that had made her hope he might be thinking of her as more than a friend… or had she imagined it? But the thought of seeing him again, of dinner, of their usual Sunday breakfast together made her smile. She couldn't wait to see him.

But in the meantime, she'd agreed to see Jordan again.

Poppy poured herself a glass of wine and picked up the phone.

Half an hour later, Rachel knocked at the door sending Angus into a spiral of barking.

'Shush, Angus, it's only Rachel,' Poppy said. She was confused and needed someone to spill her heart to. Rachel was the obvious person, and she had offered to be available if Poppy needed to talk.

'Has something happened?' Rachel asked, when Poppy had poured her a glass of wine and the two women had retired to the deck. It was early evening, and the sky was light; the sun still hadn't dropped below the horizon when it would send streaks of pink and yellow across the sky.

'You're the only person I can share this with,' Poppy said. 'I know I can trust you to keep it to yourself.'

'Of course.' Rachel gave her an enquiring look.

'I had lunch with Jordan Butler today, on *The Odyssey*. It was a long lunch, and…'

'You didn't…?' Rachel's eyes grew wide.

'No, of course not, although he did show me around the boat, including an enormous cabin containing a huge round bed. The thing is… he kissed me.'

'So?'

'It's the first time I've been kissed on the lips since Jack.'

'How did it feel?'

Poppy considered for a moment. 'It felt weird, wrong somehow. There was a frisson of something, but…' She shook her head. 'I don't know… It wasn't… I felt a sense of betrayal, as if I was betraying Jack.'

'He's not Jack, Poppy,' Rachel said gently. 'Maybe you and I will never find anyone to match the one we had. We were lucky, luckier than some.'

'That's not all.' Poppy took a gulp of wine to give her the courage to share what she wanted to say next. 'I had a text from Cam. He's coming home.'

'Oh, Gail must be feeling better. I'm glad. But…' She peered at Poppy. 'You and Cam? You spoke to me about him earlier. But Liz… I thought she was imagining things, being her usual self. Was she right?'

Poppy blushed. 'There's nothing… We haven't… He hasn't… Oh, it's so complicated, Rach.'

'Tell me. I'm in no hurry. I don't have anyone to get back to.' She took a sip of wine.

'As I think I told you, I do have feelings for Cam. He's been such a help since Jack passed, and he and Jack were such good friends, even though they were so different. At first, that was all it was. We continued to have breakfast together on Sundays, as we always did when Jack was alive – we've done it since the children were small – and he'd come into *Crossings* for lunch a few times during the week. But…' she bit her lip, '… over time, my feelings seem to have changed. I want more than the friendship we've always had. Before he went to Sydney, it seemed… I'd hoped… maybe he felt something for me too. But,' she sighed, 'he's been gone so long, I gave up hope, so when Jordan invited me on a date, I agreed. Am I so fickle?'

'Not at all. It's only natural to want some affection… and now Scarlett's gone too, I can understand how you might feel lonely, the need to fill a gap in your life. I've never felt the need myself, but I have my two terrors to keep me busy, not to mention my B&B guests.'

'I have *Crossings*. Shouldn't that be enough? It has been for the past five years.'

'Perhaps you're changing, discovering it's time to move on?'

Rachel's words were almost identical to what she'd said to Cam. But they'd fallen on deaf ears, unless… 'So you don't think I'm mad, that to even be thinking of someone else is a betrayal of Jack?'

'Of course not. I'm sure Jack wouldn't think that. He was always so full of life. Surely he wouldn't want you to grieve for ever?'

'But Cam…? He was his best friend.'

'When does he get back?'

'Tomorrow. He wants to talk.'

'There you go. Maybe he's been thinking about you, too.'

'Maybe…'

By the time Rachel left, Poppy had managed to convince herself that talking to Cam would be a good idea. She might be able to discover how he felt about her. But what if she was wrong?

Thirty

Finally, when he'd almost given up hope, Cam received the reply he was looking for from Poppy.

Glad Gail's feeling better. Will be good to see you home again.

It wasn't as welcoming as he'd hoped for, but was a reply, nevertheless. There was just one more thing he wanted to do before he left Sydney. He'd managed to contact Bill Louden, one of the guys he'd shared a house with when they were students. When Cam had returned to Pelican Crossing, Bill had remained in the city, taking up a cadetship with The Sydney Morning Herald. They'd kept in touch over the years, and now Bill was an investigative reporter, Cam had sought his help in digging into Jordan Butler's background.

His old friend had been curious as to why Cam was wanted information about the developer, but once he heard of Butler's plans for the small coastal town, his interest was aroused, and he agreed to see what he could find. A text the previous evening had suggested they meet in the city for a beer.

'Good to see you.' Cam shook his old friend's hand and glanced around the upmarket bar with the view of Sydney Harbour. It was a lot different to what he was used to. He was glad he'd worn his suit so didn't look out of place among the other suited businessmen enjoying a drink before heading home from work.

'Good to see you, too, Cam. What'll you have?'

'My shout.'

When Cam had been served with the craft beers Bill recommended, the two men headed to a booth at the side of the bar where they could talk without being overheard. After the usual small talk during which they caught up on each other's lives, Bill said, 'I think I may have something for you.'

Cam took a mouthful of beer and leant forward, hoping Bill had found something in Butler's business dealings that Cam could use to blacken his name in Pelican Crossing.

'He's been pretty clever up to now,' Bill said, 'always stayed on the right side of the law.' He rubbed his chin. 'There's just one instance where he might have strayed. Nothing was ever proved. He's too wily for that. But a couple of years ago, there was a rumour going around that he and one of his minions had put the heavy word on the owner of a small hotel, forced him to sell. Then they turned it into what's now a trendy nightclub for young people with more money than sense.'

'The owner didn't want to sell?'

'The place had been in his family for generations. It's not clear exactly what tactics Butler used. I'm still digging. Could prove to be a winner if I can crack it.'

'You'll let me know if you do?'

'Sure thing.'

Cam hoped he'd manage it in time to save Pelican Crossing. From what he had heard so far, if Butler succeeded with his development, it would change the character of the town completely, even the marina might be under threat.

'Thanks, mate,' he said, draining his beer.

'Thank you. It's been in the back of my mind for some time to look into the guy. This new information is gold.' He grinned. 'I'll keep you in the loop. And if you hear any more…'

'I'll let you know. I'm going back home tomorrow, so may be able to get a handle on what's happening. Thanks,' Cam said again, as the two shook hands and parted. By this time tomorrow, he'd be home and having dinner with Poppy.

*

Despite feeling excited at the news Cam was returning home, Poppy told herself not to get her hopes up. Even though he'd suggested dinner, he'd given no indication he had anything other than an evening with an old friend in mind. And Jordan was good company. He treated her well and it was nice to feel spoiled. Since Jack died, there had been no one to spoil her the way he had. Jordan had shown an interest in Pelican Crossing, asking about the history of the town and been very complimentary about the yacht club, the marina and several of the businesses in Main Street, including *The Grand Hotel*. And when the local paper published an article about Gary's plans to set up a dive school, he'd wanted to know more about it and about Gary too, curious about his relationship with Jamie's fishing charter business.

Tonight, he'd invited Poppy to dinner again, this time at *Addison's*, and she was looking forward to another visit to the restaurant. Even though it would bring back memories of her dinner there with Cam, she knew she couldn't continue to hope for a future with her old friend, whereas, with Jordan… there were possibilities.

Addison's lived up to the promise of Poppy's first visit. Tonight, everything was bathed in the glow of the setting sun and as she sipped the expensive wine Jordan had ordered, Poppy could almost imagine she was far away from Pelican Crossing. It came as no surprise, therefore, when Jordan began talking about his travels and comparing the evening to those he had spent in more tropical climes.

'You'd love it, Poppy,' he said, painting a picture of relaxing by the pool in a luxury resort surrounded by palm trees, being served food and drink by attentive waiters, the ocean only a stone's throw away.

For a fleeting moment, she was tempted by the vision he described, then common sense prevailed. She belonged here, not in some luxury resort, not travelling the world. What would she do away from Pelican Crossing, away from all the memories of Jack and their life together, away from her family?

'I don't think so, Jordan. It sounds wonderful, but it's not for me. I'm not like the women you normally hang around with. I'm not tempted to leave Pelican Crossing. It's where I belong, where my family is, where my grandchildren will grow up.' *And the life Jack will always be a part of.*

'You're making a mistake, you know. A big mistake. Don't say I didn't give you the opportunity.'

Poppy gazed at him in surprise. What on earth was he talking about? 'What do you mean?' she asked.

'Oh, nothing.' He leant across the table and took her hand in his. 'It's just… you're too lovely to waste away in a small place like this.' He waved his free hand around.

Their meals arrived as Poppy opened her mouth to reply, and no more was said about luxury resorts or making mistakes, but the conversation stuck in Poppy's head. It was such an odd thing to say.

They were finishing their meal with coffee and a cheese platter, when Jordan said, 'This dive school we were talking about. I'd like to see what it's about. You mentioned you were thinking of booking lessons. Maybe we could pop in together.'

Had she? Poppy didn't recall. And, for some reason, she didn't want her first visit to Gary's dive school to be with Jordan. It was Cam who had suggested it to her, and he was the one who should be with her. He knew Gary whose dad was an old mate of his. Jordan was a stranger, and despite finding him attractive and enjoying his company, the more she saw of him, the more of a stranger he seemed. He was no longer the young man who had seemed like someone from another planet when she was nineteen. He was now a wealthy businessman, and Poppy had no idea why he was in Pelican Crossing, or why he was interested in spending time with her. She wasn't the sort of woman he was accustomed to spending time with in the sophisticated circles in which he moved.

'Let me think about it, Jordan,' she said, smiling to hide her reluctance.

'Don't leave it too long.' He smiled too, but there was something in his expression which sent a shiver down Poppy's spine.

She was glad when the evening ended and she was back home again with Angus, the little dog so pleased to see her, it seemed his tail would never stop wagging.

Thirty-one

Next evening, all thoughts of Jordan disappeared as Poppy dressed to have dinner with Cam, having ensured *Crossings* could manage without her again. She'd missed him so much while he was in Sydney and, although she understood why he had gone to be of help to Gail, she hadn't expected him to be away for so long.

Gazing into the mirror as she applied her makeup, the words he'd said before he left came back to her. He'd said they needed to talk. But he hadn't said what he wanted to talk about. A shiver ran down her spine as she considered possibilities, before reminding herself that Cam had never given her any reason to believe he felt anything for her, considered her anything other than Jack's widow.

'What do you think, Jack?' she said, picking up the photo which stood on her bedside table. It was a favourite of hers, taken a few months before he died. He was standing on their deck, a glass of beer in his hand and a silly grin on his face. It was such a typical pose, him standing there with the ocean behind him, looking as if he hadn't a care in the world. She remembered that night as if it was yesterday. It was his birthday, his forty-fifth birthday and they were preparing to go out to dinner, to meet friends at the yacht club, along with the girls and their partners. Scarlett was in her bedroom getting ready and fussing that Lachlan hadn't arrived from Canberra. Jack was wearing a crazy tee-shirt the girls had bought him and which he insisted he was going to wear to dinner. Poppy smiled at the memory, wishing Jack could tell her what to do, tell her what Cam was thinking, and what she should do about Jordan Butler. She sighed and kissed the photo before replacing it.

Angus barked, a sure sign Cam had arrived and, only a moment later, there was a knock at the door. Taking one last glance in the mirror and smoothing down the skirt of her pale blue dress, Poppy went to answer it.

'Wow, Poppy, looking good.' Cam took both of Poppy's hands in his and leant over to give her a peck on the cheek. Poppy's heart dropped at the familiar greeting, realising she'd been hoping for something more.

'Good to see you back, Cam,' she said, forcing a smile. 'You've been gone a while.'

'Yeah. Gail... you know...'

'She's feeling better now?'

'Somewhat. Judy's death has hit her hard.' He dragged a hand through his hair, causing it to stand on end and making Poppy want to smooth it down.

'I'm sorry.'

'Yeah,' he said again. 'Ready to go?'

'Sure. Angus, be good,' she said to the little dog who had adopted the sad-eyed expression he assumed when he knew she was going out to leave him. She looked up at Cam and this time her smile was genuine. 'Let's go.'

*

It was so good to be with Poppy again. Cam couldn't wipe the smile off his face. When she opened the door, he'd been tempted to pull her into his arms and kiss her till she begged for mercy. But he didn't want to scare her, so he'd managed to restrain himself and give her his usual greeting, the peck on the cheek, the way he'd greeted her when Jack was alive, and which had never changed.

Once inside the car, the scent of Poppy's perfume made it difficult for him to concentrate. But his pleasure at being with her again was tainted by something Rory had said. He'd dropped into the marina before picking up Poppy, wanting to let Rory know he was back and to check all was well. He planned to be back at work on Monday and to let Rory have some time off. The guy deserved it after being in charge for so long.

'Anymore signs of Butler?' Cam had asked, his mind on what he'd discovered about him in Sydney.

'Funny you should mention him. He was in here the other day wanting to know who owned the marina. He seemed a bit put out when I told him it was the council.'

'Oh!' Cam had wondered when Butler would get around to the marina.

'Something else.' Rory looked uncomfortable.

'Spit it out.'

'Well... it's only what I've heard. It may not be true.'

'What is it, Rory?'

'Rumour is that he's been seeing Poppy Taylor.'

Cam's heart had dropped. Poppy? He remembered she'd mentioned she knew the guy, but said it had been a long time ago, before she and Jack were married. If the rumour was true – and these things didn't get said without evidence – they had renewed their friendship while he was gone.

Now, he had to work out how to bring it up, or perhaps she'd mention it first.

Their conversation on the way to the yacht club was all about Gail. Poppy wanted to know how she was coping with Judy's death and what their friends were like.

'I'm glad Scarlett and Lachlan were able to be there for her,' she said. 'I wish I...'

'No, there was no need for you to be there too. They have a wide circle of women friends who rallied round. I would have come back earlier, but Gail clung onto me. It was hard.' Cam remembered those dreadful days after Scarlett and Lachlan left, days when Gail didn't seem to care whether she lived or died. 'Maybe now...'

'Good idea. I'll call her. When I spoke to her after the funeral, she wasn't making much sense. Maybe she'd welcome a visit now.'

'I think she might. She misses Judy a lot. You can understand, having lost Jack.'

'Yes.'

Cam was silent. This conversation wasn't going the way he'd planned. All this talk of death and Jack. How was he going to bring it round to Poppy and him? And if she'd been seeing Butler – and admitted it – how was he going to reveal what he'd found out about him?

*

Poppy wondered what was wrong. After greeting her as usual, Cam had seemed different. Had something happened in Sydney... with Gail? What was it he wanted to talk with her about?

They walked into the yacht club to be greeted by Mandy, who seemed surprised to see them. Cam hadn't spoken since they left the car, but once they were seated by the window, he seemed to relax.

'It's good to be back,' he said with a sigh. 'The city's not for me. I missed Pelican Crossing. I missed you, Poppy.'

This was more like what she wanted to hear. 'I missed you too, Cam.' She gazed across the table at the man who she knew was the one in her heart. Jordan Butler couldn't hold a candle to him. What had possessed her to spend time with him, to even consider a future with him?

'That's not what I heard.'

Poppy stared at him in surprise.

'Would you like to order wine, sir?'

Poppy's eyes swivelled to the waiter standing patiently by their table, her mind a blur. What had Cam meant?

Cam picked up the menu and, giving it a cursory glance said to Poppy, 'A Clare Valley Pinot Gris okay by you?'

'Fine.' Poppy didn't care what she drank. She just wanted to know what Cam was talking about. She waited till the waiter had left. 'What do you mean? What have you heard?'

Cam seemed to hesitate, then he said, 'I dropped into the marina before I picked you up, and Rory told me you and Jordan Butler had been seen together.'

Poppy blushed. Put like that, and coming from Cam, it sounded so... She winced, feeling like she had as a child when she'd been found out doing something wrong. But she wasn't a child. She'd done nothing wrong. All she'd done was spend time with an old friend… when Cam was in Sydney comforting his ex-wife, she reminded herself. She had nothing to be ashamed of. So why did she feel like this, as if she needed to explain herself to him?

Cam was still staring at her.

'I might have had dinner with him a few times,' she said. 'He's good company. He…'

'Poppy, do you realise who he is?'

'What do you mean?'

'Let's order first.'

Mystified, Poppy picked up the menu, although she had been here so often, she knew it by heart. 'I'll have half a dozen oysters Kilpatrick followed by the barramundi Caesar salad. You?'

'I'll always be a steak man. The oysters natural and the filet mignon.'

'Like Jack,' Poppy murmured, almost to herself. It was comforting to be in Cam's presence, like coming home after the expensive meals Jordan had treated her to.

'Now,' she said, when their wine had been served, tasted and poured, 'you were about to tell me something about Jordan.'

'I was.'

But now the time had come, Cam seemed reluctant to speak.

Poppy waited. She took a sip of wine, enjoying the light, dry flavour on her tongue. It was a good choice. Cam knew his wines.

Cam took a deep breath. 'Did you know he was behind the offer to buy *Crossings*?'

Poppy stared at him in amazement. Whatever she had expected, it wasn't this. 'How do you know?' she said, her voice no more than a whisper.

Cam twirled the stem of his glass before replying. 'I always felt there was something off about him,' he said. 'It seemed strange that someone like him would choose to holiday in Pelican Crossing and to stay so long. Also, he appeared very curious about the town… unnaturally so.'

'But surely it might only be natural curiosity?' Poppy didn't want to believe what Cam had told her. She thought back over her conversations with Jordan, realising there could be some truth in Cam's words. Was this what he had wanted to talk to her about?

'Maybe. Anyway, when I was in Sydney, I decided to see what I could find out about him. First, I checked him out on the internet. Then, once I felt I could leave Gail alone, I went to Double Bay.'

Poppy swallowed. It was where Jordan had lived back then, where he might still live.

'I visited his father, Butler senior, in his office, pretended to be interested in a block of units he's building. I didn't give my real name.'

Poppy's eyes widened. This didn't sound like the Cam she knew. He must have been really worried. 'What did you discover to make you think he's behind the offer for *Crossings*?'

The old man suggested that if I was willing to take a risk, I might be interested in a project his son was working on... in a small Queensland town. He gave me some brochures. They mentioned Pelican Crossing. It's clear Jordan Butler has plans to turn Pelican Crossing into a carbon copy of the Gold Coast – casinos, nightclubs and all the rest.'

Poppy's eyes widened even further. 'But he can't, can he, not if we refuse to sell?'

'Jamie has had an offer for his fishing charter business too, and I'd be willing to bet a number of other local businesses are in the same boat. Rory told me today he was even nosing around the marina. And not everyone is like you and Jamie. Some will be swayed by an offer they can't refuse. Then...' he shrugged, '... I've heard he may not be averse to using dirty tactics to get what he wants.'

Their oysters arrived, but Poppy had lost her appetite. She had thought Jordan impossibly suave, couldn't understand what he saw in her, but this... She suddenly felt dirty... used. 'I wondered what he could see in someone like me. Now I know. It was *Crossings* he was interested in all the time.' Poppy caught an expression in Cam's eyes she hadn't seen before, an expression that made her heart leap.

'Don't put yourself down, Poppy. Any man would be lucky to spend time with you. But I'm afraid you might be right. Did he...?'

Poppy remembered now how interested Jordan had been in Pelican Crossing, how he had encouraged her to travel. She shivered at the thought of how close she might have come to taking his advice. But, she realised, she never would have. Pelican Crossing was her home. Then Cam's words sunk in. Did he mean...?

'It's what I wanted to talk to you about, Poppy. Not Jordan Butler, though what I discovered about him is important. I wanted to talk about us.'

Poppy shivered again; this time it was a different sort of shiver.

Cam took a gulp of wine. 'Jack's been gone for five years. I know you're still grieving for him. I guess you always will be, but… when you talked about making a life for yourself, I wondered…'

Poppy held her breath, her heart beating madly. She gazed at Cam, willing him to say what she wanted to hear.

'I know we've always been friends, and you've regarded me as Jack's best mate. You've always been special to me, Poppy, ever since we were all teenagers together. I'd like to think, now we're both on our own, we could begin to take our friendship to another level. I don't mean right away,' he said, 'but perhaps… in time…' His eyes met hers.

Poppy exhaled. She smiled, hoping he couldn't sense her exhilaration. 'I think that's a good idea,' she said.

Thirty-two

'I think that's a good idea.'

Cam exhaled. He'd been afraid Poppy would reject him, even laugh at him for being such a fool as to think he could take Jack's place. Not that he actually wanted to do that. He knew Jack would always have a special place in Poppy's heart... in his too. But life went on, and they were here. 'Let's drink to that,' he said, huskily, trying to subdue the burst of happiness at her reply.

Poppy raised her glass to meet his.

Neither had eaten anything, but now they made a start on the oysters.

'So, what do you propose?' Poppy asked, a wicked twinkle in her eyes.

Cam was stumped. He hadn't thought any further. 'I... I'm not sure,' he said, 'but maybe we can spend more time together, go sailing...' His voice trailed off. They'd already been doing that.

'You mentioned diving,' Poppy said. 'While you've been gone, Gary has opened his dive school. I've been thinking about taking lessons.' She grinned.

'Leave it with me. I'll check it out with him.' Cam was glad to have something to follow up. 'We're having breakfast tomorrow as usual?'

'Of course. I've missed our Sunday breakfasts.'

Cam had missed them too. For the past five years, seeing Poppy every Sunday had been the highlight of his week.

Their entrée plates were removed, their main courses arrived, and the conversation moved on to a discussion of their children. Cam was able to update Poppy with news about Scarlett and Lachlan from when he'd seen them in Sydney, while Poppy filled him in on her shopping spree with Megan.

'How's Amber?' Cam asked, remembering how Poppy's eldest daughter was eager to become pregnant like her sisters.

'Still no news,' Poppy said frowning, 'but she's optimistic this new treatment will work. We can only hope.'

'Mmm.' It was something way outside Cam's knowledge.

When they rose to leave, Cam put a hand on Poppy's waist, feeling some sort of ownership for the first time when instead of shrugging it off, she leant into him. He felt a rush of desire which he quickly stifled, remembering his vow to take things slowly.

At the door, a waitress who looked vaguely familiar grinned at them.

'It's Mandy, my friend Liz's daughter,' Poppy said. 'The last time I was here I was with Jordan. I'll be getting a reputation.'

'Well, I hope you won't be seeing him again.'

'No...oo.'

But Cam could tell Poppy wasn't being completely honest.

'He's going to think it strange if I suddenly stop seeing him,' Poppy said. 'Now that you've told me what he's up to, it might be a good idea to keep him sweet, while I try to find out more about his plans. What do you think?'

Cam thought it was a dreadful idea. He hated to think of Poppy spending any time with that creep. But he had to admit it might have some merit. 'Let me think about it,' he said.

'You have to trust me.'

'I do.' It was Jordan Butler he didn't trust.

When they reached Poppy's house, Cam hesitated, wondering if it was too soon to make a move, if he should give her the peck on the cheek which was their usual greeting and farewell. While he was wondering, Poppy turned towards him.

'Thanks for a lovely evening, Cam, and thanks for...' There was an expression in her eyes that made his knees weak. Her lips parted... waiting to be kissed.

Cam couldn't resist the invitation. He pulled her into his arms, her soft body feeling exactly as he'd imagined, and when their lips met, his senses swam. It was as if time stood still.

*

Poppy almost skipped into the house, surprising Angus who had been snoozing on the sofa. She picked up the little dog and danced around the room with him. Cam Mitchell had kissed her, a proper kiss, on the lips. And it had been every bit as exciting as she'd imagined, making Jordan's kisses fade into insignificance.

And he wanted to get to know her better, to become more than the friends they had been for what seemed like for ever. Then she came down to earth with a bump, letting a surprised Angus drop to the floor. What would Jack think?

Her joy suddenly ebbing, Poppy stepped out of her shoes and went to the bedroom where she picked up Jack's photo again. He was still smiling at her, just as he had been before she left. It was as if he was telling her it was okay, that he approved. Cam was his friend, his best mate, he trusted her with him and, if he couldn't be there, Cam was the perfect person to take care of her.

Poppy smiled as she imagined Jack's words. She didn't need taken care of, but it was what Jack had always tried to do. And, in that respect at least, Cam was like Jack. He'd never let anything bad happen to her. She remembered what he'd told her about Jordan Butler. How could she have let herself believe, even for an instant, that he was interested in her as a woman? The man had set out to exploit her, to play on their previous acquaintance, on her loneliness, on what he saw as her vulnerability, to try to manipulate things to suit his needs.

Then she smiled again and put a finger to her lips, remembering Cam's mouth on hers, reliving the way her heart had leapt, how she had wanted to stay there in his arms for ever.

*

Next morning, after a sounder night's sleep than she'd had since she could remember, Poppy awoke with a smile on her lips at the prospect of breakfast with Cam, and in anticipation of their new relationship.

Angus, sensing her mood, danced around, getting under her feet as she pulled on a pair of shorts and a tee-shirt for their morning walk along the beach. But whereas this would normally have irritated her, this morning nothing could extinguish the glow which surrounded her.

The only other person on the beach this morning was Agnes, whose spaniel was sniffing around in the shallow water. Angus joined her and the pair scampered along together, becoming thoroughly wet in the process.

'Lovely morning. You look happy,' Agnes said. 'Has Cam Mitchell come back from Sydney?'

Poppy stared at her. How did she know? And what was she implying? She couldn't know what Cam said to her last night, could she? Poppy smiled sunnily. Nothing could disturb her this morning.

'Oh, I am happy,' Poppy said and took a long inhale of the sea air. 'Just grateful for everything I have.'

The ageing hippie nodded knowingly. 'That's a good place to be,' she said with a wink, 'be sure to embrace it,' she added before walking away.

Back home, she fed Angus and filled his water bowl, then headed for the shower, humming to herself as the water cascaded over her. Afterwards, she examined her naked body in the mirror wondering what Cam would think of it if... when... they took things further. It was five years since anyone had seen her naked and in that time she'd gained a few kilos. Jack had always said how much he liked her womanly figure, but would Cam? Gail had always been slim, much slimmer than Poppy, even in their teens. What if she was a disappointment to him?

Putting that thought aside, she pulled her favourite summer outfit out of the wardrobe with Agnes's words ringing in her mind. She'd never felt happier and she was determined to embrace it. The sleeveless, peach-coloured dress with the deep v-neckline showed off her fuller figure to advantage, and she always felt good when she wore it. It was casual and perfect for breakfast at *The Blue Dolphin Café*.

Remembering her promise to call Gail, Poppy checked the time, but it was too early to call now. She'd wait till after breakfast. Then, giving Angus a cuddle and a treat and telling him to behave while she was gone, Poppy set off to walk to the café, too excited to wait any longer.

Unlike on previous Sundays, this morning she had butterflies in her stomach as she made her way along Main Street, enjoying the sight of the familiar buildings she passed on the way. What would happen to them if Jordan Butler had his way? What would happen to the newsagency with the collection of cut-price paperbacks sitting outside, the hardware store whose window didn't seem to have changed for years, *The Mousehole*, the tiny shop squeezed between two others in which a group of local women sold their art and crafts... and all the other establishments with which she'd grown up? It couldn't happen. They wouldn't allow it to happen. But, right now, Poppy didn't know how they were going to manage to avoid it. She tried to comfort herself with the thought that perhaps Cam was wrong, perhaps Jordan wasn't the monster he'd depicted, but she was afraid it was all too true.

As she walked along, she caught a glimpse of a lone pelican perched on one of the lampposts on the beach side of the road. She remembered her dad telling her that they'd designed them strong enough to hold two pelicans. She smiled, just one more thing she loved about this town.

Poppy had almost reached the café when she saw Cam walking towards it from the opposite direction. He was wearing a pair of jeans with a white short-sleeved shirt. Her heart turned over at the sight of his broad shoulders straining the seams of the shirt and his strong tanned arms. She forced herself to calm down. This was Cam. They met here every Sunday, had done for years. *But that was before he kissed you*, a little voice in her head said.

'Good morning. Sleep well?'

This morning, Cam's usual peck on the cheek felt different, more intimate.

'Very well, thanks. You?' For the first time, the question brought up an image of Cam in bed. Poppy blushed.

'Pretty good, thanks. A man with a clear conscience always sleeps well.'

Poppy laughed at his habitual reply. This morning it seemed to have implications it never had before. She must stop this... reading things into his words.

They took seats at their usual table and placed their orders, like they had every Sunday for the past five years. But today it felt so very different. Poppy wondered if Cam sensed it too. She glanced at him out of the corner of her eye, but he just looked the same as always.

Perhaps she did too, and the joy she was feeling didn't show in her face.

'Called Gail yet?' Cam asked when they were on their second cup of coffee, both unwilling to leave.

'Not yet. I'll do it when I get home. I'll go down to see her... if she wants me to.' While the thought of leaving Cam now that they'd decided to spend more time together, was difficult to bear, she knew she owed it to her friend to offer what support she could.

'I don't...'

What Cam was about to say was interrupted by a loud crash as the waitress dropped a tray of glasses. He leapt up to help the girl who had burst into tears.

'Sorry,' she said, 'I don't know what happened. I had such a shock this morning. Brad, the owner, told me he's had an offer to buy the café. If it closes and I lose my job, I don't know what I'll do.'

Poppy and Cam looked at each other. What they had feared was beginning to happen.

Thirty-three

Poppy arrived home, excited at the prospect of seeing Cam again next day. They'd gone together to see Gary at his dive school and booked her in for a lesson at ten o'clock, with Cam, as an experienced diver, agreeing to come along to hold her hand and make sure she didn't chicken out at the last moment.

But she was worried about the news the owner of *The Blue Dolphin Café* had received an offer to buy too. Before they parted, she'd promised Cam to check out the owners of other shops in Main Street. He was going to do the same with the men he knew around the bay and with the proprietor of *The Grand Hotel* which he suspected might also be in Butler's sights.

She was just working out what to do first, when her phone rang. Seeing Megan's number, she answered immediately. 'Megan, is everything all right?'

'Everything's fine, Mum. Gav's at work. I'm on my own and I wondered if you'd like some company. Everyone else is at work too.'

Poppy stifled a smile. Megan had always got bored easily, and now she was pregnant she seemed to want company more than ever. 'Of course,' she said. 'Why don't you come over here. There's something you can help me with.'

'Sure, see you soon.'

As soon as the call ended, Poppy keyed in Gail's number, remembering her promise. It would be difficult to make time to visit her in Sydney, and she didn't want to leave Cam so soon, but a promise was a promise and if Gail needed her, she'd make the trip.

'Gail, how are you?' Poppy asked, as soon as her friend answered.

'Oh, you know. Not great.'

'Cam said...' She bit her lip.

'Cam was great. Such a support. I don't know how I'd have managed without him. Jude and I have a lot of friends, but none of them knew what to do. Now he's gone back to Pelican Crossing...'

'That's why I'm calling. Last time we spoke, when I suggested coming down, you said the time wasn't right, to wait till after. Would you like me to come now?' She held her breath waiting for Gail's reply.

For a few moments there was silence, and Poppy began to wonder if Gail was still there, then, 'Oh, Poppy. It's good of you to offer, but... perhaps not. What I would like... I've been thinking a lot about Pelican Crossing since Jude passed, of the happy times we had there. I know we can't turn back time, and Jack's gone now too. But I wondered... could I come for Christmas? Jude's everywhere I look here in Sydney, in the home we shared, in the places we went together. I don't think I can face Christmas without her here. We always made it a special time for us.' She began to sob.

Poppy didn't hesitate. 'Of course you can. I have plenty of room. And Scarlett and Lachlan will be here too. It'll be perfect. Why don't you come a few days before Christmas to give us plenty of time to catch up? Maybe we can persuade Cam to take us sailing.'

'Thanks, Poppy. I'd like that. It's only a few weeks away. It'll give me something to look forward to.'

'Great. Let me know when you plan to arrive.'

Poppy couldn't hide her relief that she wouldn't need to make the trip to Sydney with its memories of her first meeting with Jordan, but she felt a niggle of concern. How would Gail react to seeing her and Cam as a couple? She'd left him, had been married to Judy, but Poppy had the feeling Gail still felt possessive of her ex-husband.

She was still processing her thoughts when Angus's bark signalled Megan's arrival.

'Wow, look at you,' Poppy said. In the few weeks since she'd seen her, Megan had ballooned.

'I know,' Megan said. 'I can't wait till this one's born.' She rubbed her belly. 'Gav says it must be a boy... another footie player,' she said, referring to the fact her husband played for the local team. 'He'll be disappointed if it's a girl, but I don't care. As long as it's healthy. I can't wait to see Scarlett at Christmas. They are coming here for Christmas, aren't they?'

'They are, and your Aunt Gail will be here, too. I've just been speaking to her on the phone. She doesn't want to spend the holiday in Sydney where there are so many memories of Judy.'

'That figures. Though it's never bothered you, has it... the memories of Dad here in Pelican Crossing?'

'Not at all, but everyone's different.' Poppy loved all the memories of Jack, both in their home and in the town. It was as if he was still with her, or at least his spirit was, keeping an eye on everything she did, making sure she was safe. It was a comforting feeling, one she might have to let go if she and Cam... But there was plenty of time to think about that.

'How will Uncle Cam feel... about her being here for Christmas?'

He'll be fine. They're good, Megan. He's just spent a few weeks with her helping arrange Judy's funeral.'

'Oh!' Megan looked thoughtful. 'Do you think, her and Uncle Cam...?'

'What?'

Megan shifted uneasily. 'It's just... now she's on her own again...'

Poppy stared at her, her mind going into overdrive. What made her think that? Had Scarlett said anything? Had Gail said something to Lachlan? Gail had been married to Judy... but she did seem to have become dependent on Cam while he was in Sydney.

'What did you want me to help you with?' Megan asked following Poppy into the kitchen. 'Oh, I'd love a cup of tea and is that your banana bread I can smell?'

Poppy smiled, deciding to put her daughter's comment to the back of her mind to be considered later. It probably didn't mean anything. She couldn't know about her and Cam, even though both she and Amber had earlier suggested they'd be a good match. 'It is,' she said. Megan had always loved her banana bread, made to the special recipe handed down by her mother. She'd baked it the day before, but the aroma still filled the kitchen. 'Trust you to detect it. It's in the tin with the blue lid. Why don't you cut yourself a piece while I make us tea?'

'Yum! I am eating for two, though Gav says I might as well be having a clutch of babies the amount I manage to eat. No, there's only one in here.' Megan patted her stomach and grinned at Poppy's expression.

Poppy waited till they had taken their tea and slices of banana bread out to the deck, Angus following them in the hope of some titbits, before she answered the question which Megan had asked earlier and seemed to have forgotten. 'You wanted to know what I needed help with.'

'Mmm. Oh, Mum, this is divine.'

Poppy grinned. She hadn't lost her touch. 'It's complicated. I didn't tell you I received an offer for *Crossings*.'

Megan stared at her, wide-eyed. 'Someone wants to buy *Crossings*? You wouldn't sell Dad's restaurant.'

Poppy managed to hide her annoyance. The restaurant was just as much hers as it had been Jack's. And it had belonged to her parents before she and Jack had taken over. But what did it matter? 'Of course not. I refused.'

'That's okay then.' Megan took another bite of the banana bread.

'That's not all. It seems this Sydney developer is behind it. A man called Jordan Butler. He owns that big motor cruiser sitting in the marina.'

'Oh, I think Gav mentioned him… and Mandy. She said you and him…'

'Mandy needs to mind her own business.' Poppy's lips tightened, remembering how he'd fooled her.

'Wasn't his boat one of those that were vandalised?'

'Yes, it was.' Poppy was beginning to think Jordan might have been behind that too. But why vandalise his own boat? 'Cam was suspicious of him and when he was in Sydney, he did a bit of digging. This Jordan Butler has plans to buy up part of Pelican Crossing and turn it into some mega tourist spot.'

'He can't do that!'

'Not if we manage to stop him.'

'How can we?'

'First, we need to make a list of all the shopkeepers on Main Street and the neighbouring area. That's where you can help me. So far, we're only aware of offers on *Crossings* and *The Blue Dolphin Café*…

and Jamie's fishing charter business. If we can get everyone to agree to stand firm, refuse to sell, then we'll be right. Otherwise, Pelican Crossing as we know it will cease to exist.'

'Okay, let's do it. I need something to take my mind off the sinker.'

Poppy grimaced, wishing she wouldn't call her baby that, but this time made no comment.

The rest of the morning was spent with Poppy listing the properties, and Megan the owners, most of whom they knew. Poppy lost count of the number of cups of tea she made, and the banana bread was all eaten by the time they finished.

'What's next?' Megan asked with a sigh of relief. 'Are you going to talk to all of them?' She gazed at the list with dismay.

'Cam and I will do it between us. You can help if you want... though perhaps not,' she said, noting how tired Megan appeared to be. 'Best you concentrate on staying well for the bub.'

'What about this Jordan guy? Was Mandy right? Are you really seeing him? Are you going to confront him about it?'

Poppy blushed. This was where it was complicated. She knew Cam didn't approve of her plan to continue to see Jordan in an attempt to find out more about what he was planning.

Thirty-four

Cam was glad to be home in Pelican Crossing, and to have found a new happiness with Poppy. But the spectre of Jordan Butler was hanging over him and the town. While Poppy had promised to check on the retail establishments, he had undertaken to approach Jamie, a few others he knew at the boatyard which was located to one side of the marina, and Troy at the hotel. He had no idea just how many local businesses had been approached by the realtor Butler had engaged, but he meant to find out.

After breakfast with Poppy yesterday, he'd had to spend the day at the marina, catching up on everything that had happened while he was gone. Rory was a good man, but he didn't have the overall view of the business that Cam had developed over the years, and Cam was responsible to the council for the running of the marina. At least that was safe from Butler's machinations.

He was looking forward to helping Poppy get started with Gary this morning, sure she'd be as skilled at diving as she was at everything else she'd taken on. And, once she'd learnt the basics, it was one more activity they could do together. The prospect of a future with Poppy sent a warm glow through him. It was more than he could have hoped for.

'Got a minute, boss?' Rory's voice interrupted Cam's thoughts.

'Sure. What's up?'

'Nothing, really, but… that Butler guy's been nosing around again. He was in yesterday and wanted to know about the boats we have for sale.'

'Is he interested in buying?'

'That wasn't the impression I got… It was more that he wanted to find out how we sourced and advertised them. I told him I wasn't privy to that part of the business, and he wasn't pleased.'

Cam's lips tightened. The boat business, along with the boat chandlery was something he'd added to the marina when he took charge. He ran Pelican Marine as a separate business with the council's permission, and it had proved profitable both for him and the council to whom he paid a percentage of all sales. If Butler had his sights on that too, nothing was safe. He stared out the window at the large motor cruiser still sitting there as if it belonged. He wished he could put a bomb under it – and Jordan Butler – but knew he'd have to find a more legitimate way to foil his plans.

'Thanks, mate. I'm going to be out for a bit this morning. Have something to check at your brother's dive school and I want to catch up with your dad. I'll be back before lunch to let you have a break.'

'No worries. Give my best to Gary. Things seem to be going well for him, though he did have an attempted break-in a few days after he opened. Lucky Dad had a good security system put in.'

'Lucky.' But it was another cause for concern. There had been too many things like this happening for them to be a coincidence. Maybe Cam should have a word with the police again though without any concrete evidence, there was little they could do. To date, they seemed to be putting all those incidents down to teenagers misbehaving. But Cam suspected it was more than that.

Seeing Poppy's familiar figure walking towards the boatyard, Cam closed his computer and, telling Rory again that he wouldn't be gone for long, made his way across the yard to join her.

'Good morning,' he said, greeting her with a hug and a kiss. It felt odd, if good, to be on such affectionate terms with her after so long.

'Morning, Cam.' Poppy smiled, sending a wave of pleasure through him. Despite Jordan Butler, life was good. Cam's relationship with Poppy was one thing he couldn't destroy.

'Hey Cam… and Poppy too,' Jamie came out to meet them. 'How are you both? Come to see me or Gary?'

'Gary first. Poppy's here to visit the dive school. Then I want to catch up with you if you can spare the time.'

'Sure thing. The young fellow's been busy since he opened up the school and managed to get time in the local pool.' He gestured to the council-owned ocean pool located on the rocks at the end of the beach. 'See you in a bit then.' He wandered off, and Cam and Poppy headed to the door above which was the sign, *Pelican Crossing Dive School* in large letters.

Poppy shivered.

'Nervous?'

'More excited, I think. I can't believe I've lived by the ocean all my life and never learned to dive.'

'It's never too late.'

'So you say.' But she smiled, her eyes twinkling, as if sharing a joke.

Once inside, Gary came to greet them. He was a younger version of his dad, reminding Cam of his own younger days. Wearing a pair of board shorts and a tee-shirt with the dive school logo, his blond hair tied back in a ponytail, he exuded confidence.

Cam introduced Poppy who said she could remember him when he was at school with Megan, then Gary took over. 'No need for you to hang around, Cam. We're going to be working on the theory today. All going well, Poppy, next week we'll get you into the pool, then we'll head out on the dive boat. That's when Cam can come along and make himself useful.'

'Right. So...' She gave Cam a pleading look.

'You'll be fine,' he said. 'Gary is the expert here. I'm going to have a word with Jamie then I'll go back to the office. Drop by when you finish here, and we can maybe get a bite of lunch.'

'Okay.' Poppy looked more subdued than usual. She was clearly out of her comfort zone. Cam was tempted to pull her into his arms and carry her off. But he knew she'd love it when she got going. He wished he'd thought of introducing her to diving before now. Even though Gary had only recently opened this school, there were others up and down the coast.

Leaving Poppy in Gary's capable hands, Cam went back to the office where Jamie was huddled over a computer.

'Too early for a beer?' Jamie asked.

'Too early for me, but a coffee would go down well.'

'No problem.'

A few minutes later, both men were leaning against the seawall at the edge of the boatyard, with mugs of strong black coffee.

'What's on your mind?' Jamie asked, taking a gulp of his drink.

'Jordan Butler.'

'I wondered if it was him. What's he been up to?'

'I did a bit of digging when I was down in Sydney. Seems he's behind the offers to purchase your business and *Crossings* – and I don't know how many other local businesses. I just heard yesterday about *The Blue Dolphin Café*.'

'Yeah, I heard Brad was considering selling. He must be close to retirement. I guess an offer to buy might have been welcome.'

'We can't let it happen, Jamie. With what Butler has in mind, Pelican Crossing would lose its uniqueness, would turn into another tourist hotspot with no character.'

Jamie rubbed his chin. 'Not sure what you have in mind.'

'I'm not too sure, either. I do know you've refused to sell, as has Poppy. She's agreed to check on the other retailers on Main Street… and I wondered if we could get the council involved.'

'Hmm. It's a thought. The guy would need planning permission if he aims to demolish and rebuild. How about a town meeting? My guess is, that if businesses have been approached separately like Poppy and me, people have no idea there's an overall plan.'

Thirty-five

By the time Poppy finished her session with Gary, she was hooked. She couldn't wait for her next session in the ocean pool, then it would be out into the bay.

'You're looking pleased with yourself.' Cam grinned when she walked into the marina office. 'I guess it went well?'

'A lot of theory. I can't wait till next week. Oh, Cam, you were right. I know I'm going to love diving.'

Cam grinned again. 'Ready for lunch?'

'I am.'

'Me too. I'll speak to Brad while we're there.'

'How did you go with Jamie?' she asked, as they made their way to the café.

'I told him what I'd found out about Butler, and he suggested a town meeting. Might be a good idea.'

'Oh, I hadn't thought of that. Maybe I can sound out the people I talk with. I'm guessing not all of them will have been approached with an offer to buy.'

By this time, they had reached the café and were seated at their favourite table. Chloe, their usual waitress arrived and handed them menus. She had lost her customary bounce, seeming as downcast as she had been the day before.

'Brad around?' Cam asked, sending Poppy a sidewards glance.

'In the kitchen.'

'Won't be long. Can you order for me?' Cam said to Poppy, sliding out of his seat and heading towards the café kitchen.

'What's that about?' Chloe stared after him.

'He wants to have a word with Brad about the offer for the café. Nothing to worry about.'

'Easy for you to say. I need this job. What if the new owner doesn't want to keep me on?'

'There may be no sale. It's something Cam and I are working on.'

The girl looked sceptical but only said, 'I'll come back when you've decided on your order.'

'I can give it to you now,' Poppy said, quickly scanning the menu. When she came here for lunch, she always ordered the Blue Dolphin sandwich – avocado, feta, mushrooms, olives, hummus and greens with dressing served on rye. She ordered the same for Cam along with two coffees, one black, one iced latte.

She was checking her phone and smiling at a text and photo from Scarlett when Cam returned. She looked up and raised an eyebrow.

'It's what we thought. An offer from the same Sydney realtor as contacted you, seeming too tempting to refuse. But Brad's no fool. He sensed there might be something dodgy about it, so hasn't replied. He's on board with the idea of a town meeting, and says he'll check with a few others he knows who might have been targeted too.'

'So what's next? I could sound Jordan out re…' Poppy's voice trailed off at Cam's shocked expression.

'What? He doesn't know we're onto him and he's expecting to see me again.'

'I don't want…' Cam leant forward and covered Poppy's hand with his. 'I know I have no right to tell you what to do or who to see, Poppy, but… Jordan Butler… I don't trust the man.'

'What do you think he's going to do?' Poppy asked, but a warm feeling unfurled in the pit of her stomach at Cam's concern. 'He'll suspect something's up if I suddenly refuse to see him. Isn't it better to keep him in the dark?'

'I suppose…'

'Don't worry, Cam. It'll be fine.' Poppy turned her hand to entwine her fingers with Cam's, only releasing them when their food arrived. She was pleased to see Chloe looked happier. Perhaps Brad had said something to put her mind at rest.

'Maybe it's not such a bad idea… you continuing to see Butler,' Cam said when they had finished eating, 'but be careful, won't you?'

'Of course, aren't I always?' Poppy grinned, remembering times when she'd been the risktaker of the group... when they were all teenagers. Judging by Cam's expression, he was remembering, too. 'I'm a lot older and wiser than I was at sixteen,' she said.

'Just the same. Take care. You're precious to me.'

Poppy felt that warm glow again.

'Now that you've started the ball rolling with Jamie and Brad, I'll drop into a few of the businesses in Main Street on the way home, see how many have been contacted. Not all of them would own their premises, so it might be difficult to figure out who the owners are.'

'I can check with the council.'

'Right.' Poppy stared into space, lost in thought as she pictured Pelican Crossing's Main Street. Most of the buildings were of the same vintage as *Crossings*, some renovated, some not. And there was *The Mousehole*, the aptly named little shop which was the outlet for the group of local artisans and their unique collection of goods. What would happen to them if Jordan succeeded?

Cam farewelled Poppy with a hug and a kiss on the lips which sent her heart racing. Then he was off, back to his office, and she was left to approach the shopkeepers, many of whom she'd known all her life.

*

By the time Poppy returned home, she had discovered that all of the shopkeepers who owned their premises had been approached, and the others were mystified by her question. She was exhausted and ready to have a rest, but the sight of Angus waiting to greet her, changed her mind and, after drinking down a glass of water, she picked up his lead and they headed to the beach.

Once there, as usual, the sea air and the sound of the waves lapping on the shore, helped to change her mood and she was feeling more optimistic when she arrived back to find Amber waiting for her. Her heart dropped at the sight of her oldest daughter standing on the doorstep, her eyes red and puffy.

'What's the matter, darling?' she asked. She unclipped Angus's lead to allow him to run into the yard.

'Oh, Mum! It didn't work,' Amber sobbed.

Poppy winced. She tried to mentally count back. Amber had told her the IUI process took four weeks and she'd know if it had been successful in another two. It was time. 'Oh sweetheart, I'm so sorry.' She pulled the sobbing young woman into a warm hug. She and Chris had been so optimistic this process would work for them. 'Have you told Chris?'

Amber shook her head. 'I came straight here. I needed...' she gulped, '... I needed to see you.'

Poppy hugged her again. She might be in her late twenties, but Amber was still her little girl, and right now, she needed her mother. The thought that her daughter might never become a mother flitted through Poppy's mind, but she didn't want to think of that, not yet anyway.

'Come in and we'll have some tea.'

Inside the bright kitchen, Amber took a seat at the table and scrubbed her eyes with a tissue, while Poppy filled the kettle and took a couple of mugs and camomile teabags from the cupboard, hoping the tea might help calm Amber. She wished there was more she could do to help.

'Thanks, Mum. It's good to be here.' Clasping the mug in both hands she gazed around the room which hadn't changed much since she and her sisters had been growing up here. 'Sorry to be such a misery.'

'Nonsense. It's okay to be sad, and it's healthy to have a good cry. Your dad always told me that when I was miserable about something.'

'I don't remember you ever crying,' Amber said, looking up.

'I did it in private,' Poppy said with a smile. 'Made sure none of you girls saw me. We all have our moments, and a good cry always helps.'

'Thanks,' Amber sniffed and took a sip of tea. 'This helps too, Mum.'

'Why don't you stay for dinner? Chris, too. You can call or text him. It'll be good to have someone to cook for. I sometimes wonder if it's worth it just for myself.'

'I did suggest this house was too big for you,' Amber said, sounding more like herself.

'And I said I'd never move,' Poppy countered.

'You need someone in your life, not someone to replace Dad – no one could do that – but someone to look after you.'

'In my old age?' Poppy asked with a grin, wondering what Amber would say if she knew about her and Cam. It was all too new to share, but if they continued to see each other, her girls would have to know. She thought they'd be pleased, more so than if it had been a stranger like Jordan Butler. She shivered at the thought of how close she might have come to making a huge mistake.

'No, but someone like... like Uncle Cam.'

Poppy felt herself redden. She almost choked, but managed to stop herself from blurting out the news that she and Cam were seeing each other.

'Why don't you contact Chris, while I feed Angus and see what I have for dinner,' she said to cover the silence after Amber's remark.

'Okay.' Seemingly unaware of Poppy's blushes, Amber took out her phone, and Poppy busied herself with filling Angus's bowls.

When Chris arrived looking worried, Poppy poured two glasses of wine and sent the young couple into the living room to give them some privacy, while she set about defrosting a dish of lasagne and putting together a salad.

'It's going to be all right,' she said to Angus, hoping she was right. She hated seeing Amber so upset and knowing there was nothing she could do to help.

When she called into the living room to say dinner was ready, the couple were together on the sofa, Amber's head on Chris's shoulder, his arms around her. It was good to see them comforting each other. Chris was a good man. Amber had made a good choice of husband – all the girls had.

'Mum.' Amber, sensing her mother's presence, raised her head. She was smiling. 'We're going to try again,' she said. 'They suggest three cycles before going to IVF. We may be lucky next time.'

Thirty-six

When Cam returned to the office, he was fired up with the idea of a town meeting, but unsure how to go about it. Then he remembered his old schoolfriend who was now the mayor. Joe would know how to get things moving. But the afternoon proved busy with several enquiries about boats which were for sale, so it wasn't till after he closed for the day that he had time to contact him.

It was after six, but Joe was known for being a workaholic since his wife died, so Cam drove round to the council chambers, relieved to see Joe's car still parked in its usual place. The door was open, so he walked in, and seeing the reception desk empty, went straight upstairs to the mayor's office.

As he approached, Cam heard the sound of raised voices, then a young man pushed past him. He knocked on the open door.

'What is it now?' Joe's angry voice echoed into the corridor.

'Joe?' Cam peered around the door.

'Cam! I thought it was that fool back again. I don't know why we hired him. Anyway,' his voice softened, 'good to see you. What brings you here?'

'Do you have a minute? There's something I want to ask you about.'

'I always have time for you. We don't see nearly enough of each other. Since Barb passed…' He sighed. 'Take a seat. What can I offer you? Tea, coffee… or I have a passably good bottle of Scotch.'

'A glass of Scotch would be most welcome.' Cam sensed it was what Joe wanted himself.

'Good man,' Joe said, confirming Cam's suspicions.

'Now,' Joe said, when he had poured two generous servings of the tawny liquid, 'how can I help you?'

'It's a bit of a long story.'

'I have plenty of time… too much these days. Why don't you start at the beginning?'

Cam took a sip of whisky. 'It's like this,' he began.

By the time he'd finished, both men's glasses were empty.

'Another?' Without waiting for an answer, Joe refilled their glasses. 'So, you want to organise a town meeting? You do realise, if you do that, this Butler guy will know you've been looking into him and if he's as ruthless as you seem to imagine, he might well retaliate?'

'I do realise that, yes. But I can't think of another way to let everyone know and to get support. Otherwise, I'm afraid a few might agree to sell and create an awkward situation.'

'Hmm. I can see that. Even if the council refuses him permission to demolish or revamp existing buildings, they could suddenly catch on fire, forcing others to give into his demands. That what you're afraid of?'

Cam hadn't thought that far ahead. Joe painted a frightening picture. While he'd thought Butler would stop at nothing to get what he wanted, surely even he wouldn't go that far? Then he remembered what Bill had told him in Sydney. A chill ran down his spine. 'I hadn't imagined… but you could be right.'

'However, I do think you're on the right track. The community needs to know who they're dealing with… not an anonymous realtor in Sydney but an interloper on their own doorstep, so to speak. I can alert the appropriate bodies in the council to be on the lookout for planning applications, while you set the wheels in motion on the ground. You should talk to Finn Hunter. He recently moved up the coast from Bellbird Bay to take on the editor's role at *The Crossing Courier*. From what I've heard, he's pretty community minded. He'd be your best bet to get the word out there.'

'Thanks. There's not much time before Christmas, but I'd like to have it as soon as possible.'

'Good idea. Catch everyone before they get bogged down with Christmas shopping and the tourist rush.'

'Mmm.' Cam hoped it wasn't already too late.

'Where did you have in mind to hold it?'

'I thought of the hall in the new sports centre. It's a council building, so would need council approval.'

'You've got it. I'll send a memo to the caretaker to let him know you'll be in touch, and if there's anything else I can do…'

'Thanks, Joe. I've taken up enough of your time.' Cam rose to leave.

'Not at all. This concerns us all. If Butler has his way, it would be a disaster for the town. Thanks for coming.'

The two men shook hands.

'I'll look out for your announcement in the paper and do keep in touch. It's so easy to lose contact.'

'Will do.' As Cam left, he thought about Joe's last remark. Had he been guilty of losing touch with many of his old friends after Gail left, embarrassed she'd chosen a woman over him? It wasn't too late to put things right, especially now he and Poppy were… what were they?

Too unsettled to go home where he'd no doubt heat up one of the frozen dinners which filled his freezer, Cam decided to treat himself to a meal at the local Thai restaurant. He'd always enjoyed Asian food after a holiday he and Gail took before Lachlan was born. He sometimes bought a takeaway meal from this restaurant, but tonight he felt like being with other people.

He pushed open the door to be greeted by the enticing aroma of spices. The restaurant was busy, being one of the few open on a Monday evening, and he was looking around for a table when he heard someone call out, 'Uncle Cam!'

He looked across to where Megan and Gavin were seated at a corner table and were waving to him. Wondering if Megan knew about him and her mother, he took a deep breath before heading across to join them.

'We were just talking about you,' Megan said.

Cam blushed, but Gavin's next words reassured him.

'We haven't managed to identify the culprits of the vandalism at the marina,' he said. 'It doesn't appear to be the work of the usual groups of teenagers. We can't figure it out.'

Cam gave a sigh of relief, though why he was worried about Megan knowing he and her mother had become more than friends, he wasn't sure. 'I think I may have the answer for you,' he said, Gavin's eyes widening as he explained what he had learned about Jordan Butler and his suspicions he was behind the damage.

'But his own boat was one of those targeted,' Gavin said.

Cam nodded. 'He's devious, I wouldn't put it past him....'

'Ah, I see,' Gavin said

Megan, who had been silent during their exchange suddenly spoke up. 'He's the one Mum's been seeing, isn't he? She hasn't said much about him but my friend, Mandy, saw them at the yacht club a couple of times.'

Cam stared at her. He knew Liz's daughter, Mandy, had seen him there with Poppy, too. Did that mean...? He was relieved by what Megan said next.

'I know you and Mum have had dinner there too, but you're different. You're family.'

Cam squirmed. If only Megan knew. His dearest wish was to *be* part of their family, not to be regarded as such because of his friendship with Jack. He wondered when Poppy intended to tell the girls about them. 'I think your mum knew him a long time ago... before she married your dad,' he said.

'Oh! Does she know about all this?'

'She does. We're on it together.'

Megan laughed. 'You make it sound like one of those American cop shows Gav likes to watch on Netflix.'

'Not exactly,' Gavin said. 'This Butler guy hasn't committed a crime, not yet anyway. And it sounds as if he takes care to keep on the right side of the law. I think a town meeting's a great idea, Cam. Count me in if you need any help.'

'Thanks, Gavin.'

'Oh, good,' Megan said as a waitress appeared with a selection of dishes, their delicious aromas wafting across the table and making Cam's mouth water.

'Why don't you share with us?' Gavin asked. 'I think Megan got carried away when we ordered. We'll never get through all this on our own, not even if you're eating for two, honey.' He grinned at Megan who pouted.

Then she smiled. 'You're probably right, Gav. I do tend to go overboard. Do say you'll help us out, Uncle Cam.'

'Since you put it like that...' Cam smiled as the waitress reappeared with another bowl and cutlery for him. 'At least let me order the wine. Gavin?'

'Good of you. I wasn't going to indulge, since Megan isn't drinking during her pregnancy, but I'd be happy to join you.'

During the meal, the conversation veered from Jordan Butler and the town meeting to Megan and Gavin's preparations for the new baby.

'It can't come soon enough,' Megan complained. 'These hot nights... I'm not getting much sleep. And it's only going to get worse.'

Cam murmured sympathetically. He remembered what it had been like when Gail was pregnant, how she had often got up in the middle of the night to wander around the house. 'You'll consider it's all been worth it when the baby's born,' he said.

Megan grimaced. 'You think?'

Cam smiled. Thinking of Gail reminded him that Poppy had told him Gail wanted to come to Pelican Crossing for Christmas. He wasn't sure how he felt about it, if it would interfere with the new situation between him and Poppy, though why should it?

All was going well until they left the restaurant. As Megan hugged him farewell, she whispered into his ear, 'I wish it was *you* Mum was seeing, Uncle Cam. I'm sure Dad would approve.'

Thirty-seven

Poppy rushed out to pick up the local paper as soon as Angus's bark told her it had been delivered. Taking it into the kitchen she sat down beside her half-drunk cup of coffee, opened it and flipped through the pages till she found what she was looking for. She gave a sigh of pleasure when she saw the headline – *Town meeting to discuss proposed development*. She read the article, which outlined Jordan Butler's proposal for Pelican Crossing without mentioning his name. It was very detailed, and Poppy realised Cam must have given Finn the brochures he'd obtained from Jordan's dad in Sydney. She hadn't seen them, but Cam had told her all about it. Still, it was a shock to see it there in black and white. She wondered what Jordan's reaction would be when he read it, as he was bound to do.

She'd find out soon enough. Despite Cam's warnings, she had continued to see Jordan. They were to have lunch today at a restaurant he claimed to have discovered along the coast from Pelican Crossing and, although she felt guilty about going ahead regardless of Cam's disapproval, she was looking forward to it.

'It won't be for long, Angus,' she told her pet whose expression seemed to mirror Cam's disapproval. 'Just till the town meeting when he'll see where I stand.' *Then maybe he'll leave town and leave us all alone.*

Dressing in a smart beige and white linen dress – Jordan didn't do casual – Poppy took particular care with her hair and makeup. Ever since Cam had told her what Jordan was up to, she'd made sure she always looked her best for him. She was going to give him no reason to dismiss her as some dull, small town, middle-aged woman. She couldn't forget how he'd managed to fool her into thinking he was interested in her.

'Hi, Poppy. You're looking beautiful as usual,' Jordan said, giving her a kiss on the cheek.

Poppy smiled, this time his words failing to move her. Cam was worth at least ten of him. How could she ever have contemplated having a relationship with him? But that was when you thought Cam wasn't interested, she reminded herself, feeling the familiar glow at the thought of her old friend. 'Thanks,' she said.

The restaurant was one Poppy hadn't been to before. It was situated on a low-lying piece of land overlooking the ocean – so close you could almost imagine you could step right into the water. As with all her previous dates with Jordan, the meal was expensive and exquisite, but Jordan wasn't his usual self. There was a tension about him that hadn't been there before. It wasn't till they had finished the luscious dessert of mangomisu – a tropical version of tiramisu made with mangoes – and had been served coffee, that he said, 'I suppose you saw the local paper?'

Poppy took a deep breath. 'You mean the article about a town meeting? Is it something that concerns you?'

'How did that pipsqueak of an editor get his hands on the information? I made sure no one in Pelican Crossing knew about my plans.' He pounded his fist on the table, his lips tightening.

'*Your* plans?' Poppy pretended surprise. 'Do you mean you're behind the proposed development. You…' she deliberately widened her eyes, '… you mean you were behind the offer to buy *Crossings*?' She thought she did it rather well. Perhaps she should have taken up acting as a career.

'You should have accepted the offer,' he said. 'You'll never get a better one. What do you want with a restaurant in an old building when you could be travelling the world, seeing all the places you've only dreamt about?'

'Is this what it was all about – all the wining and dining and compliments? Were they all a ploy to try to force me to sell?'

'Oh, Poppy, how could you think that? Can't you see how I feel about you? I just want you to be happy instead of wasting away in a place like this.'

At his words, Poppy forgot her vow to keep him sweet in order to find out all she could about his project. A rush of anger shot through her. 'That's my home you're talking about, the town where I grew up, the place I love and where I intend to spend the rest of my life. You say you want me to be happy, but you've never taken time to find out what I want with all your talk of travel and faraway places. I don't know where Finn got his information,' she lied, 'but I'm glad he did. The people of Pelican Crossing deserve to know what you're up to.'

'And they will, and you may be surprised how many will agree with what I propose for the town.'

Poppy gazed at him in surprise.

'I intend to attend this town meeting to put my case, to describe my vision for the future of Pelican Crossing. We'll see how many disagree with me. Now, I think we're done here.' He asked for the bill, paid and escorted a shaken Poppy out of the restaurant.

Could he be right, she wondered as she settled into his car to return home. Surely the residents of Pelican Crossing, the people she'd grown up with, and those newcomers who'd chosen to live there because of its laid back atmosphere, wouldn't back Jordan's plans?

'I'll see you at the town meeting,' she said, when his car stopped outside her house, 'and you'll find out what the residents of Pelican Crossing think of your plans.' She stepped out of the car, slamming the door behind her, relieved when she heard it drive off.

*

'And he intends to be at the meeting to "put his case",' Poppy said, her voice rising in anger.

As soon as she'd returned home from the lunch with Jordan, Poppy had called Cam, eager to share her news. Unfortunately, she'd called at a bad time. He'd been about to take a prospective purchaser out on one of the yachts for sale. But he'd agreed to call round after work.

Now, they were seated on her deck with a bottle of wine and two glasses, and she had recounted her conversation with Jordan.

'Good.'

'Good? Is that all you can say? It's a disaster.'

'Not at all. We've forced him to be open about his plans.'

'But what if… He seems to think there will be some who agree with what he calls his *vision for the future of Pelican Crossing.*'

'Do you really think that, after talking to all those shopkeepers? The residents of Pelican Crossing are smarter than that, too smart to be taken in by his schemes, no matter how charmingly he may wrap them up. I guess your lunch didn't end well?'

'Not exactly. I lost my temper,' Poppy admitted ruefully. 'I doubt he'll invite me again.'

'That's good too. You know I didn't want you to keep seeing him.' His eyes twinkled, and he reached over to squeeze Poppy's hand, sending a shiver of excitement right down to her toes.

'Would you like something to eat?' She started to rise, feeling uncomfortable with these new feelings, unsure what was going to happen next and if she was ready for it.

'Later.' Cam pulled her back down, moving to take her in his arms, and planting butterfly kisses on her forehead and eyelids. 'First, I want to show you how much I care for you.' He pulled Poppy closer, his lips meeting hers as she felt her passion rise.

Poppy relaxed into him, wondering what she had been worrying about. This was Cam, the man she'd known all her life, the man she'd hoped had feelings for her.

It was sometime later before they parted.

'I suppose we'll have to tell the girls now,' she said with a laugh.

'I think we'd better. I don't expect they'll be surprised.'

Thirty-eight

It had been a week since the announcement appeared in the paper, and now the town meeting was about to begin.

Cam stared around the room into which most of the residents of Pelican Crossing had crowded. All the shopkeepers were there, along with many others, most of whom he knew but some of whom were strangers to him. Amber and Megan were there too, with their husbands. They waved to Cam when he caught their eyes. As he'd predicted, neither had been surprised at the news he and Poppy had become closer, Amber saying, 'It's about time' and Megan giving them both a knowing grin.

He knew Poppy was surprised he'd refused to take a major role in the evening's proceedings, but he preferred to leave it up to Joe as mayor to chair the session, and Finn to reveal details of Butler's proposal, based on the information Cam had provided. Since returning from Sydney, he'd been back in touch with Butler senior – as Jack Taylor – and had managed to glean additional information about the project. He'd also contacted Bill again, and his old friend had been happy to dig up more dirt on Jordan which could be used for future articles in *The Crossing Courier* if required. Butler himself had insisted on taking part, as he'd told Poppy he would. It should be an interesting evening.

Cam felt Poppy tremble. She was sitting next to him in the front row of the audience. He squeezed her hand. 'It's going to be fine,' he said, mentally crossing his fingers. Surely Butler wouldn't manage to sway the audience to his point of view? When he and Jamie had considered the idea of having a town meeting, they had envisaged it as a sort of protest. They had never imagined it would turn into a debate.

Joe stood up and the chatter died down. Cam was suddenly conscious of Butler's eyes on him. They moved to focus on Poppy, then back to him again. He gave a snide smile, and Cam felt his gut churn. Jordan Butler wasn't someone to cross. He was glad he'd decided not to put the case for the town. Finn was a relative newcomer to Pelican Crossing and could be regarded as neutral by the community though perhaps not by Butler. But the editor assured him that he'd dealt with worse than Jordan Butler before now, having cut his journalistic teeth in Sydney and Melbourne.

The mayor welcomed everyone and stated the reason for the meeting, attracting a few muttered comments when he mentioned that many might have received offers for their properties. He then introduced Finn and Jordan, the latter receiving a few jeers when he was identified as the developer behind the offers to purchase. Cam saw him flinch. It must be unusual for him to be faced with an antagonistic audience.

A deathly hush fell on the room when Finn rose to speak. During his short time in Pelican Crossing, he'd managed to rejuvenate their failing newspaper which now had a healthy following and had gained the respect of the community. Not only did he edit the local paper, he was active in a number of local organisations and charities. He clearly laid out Butler's proposal, finishing with, 'Do we want Pelican Crossing to become a carbon copy of the Gold Coast?' generating a resounding, 'No!' from the audience, followed by cheers and a standing ovation.

Next, it was Butler's turn, and Cam was pleased to see he appeared to have lost some of his customary confidence at the crowd's reaction to Finn's presentation.

However, once he stood up, his usual arrogance reasserted itself as he proceeded to give a polished address, accompanied with a PowerPoint presentation. He was a gifted speaker and brought all his undoubted charm to bear on his audience. Cam could understand how he had managed to charm Poppy and was doubly glad she'd seen through him.

At the conclusion of his presentation – which received none of the accolades Finn's had – Joe called for questions. When Cam twisted round, he saw a flurry of hands go up. It was going to be a long evening.

Most of the questions were directed to Butler, and while it was clear he was accustomed to dealing with objections, it was obvious he hadn't expected the degree of antagonism towards his project. As one after another questioned why he wanted to despoil their town, he began to visibly wilt. The final straw came when Agnes, the woman who ran the pelican rescue centre, rose to her feet, her white hair flying wildly and making her look like a madwoman. She pointed a finger towards Butler and yelled, 'We don't want you here. The sooner you leave Pelican Crossing the better.' Her words were met by applause and a loud cheer.

Butler sat down, his arrogant demeanour undiminished. What had Poppy seen in him?

The town's feelings were clear, but Cam knew it would take more than that to defeat a man like him. But maybe. just maybe, he would choose somewhere else for his development, and Pelican Crossing would be spared.

Cam turned to Poppy who had a smile on her face. 'That went well, don't you think?'

'Better than I expected, but I doubt Jordan is convinced. He's pretty thick-skinned and I have no doubt he's met opposition, even hostility, before now. But I was proud of our community. And Agnes… Who'd have thought she'd have the guts to stand up like that?'

'She's a pretty amazing woman… not unlike another one I know.' He smiled at Poppy. 'Why don't we head off home and celebrate what seems to be a victory for the future of Pelican Crossing.'

'Seems is the word, but I'm happy to go along with you. Sounds like a good idea.'

Once outside the hall, Cam and Poppy squeezed through the groups of people who had congregated there to discuss the evening. It appeared everyone wanted to talk about what they had heard and be reassured none had accepted Butler's offer. If a few had agreed to sell, it could put everyone else's future in jeopardy.

Although tempted to hang around to hear what was being said, the warmth of Poppy's hand in his, and the prospect of the private celebration awaiting at the house on the clifftop, made it an easy decision to keep moving.

Back at Poppy's, they were greeted by Angus, delighted to have them home. He cavorted around them, getting underfoot while Poppy took a bottle of prosecco from the fridge and a couple of glasses from the cupboard. She handed Cam the bottle to open and carried the glasses through to the living room, Angus padding along behind her.

Once they were settled on the sofa, Angus lying happily at their feet, Cam poured two glasses. 'To us,' he said raising his glass. 'To the future of Pelican Crossing, and to it never changing.'

Poppy raised her glass to his. 'To it never changing too much,' she said. 'Some change is inevitable, and we have to move with the times. But we can do that without the machinations of a Jordan Butler, and we can maintain the unique nature of our town.'

'I'll drink to that.' Cam tipped up his glass.

They had demolished most of the bottle, and Angus was snoring peacefully when Cam reached an arm around Poppy's shoulders. 'You made the right decision, sweetheart. Butler was no good for you.'

'I knew that from the start, but you were gone for so long and I didn't know how you felt about me. It's been five years since Jack passed. It was time for me to move on. I wanted something more than a friend in my life, and it seemed you...'

Cam put a finger on her lips to stem her words. 'Let me show you how I feel about you.' He took the glass from her hand, placed it carefully on the coffee table, and proceeded to do just that.

Thirty-nine

Poppy opened her eyes, almost blinded by the early morning sunlight shining through the window. *Why hadn't she closed the shutters last night?* Then she remembered and turned her head to look at the man lying beside her. He was so familiar, yet it was strange to see him lying in the same spot Jack had for so many years. A warm glow enveloped her at the realisation he now belonged there too.

Last night had been amazing. It had been such a different experience for Poppy who had only ever made love with one man, with Jack. Cam had understood that, and had treated her gently, kissing and caressing her till she almost cried out as a surge of desire overtook her. After living without a man for five years, it had come as a surprise to discover how much she had missed both the passion and the comfort of having a warm body close to hers, and to her relief, he appeared to enjoy her fuller figure.

'Poppy?' Cam's eyes opened. He smiled, moved closer, and their lips met in a gentle kiss. 'Good morning, beautiful.'

Poppy's heart leapt. It had been so long since anyone had called her beautiful. Jordan's casual blandishments had slid off her like water from a duck's back, but Cam's compliments were different. They were honest, like the man himself. 'Good morning, you. I guess we should get up,' she said as she heard Angus scratching at the door. At least they'd remembered to close that.

'I suppose. I do have to go to work today. What will you do?' He pulled her into a hug.

'Let me see.' Poppy pretended to consider. 'Make breakfast, take Angus for a walk along the beach, bake something to take to lunch...'

'Don't tell me. It's one of your witch's lunches today. You'll have plenty to talk about after last night.'

'You're as bad as Jack, calling us names,' she said but she smiled. It was fun to be teased, the sign of a good relationship in her opinion, and she and Cam had always been on these terms. The difference was that now they were on more intimate terms too. The warm glow she'd felt earlier returned. 'But yes, lots to talk about.' About her and Cam too, Poppy realised. So much had happened since their last lunch. Rachel already knew about her and Cam, and she was pretty sure Liz had her suspicions – she'd made enough comments about Cam – but Poppy wasn't sure about Gill. She often suspected the divorce lawyer's job had prejudiced her against men, and her own experience with marriage hadn't helped. Poppy hoped they'd all be happy for her, as happy as she was herself, and she was fairly bursting with happiness.

After a breakfast of scrambled eggs on sour dough toast, followed by more toast with marmalade for Cam, washed down with two cups of coffee, Cam rose to leave. 'Wish I could stay and join you and Angus on the beach,' he said, prompting a short bark from Angus at the sound of his name.

'I wish you could, too.' Poppy wound her arms around his neck, happy in the knowledge she now had the right to do this.

'Don't do that, or I might never leave,' he groaned with a laugh. 'See you tonight?'

'Can't wait.'

With another hug and kiss, Cam was off, leaving Poppy with a smile on her face.

'Just us again, Angus,' Poppy said, but she was aware of a lilt in her voice that had been missing for some time. It was amazing what a difference a good man could make, she thought as she popped on her hat and picked up Angus's lead.

On the beach, Poppy breathed in the scent of the ocean, the sound of the waves and the shrieking of the seabirds as familiar to her as her own face in the mirror. When she saw Agnes coming towards her, her old dog padding alongside, she stopped. 'That was a brave move last night, Agnes. You said what we were all thinking. I'm sure everyone will be talking about it this morning.'

'Someone had to say it. We don't want people like that coming here and destroying our lives. I'm glad you've seen sense at last too.' She peered at Poppy, giving her the impression Agnes could see right through her and knew Cam had spent the night in her bed. Poppy blushed.

Back home again, Poppy set about baking the White Christmas she'd promised to take to lunch. Although Liz was providing lunch, Poppy had offered to bring along a batch of this confection made from her mother's special recipe. It was the closest thing to a white Christmas they could get in this part of the world.

She found a selection of Christmas songs and carols on YouTube to keep her company as she mixed the ingredients together, planning to put up the Christmas tree on the weekend as she sang along with *Jingle Bells*, *Deck the Halls* and *The Twelve Days of Christmas*. Once she had placed the mixture into the freezer for the requisite fifteen minutes, she headed to the shower. It was a hot morning, and a relief to take a cool shower before getting ready for lunch.

*

Poppy always enjoyed visiting Liz's small apartment, there was something about it that provided a sense of peace. But today she was fizzing with excitement. She wondered if her friends would sense the difference in her as Agnes had. Did her face give away the fact she'd slept with Cam last night?

'You're first to arrive,' Liz said, greeting her with a hug and kiss, the sound of Christmas carols pouring out from the room behind her. 'I'll turn that down now. I put it on to get me in the mood.'

'It's that time of year. I played some too, while I was baking.' Following Liz into the kitchen, she put the container of White Christmas down on the benchtop.

'Oh, good, you remembered.'

'Why wouldn't I?'

'I thought you might have had other things on your mind.' Liz grinned.

'Mandy's been talking again, and you've put two and two together to make five?'

'And last night... you and Cam... You can't tell me there's nothing going on.'

'No.'

'No there isn't, or no you can't?'

'No, I can't,' Poppy said with a sigh.

'I knew it! I'm happy for you. Cam's so exactly right for you – old friend, husband's best mate, related through your children's marriage...'

'Thanks, Liz. You know how to make me feel good. All these reasons and no mention that we might care for each other.'

'That too! Wine?'

As soon as Liz had poured the wine, the doorbell rang and Rachel and Gill arrived in quick succession so to Poppy's relief, there was no time for Liz to ask more about her and Cam. But she knew she wasn't off the hook; it was only a delay.

Liz poured wine for the newcomers, and the group moved into Liz's living area, already decorated for Christmas with a tall gold Christmas tree in pride of place in one corner, its lights twinkling.

'Presents first,' Liz declared, and the women each produced the gift they'd purchased and brought along for their Secret Santa. With the limit of $20 they'd set for their gifts, Poppy had found it difficult to decide what to buy. But on her visit to *The Mousehole* to talk about the proposed development, she'd spied a lovely small cat carved from a piece of wood and painted white. It was something she'd have loved to own herself and hoped whoever received it, would love it too.

Liz produced a large bag into which they all place brightly wrapped parcels of different shapes and sizes, then they took turns to fossick around in the bag and pull one out. They did this every year, and Poppy sometimes wondered what would happen if one of them pulled out her own gift. So far, it hadn't happened. She assumed that like her, the others could all recognise the feel of the gift they'd wrapped.

When it was her turn, she pulled out a book-shaped package wrapped in gold paper. Pleased, she unwrapped it and was delighted to discover it was the latest release by one of her favourite authors, one which she could curl up with over Christmas. While she was unwrapping her gift, the others were doing the same to a chorus of oohs and aahs.

'Oh, a cat. I love it!' Liz's voice sounded over the others.

Poppy was thrilled she'd been the one to get this gift. Liz loved cats but was unable to keep one in her apartment. It was perfect for her.

The others were equally pleased with their gifts, Rachel scoring a scarf in various shades of blue, and Gill a bottle of body lotion.

Now the gifts were all opened, Liz ushered them to the table which was set with a Christmassy theme, and lunch began.

After demolishing the chicken breast stuffed with camembert and wrapped in prosciutto, served with roast potatoes and a roast pumpkin salad, all washed down with prosecco, Liz brought out dessert consisting of tiny slivers of Christmas pudding served with a honey yoghurt. They finished the meal with coffee and Poppy's White Christmas.

There hadn't been much conversation during the meal, apart from compliments to Liz on the food. But now they had moved on to coffee, it was time to chat.

Rachel was first to speak. 'Didn't it go well last night?' she asked. 'That bastard Jordan Butler really got what he deserved. The way Agnes spoke up at the end…'

'It was a gutsy thing to do,' Gill said, 'but maybe unwise. She may have made an enemy of him, and I'd guess he can be pretty ruthless when he's thwarted.'

'You don't think…?' Poppy was stunned to consider that, by speaking up, Agnes might have put herself at risk. 'She's an old woman, no danger to anyone, least of all Jordan Butler.'

'A man like him probably doesn't care about any of that,' Gill said.

'You know him better than any of us, Poppy. Is he capable of harming her?'

Poppy thought for a few moments, thought about the man who'd charmed her all those years ago, the man who more recently had tried to use his charm to persuade her to sell *Crossings*, who had gone about it an underhand way. 'I don't really know,' she said. 'I hope not.' But she wasn't sure, mindful of what Cam had discovered about him.

'Poppy has moved on,' Liz said, causing the others to turn to look at Poppy.

Poppy blushed, wishing the floor would open up and swallow her. She'd known Liz would bring up Cam.

'Who?' Gill asked.

'It's Cam, isn't it?' Rachel said. 'I'm so pleased for you.'

'Cam... Cam Mitchell?' Gill asked. 'Wasn't he...?'

'Jack's best friend... yes,' Poppy said. 'We were all friends, ever since we were at school together – Jack and Cam, Gail and me. Now Cam and I are both on our own, and...'

'And Scarlett and Lachlan are married and about to give Poppy and Cam a grandchild. It's perfect,' Liz said.

Poppy shifted uncomfortably in her seat, wishing Liz hadn't brought it up. She smiled awkwardly, hoping they'd change the subject. Her relationship with Cam was so new, she wanted to keep it to herself, not have it bandied about over lunch. Even if these three were her friends, there were some things she preferred to keep private.

Seeming to sense her discomfort, Rachel asked, 'Are Scarlett and Lachlan coming for Christmas?'

'Yes,' Poppy said with a sigh of relief. 'Gail's coming too.'

'That's nice for you, and for Lachlan,' Rachel said.

'Won't it make things difficult?' Liz asked. 'She and Cam...'

'Not at all. They've remained friends, and he went down to Sydney to help when her partner died,' Poppy said.

'You don't think...?' Gill asked. She'd remained silent until now.

The other three looked at her.

She appeared embarrassed, but continued, 'You've told us how helpful Cam was to her when her partner died, and now she's coming here for Christmas. You don't think she'd like her and Cam to get back together?'

'Don't be silly,' Rachel said, but Poppy thought she could detect a hint of doubt in her voice. 'Didn't you hear what Liz said?'

Had her friends always been such gossips, or was she only noticing it because she and Cam were the subjects?

The conversation became more general, and Poppy was able to relax. It wasn't till she was driving home that she remembered Liz's question... and Gill's comment which echoed something Megan had said. Of course having Gail here for Christmas wouldn't make things awkward between her and Cam... or would it?

Forty

Cam made time to go home and change before heading to the marina. Although he hadn't intended to spend the night with Poppy, he was glad things had turned out as they did. Last night had surpassed all his wildest dreams. But he didn't want to turn up to work in the same outfit he'd worn to the town meeting.

After a quick shower and change of clothes, he was ready for another day at work, already looking forward to the evening ahead with Poppy. Why had he waited so long?

As Cam approached the marina, his attention was caught by the sound of a helicopter hovering overhead, then the sight of several police cars, emergency vehicles and a fire engine at the entrance to the marina. What was happening? He broke into a jog, coming to a stop when he saw Gavin directing traffic.

'What's up?' he asked, trying to peer through to see what was causing the trouble. He could see flames and a spiral of smoke coming from one end of a line of vessels.

'Explosion,' Gavin said. 'I'm not sure I can allow you to pass.'

'I need to get to the office,' Cam said. 'Rory will be there already. I'm responsible for the safely of all the boats there.' His heart sank, a feeling of dread overtaking him. If an explosion had occurred, he could be held responsible.

He waited with bated breath while Gavin consulted his superior. 'Okay,' Gavin said, when he returned, 'but take care. There could be more explosions. We don't know what happened.'

As soon as Cam reached the marina office, his eyes went as usual to the array of boats berthed there. It took him only a moment to realise that the flames and smoke were coming from the large motor cruiser which had dominated his view for the past few weeks, or from where it had been berthed. The vessel itself seemed to have vanished.

'It's *The Odyssey*,' Rory confirmed as he greeted him. 'It was pulling out around five. I was heading out to check my lobster pots before starting work, when I heard a loud bang and saw the flames. I called triple zero, but by the time they got here…' He shook his head.

'Butler?'

Rory shook his head again.

Cam dragged a hand through his hair. Last night must have rattled Butler more than he thought if he had started to pull out this morning. He hadn't expected him to give in so easily.

'Last night went well,' Rory said. 'Must have scared him off. I thought I was going to piss myself when old Agnes stood up and said what she did.'

'Hmm.' Cam decided not to share his suspicion that Butler might not have been finished with Pelican Crossing. But he needed to find out what had happened to the man, and there had been some crew members, too. 'Give me a few minutes, Rory,' he said, heading out to check with the emergency service personnel.

Cam returned to the office no better informed than when he left. He hadn't managed to obtain any information about the occupants of the vessel, so had no idea if Butler had been on board. That section of the marina had been cordoned off to everyone including Cam. Luckily it appeared that the boats on either side of *The Odyssey* had only received minimal damage, thanks to Rory's emergency call.

There was nothing more Cam could do.

'What now?' Rory asked.

'Busy day. It seems we're going to be allowed to continue to operate. We have a couple of people coming up from Brisbane to check out that catamaran we have for sale, and a few yachties have booked in for the weeks leading up to Christmas.' This was their busiest season, the time when many southerners decided to head up to Queensland for the Christmas holidays, and Pelican Crossing marina was a favourite stopping off place. It provided good business for the town, too, and Cam knew Poppy would reap the benefit at *Crossings*.

Thinking of Poppy reminded him again of last night. It had been a long time since he'd been with a woman, and it had felt so good to hold Poppy's naked body close to his, and to hear her groan with pleasure as he stroked her soft skin; to know she was enjoying their time together as much as he was.

The office door opened, and Cam thrust all thoughts of Poppy aside as his working day began. But he couldn't dismiss the worry about Jordan Butler and wonder what had happened to him.

*

It was almost time to close up for the day. There had still been no more news about *The Odyssey* and its occupants, and Cam was looking forward to going home to shower and change before heading to Poppy's. He had texted her to suggest he pick up a bottle of wine and a takeaway and had asked whether she'd prefer Thai or Italian, deciding to keep the news about Butler's boat till he saw her. He hadn't received a reply, so when his phone rang, he assumed it was her and didn't check before replying, 'Hey, you!'

There was an awkward silence then he heard a chuckle. 'I don't think you were expecting me to be the caller, Cam,' Joe said.

'Joe. Sorry. I thought… Never mind. What can I do for you?'

'I thought you'd want to know. The explosion at the marina this morning. There was a small fishing boat nearby and they were able to pick up three men. It seems one of them may be Jordan Butler. It was his vessel?'

'It was. They survived – the three who were picked up?' While Cam had no time for the man, he wouldn't wish him harm.

'It appears so. My information is that they were airlifted to hospital in Brisbane. I understand the cruiser is a write off. It must have been a shock. If you want more information, I can…'

'No, that's not necessary. Thanks, Joe.'

'Problem?' Rory walked through just as the call ended.

Cam's forehead creased. 'No, it's Jordan Butler. Seems he and his crew have been picked up and taken to hospital in Brisbane.'

'Good news. How bad are they?'

'That was Joe on the phone. He didn't have any details.'

'Pity about *The Odyssey*. It was a beautiful piece of work.'

'It was. Can't say the same about its owner, but I'm sorry he's been injured.'

'Hmm.' From Rory's expression, it was clear he didn't share Cam's opinion. 'At least he'll be out of our hair for a while, hopefully for good.'

'You're not wrong there.'

'You leaving now?'

'Yeah.' Joe's call had been something of a relief. Cam had been wishing Butler at the bottom of the ocean, and now he'd lost his boat and sustained goodness knows what sort of injuries. It was a shock, not one he'd forget in a hurry. But there was Poppy, and the evening with her ahead. His phone pinged with a text.

Sorry not to reply earlier. Italian would be good. Can't wait. P xxx

He started to reply... *See you soon. Love you.*

Then he pulled himself up. The news about Butler had affected him more than he'd thought. There had never been any talk of love between him and Poppy. It was too soon. He deleted the text and tried again.

See you soon. Italian it is. Cxx

An hour later, having showered and changed into a pair of newly pressed jeans and a short-sleeved pink linen shirt, Cam was at Poppy's door, an Italian takeaway in one hand, a bottle of Chianti in the other. When Poppy opened the door, he leant in to kiss her, wishing he had a free hand.

Once inside the kitchen, he put down the wine and food and took her into his arms, kissing her warmly on the lips. Suddenly all the hassles of the day disappeared with the feel of her soft body and tender lips. 'I've been waiting all day for this moment,' he murmured when they drew apart.

'Me too,' Poppy whispered.

Angus, who was waiting impatiently to be noticed, gave a short bark as if to say he'd missed Cam, too.

'Mmm, what have we here?' Poppy opened the box from the Italian restaurant to unleash a delightful aroma. 'Chicken Parmigiana... my favourite. You know me so well, Cam.'

Cam shrugged. They'd eaten out together so often over the years, it should be no surprise he knew her taste.

'I've prepared a salad and I thought we could eat on the deck.'

'Sounds good. I'll pour the wine and we can take it all out. What about Angus?'

'He can join us. I'll give him a treat, so he won't expect to share any of ours.'

It was beautiful on the deck, a cool breeze wafting gently over them after the heat of the day, the sky so clear Cam could see the stars sparkling, the distant sound of the ocean adding to the atmosphere.

'What's bothering you?'

They were halfway through their meal, and Cam had been trying to forget the news about Butler, when Poppy asked the question.

'You didn't hear the news?'

'What news? I've been busy all day – Christmas shopping, putting up the tree…'

'It looks very nice.' The tall, gaily decorated Christmas tree was sitting by Poppy's front window, its lights flashing. He should have mentioned it.

'What news?' Poppy repeated.

'Butler. *The Odyssey.* There was an explosion.'

The colour left Poppy's face. Her hand went to her mouth. 'Is he…?' she asked, her voice trembling.

'He and the crew survived. They've been taken to hospital in Brisbane. Are you all right, Poppy?'

*

Cam's voice seemed to come from a long way away. Poppy began to shake. Angus, sensing her mood, moved closer, rubbing his head against her ankles.

'Poppy?' Cam said again.

Everything came back into focus. 'Sorry. Did you say Jordan's boat exploded and he was injured?' She couldn't take it in.

'That's what I heard. I saw the damage when I arrived at the marina this morning, then Joe called me just before I left the marina to say Butler and his crew had been picked up and airlifted to hospital. I don't know any more.'

'Oh!'

'You've had a shock. Sorry, I should have broken it more gently. I didn't think…'

'No, you're right. I'm okay now, but…' Poppy looked at the food on her plate and pushed it away. 'I don't think I could eat any more. I liked Jordan until I discovered how he tried to use me to buy *Crossings*, then I changed my mind about him, but this…' She shook her head. 'It's difficult to believe. I'm sorry he's injured. You don't know how badly?'

Cam shook his head. 'I don't think Joe knew either.'

'Maybe it'll be on the news.'

Cam checked his watch. 'The late bulletin should be on shortly. Shall we watch it?'

'Would you mind?' Poppy didn't know why but she had an urge to find out more about what had happened.

'You go through and turn the television on. I'll take care of all this.' Cam gestured to the plates, glasses and the half-empty wine bottle.

'Thanks.' Poppy made her way inside, Angus trotting after her. She was annoyed with herself for spoiling the mood of what had been a romantic evening, but she had to know.

'Here, you look as if you need this.' Cam handed her a glass of wine and took a seat beside her on the sofa, winding an arm around her shoulders. It felt good to have him close… comforting.

Poppy took a sip of wine, then heard the familiar music heralding the latest news. She held her breath. She'd wanted him to leave, but not like this. What if…?

The newsreader began to speak.

'In the latest news, police and fire investigators are looking into the cause of a blaze that destroyed a luxury motor cruiser at a marina on the Queensland Coast. The vessel which is believed to be owned by Sydney developer, Jordan Butler, had been berthed in the marina in the small town of Pelican Crossing. The occupants, said to be the owner and two crew, were picked up by a passing fishing boat and have since been airlifted to hospital in Brisbane.

'Police said emergency crews were called to the fire early this morning to find the twenty-seven-metre vessel fully engulfed. Crews worked to extinguish the fire, but the vessel was destroyed, with only debris left floating on the water. The cause of the fire is being investigated.'

When the newsreader stopped speaking, Poppy found she was clutching Cam's hand so tightly her nails were digging into his skin. 'Sorry,' she said, removing her hand, only to have him take it in his again and squeeze it. 'It's so terrible. What could have caused it?'

'Difficult to say. Usually fires like that are caused by a build-up in fuel vapours, maybe even a leaking gas bottle.'

'I wanted him to leave, but not this way.'

'I don't imagine any of us wanted this.' Cam pulled her into his arms.

Poppy relaxed into his embrace, comforted by his nearness, glad of his support. But she couldn't dismiss the image of Jordan lying in a hospital bed suffering from horrific burns. 'It's not as if I care about him but...'

'I know. It's a dreadful thing to happen to anyone, not something you'd wish, even on your worst enemy.'

'The town will be safe now, though, won't it?'

'I'd assume so, though I think after last night it was a foregone conclusion. It seems he did intend to leave this morning.'

'Oh!' Poppy laid her head on Cam's shoulder. He made her feel safe.

Cam pulled her close, his chin on her head. 'Maybe I should tuck you up in bed. You've had a long day and a huge shock. You need to rest.'

'Mmm.' Poppy wasn't sure what she needed, but the thought of her soft, warm bed was tempting. She allowed herself to be led into the bedroom.

'Hold me,' she said, when they were lying side-by-side. She didn't know if she wanted to make love tonight. After thinking about it all day, it didn't seem right when Jordan was lying in a hospital bed. But she did want the comfort of Cam's warm body next to hers.

However, once she was lying in his arms, and he began to stroke her gently, a rush of desire took her by surprise, and she lifted her lips to meet his.

Forty-one

Poppy awoke with a smile on her face to the raucous sound of a pair of kookaburras on the fence outside her window. She turned to receive Cam's kiss. Then she remembered. She stiffened.

Seeming to sense her withdrawal, Cam said, 'There may be more news this morning. Why don't we check while we have breakfast?'

Poppy filled Angus's bowls, then she and Cam took their coffee and toast through to the living room and turned on the television. There were the usual reports of fighting overseas, road fatalities, bushfires in parts of the country, warnings to take care in the lead up to Christmas, then the item they were waiting for.

'In relation to the explosion of a motor cruiser on the Queensland Coast yesterday, we can report this morning that the three people injured in the incident are all suffering severe burns and are presently in The Royal Brisbane and Women's Hospital in a critical condition. It is believed at least one of the patients has burns to more than sixty per cent of his body.'

Poppy stared at Cam. 'Do you think it's Jordan?'

'Hard to say. I guess there may be more in a later bulletin… or in the newspapers. We can check online later in the day. Someone like Butler will be big news, in the Sydney papers at least. But there's nothing we can do, Poppy.'

'No.' She bit her lip.

'When does Gail arrive?'

'On Tuesday.' Only three more days, and she had a lot to do before then. She needed to try to forget about Jordan Butler and concentrate on her own life. It would soon be Christmas, and she had been looking forward to it so much. Cam was right. What was happening to Jordan was out of her hands. She had her life to live, a family to care about and Christmas to prepare for.

'Will you be okay?' Cam asked as he kissed her goodbye. 'I need to go to work but I'll see you again tonight. If you don't need to be at the restaurant, why don't you come over to my place and I'll throw a steak on the barbie? Bring Angus if you want.'

'Thanks, Cam. I will. It's a good idea.' She'd been going into *Crossings* less and less, but knew, as Christmas approached, she'd have to spend more time there. A night at Cam's, away from everything, might be just what she needed. Angus would enjoy the change too. Cam was so thoughtful. She stretched up on her tiptoes to give him a kiss. 'I'll see you then.'

After Cam left, Angus began to whine.

'You want a walk, don't you? Come on then.'

The little dog danced around Poppy's feet as she popped on her wide-brimmed hat and took his lead off its hook. Then the pair set off for the beach.

This morning, several of the early morning swimmers were still around, sitting on some rocks chatting. She couldn't see Gill, but one of the group who recognised Poppy waved to her. She waved back and continued on her way; she wasn't in the mood for small talk this morning, and no doubt the explosion on Jordan's boat would be the main topic of conversation. It was unusual for an accident like that to happen in their small town.

When she reached the edge of the water, she unfastened Angus's lead and the little dog ran off, his nose to the ground. Poppy laughed. Angus never changed. He had been such a comfort to her for the past five years. She was glad Cam understood their bond and was willing to share it. She took off her sandals, paddled along in the shallow water at the edge of the ocean and thought about Jordan. While he might be a devious monster who set out to manipulate her into selling, he didn't deserve what had happened to him. They had enjoyed some good times together, and she couldn't fault his generosity – though she would have been happy with a beach picnic and a walk along the sand.

Then her mind drifted to Cam, to their time together, to how he made her feel so happy and secure. She knew Jack would approve of their relationship – and was glad he had never known about Jordan. He wouldn't have understood and would have been overtaken by jealousy. Unlike Cam whose acceptance of her dating Jordan when he was in Sydney was a relief.

Feeling more settled, she called to Angus and turned to walk back.

*

The police tape was still around the section of the marina which had housed the burnt-out vessel, but the crowd of emergency workers from the day before were nowhere to be seen. Cam was opening up his computer when Rory burst through the door.

'Did you hear the news?' he asked, bubbling with excitement.

'Is there something new? You were here when Joe rang me yesterday, and we watched the news last night and this morning.'

'It seems a couple of Brisbane detectives flew in this morning. There's talk of sabotage.'

'Sabotage? Who...?' Cam stopped. Anyone who had been at the town meeting knew how strong the community's feelings were against Butler. But sabotage...? 'Surely not.'

'It's what I heard when I was buying coffee this morning. It's the talk of the town. They plan to interview everyone who might have had reason to want Butler dead.'

'Whew, that's heavy. It could be all of Pelican Crossing.' Cam wondered if Poppy knew, if he should call her, prepare her. He took his phone out of his pocket, them put it back. She'd said she was planning to have coffee with Rachel this morning, then go into the restaurant for a bit to check on things. Maybe he'd try to catch her there at lunchtime.

Sure enough, an hour later, two men dressed in suits, walked into the office.

'Cameron Mitchell?' one asked.

'That's me.'

'You manage the marina?'

'I do.'

'Detectives Ron Jeffries and Adam White,' the taller one said. They showed Cam their badges. It was just like he'd seen on the cop shows on television, but this was real. 'We'd like to ask you a few questions. Is there somewhere private?' He glared at Rory who was staring at him, his eyes wide.

'Sure. We can go through here.' Cam led the two men into the back office and gestured to them to sit before taking a seat himself.

'Now. Mr Mitchell, you'll be aware of the explosion which took place here on the marina yesterday.'

Cam nodded.

'We understand the boat had been moored here for some time.'

'That's right. The owner, Jordan Butler, booked a berth here in the marina for several months. It seems he decided to leave yesterday.'

'Did he give any reason for that?'

'I wasn't here at the time. No one was. My assistant saw the explosion on his way to work. It was him who called triple zero.'

'Right.' The detective glanced at his companion. 'We'll want to talk to him too. Now,' he leant back in his chair, 'it's also my understanding there was some sort of town meeting the previous evening at which Mr Butler spoke.'

Gosh, they were well-informed, but Cam supposed it was public knowledge. 'That's right. A number of local businesses had received offers to purchase their properties. We discovered Butler was behind them, that he intended to buy up the place and turn it into a replica of the Gold Coast.' Cam couldn't keep the bitter note out of his voice.

'You didn't like the idea?'

'No one did. It didn't affect me personally. The marina is owned by the council. But most of the residents in Pelican Crossing have lived here all their lives. They didn't want what he was proposing.'

'And they made their feelings plain?' The detective – Cam thought it was Ron Jeffries – leant forward.

'There were a lot of questions and disagreements. It was clear to him that no one wanted what he was planning to do.'

'Anyone in particular?'

Cam thought of old Agnes, but the idea she might have sabotaged the cruiser was ludicrous. He shook his head.

'And who has access to the marina?' His companion rose to gaze out the window at the lines of craft berthed there.

'Anyone can walk in during business hours. After hours, access is only by the keypad on the locked gate. All the boat owners have an access code, as do Rory and myself.'

'Right. Thanks, Mr Mitchell.' The detective closed the notebook he'd opened earlier, but hadn't written in. 'That's all for now. We may want to talk with you again later. If we could talk with your assistant now?'

'I'll send Rory in.' Cam got up and left, glad to have the session over. As soon as he returned to the main office, he sent Rory to talk with the two detectives and picked up his phone to call Poppy. This couldn't wait till lunchtime. To his annoyance, the call went to voicemail. He sent a quick text.

Detectives in town. Suspect sabotage. Expect a visit. Call me. Cxx

Forty-two

Poppy was driving to meet Rachel when her phone rang. She glanced at the device lying on the passenger seat and saw it was Cam calling, but she was driving so couldn't take the call. It was followed by the ping of a text. She smiled. She loved the way he kept in touch, and now things had changed between them, his frequent messages meant more than ever. She waited till she had parked outside Rachel's house, then read the text, her smile quickly disappearing. *Detectives? Sabotage?* She pressed Cam's number, only to be frustrated when it went to voicemail.

'I heard the news.' Rachel greeted her with a hug. 'How do you feel about it? I know for a time, you and he…'

'I'm still in shock, Rach, but that's not all.' She opened her phone to show her friend Cam's text.

Rachel's eyes widened. 'Wow! I think we may need something stronger than herbal tea this morning.'

Poppy managed to smile. 'No, tea will be fine, and what do I smell? You've been baking?'

'Only a few trays of gingerbread cookies for the grandkids. I'll make a gingerbread house with them closer to Christmas. It's become something of a tradition with us.'

Poppy saw Rachel's eyes light up at the mention of her granddaughters. It would be a few years before *her* grandchildren would be old enough to make a gingerbread house for Christmas, but this time next year, she'd be a grandmother twice over. She needed to focus on that instead of Jordan Butler and the suspicion of sabotage. Surely they'd discover it had been an accident?

As if reading Poppy's mind, Rachel said, 'It won't be long before you're making gingerbread houses, too.'

'A few years yet, Rach.'

'It'll pass in a flash. They don't stay little long enough. Remember when Amber and Jess were that age? It sometimes seems like yesterday, then I look at the two little ones...' She laughed. 'Ginger and lemon tea okay for you?'

'Perfect.' Poppy pulled out a chair and sat down. She always felt at home in Rachel's large family kitchen. 'No guests?'

'No, thank goodness. I'm free of them till after Christmas. Then they arrive in droves. I'm fully booked through January and February, then a break till Easter. But it keeps me out of mischief.' She laughed again.

Poppy was glad she had arranged to see Rachel this morning. Her friend was always positive, though Poppy suspected she had her sad moments too. She must miss Kirk as much as Poppy missed Jack. Even though the initial grief lessened, it never completely disappeared, and this time of year was when she felt it most. But now she had Cam, who understood how she still felt about Jack. She was doubly blessed.

'So,' Rachel said, when they were both seated with cups of tea and a plate of gingerbread cookies, 'these detectives. Do you think they'll find anything or are they just going through the motions because of who he is?'

'I don't know. There was a lot of ill feeling at the town meeting, but I can't imagine anyone we know going so far as to sabotage his motor cruiser.'

'You've been on it. Was it as luxurious as people say?'

What people, Poppy wondered, but said, 'It's certainly bigger than anything else I've ever been on. It's... was... around twenty-seven metres with several cabins, all with ensuites. I didn't see all of them, but there was a large saloon, a lounge and a large rear deck. It was a floating hotel. He said there were two crew, but I didn't see either of them. I can't help thinking about him, Rach. I know what he intended to do here, and I'm pretty sure he was never really interested in me as anyone but the owner of *Crossings*, but to experience that... it must have been terrifying. They say one of them is badly burned. Jordan was so proud of his looks. What if...?'

'There's nothing you can do about it,' Rachel said, echoing Cam's words. 'Maybe, if the detectives talk with you, they'll have more information.'

'Maybe. I expect they *will* want to talk to me. He wanted to buy *Crossing*s, and I probably knew him better than anyone else here.' A thought suddenly struck her. They couldn't think *she* had anything to do with it, could they? 'You don't think they might suspect me, do you?'

'Of course not. But they'll no doubt want to interview you.'

'Mmm.'

'How are you and Cam getting along?'

Poppy blushed. 'We're good. If it wasn't for all this, I'd say everything is looking up for me. I have so much to look forward to.'

'Concentrate on that. This will be over, and you'll soon forget all about it.'

'Hmm.' Poppy hoped Rachel was right.

'Now, let me show you what I've bought my granddaughters for Christmas.'

The rest of Poppy's visit was spent more pleasantly admiring the collection of gifts Rachel had managed to collect, from stocking fillers to dolls and two small scooters.

All too soon, it was time to leave and make her way to the restaurant. In the car, she tried Cam's number again. This time, he answered.

'Where are you?'

'I've just left Rachel's. I'm on my way to *Crossings*. Why?'

'I've just spoken to Jamie. The two detectives went to see him after they left the marina. Seems they have a list of all the premises Butler wanted to buy. *Crossings* will be on the list.'

Despite the sun streaming through the car windows, a shiver ran down Poppy's back. 'What are they like?'

'Nothing like what you see on TV. They're just a couple of ordinary guys doing their job. My guess is they're only going through the motions before confirming it was an accident. But they've heard about the town meeting, that there was a lot of ill-feeling towards Butler, and need to make sure. You've nothing to worry about if you tell them the truth.'

'It's all very well for you to say that. They probably already know about my seeing him, and I was actually on *The Odyssey*.'

'You've nothing to worry about,' Cam repeated. 'I'll see you tonight and we can laugh about it together.'

Laugh? Poppy didn't imagine there would be much to laugh about. 'See you then,' she said and ended the call.

Poppy sensed the tension in the atmosphere as soon as she entered the restaurant.

'There are a couple of detectives waiting to speak to you,' Michelle said in hushed tones. 'I put them in your office and gave them coffee. I hope that was all right.'

'That's fine, Michelle.' Poppy had hoped to have more time to prepare, though what sort of preparation she could do, she wasn't sure. She took a deep breath, walked through the restaurant and pushed open her office door to see two men in suits looking quite at home and drinking coffee. 'Gentlemen,' she said.

At the sound of her voice, they both rose. 'Ms Taylor?' one asked. 'We are Detectives Ron Jeffries and Adam White. Thanks for seeing us.'

What choice did she have? They were sitting in her office. 'No problem. What can I do for you? I presume it's about this terrible tragedy?'

'The explosion which destroyed *The Odyssey*, yes,' the taller man said, as they both resumed their seats. He took out a small notebook and referred to something written there. 'From what we understand, you were made an offer for your restaurant which you refused, and you were personally acquainted with Mr Butler.'

Poppy took a seat behind her desk, feeling more confident in the familiar setting. 'That's correct. Two offers actually, both of which I refused. I had no intention of selling. I grew up in this restaurant. My husband and I took it over from my parents and made it what it is today.'

'And your acquaintance with Mr Butler?'

'We were friends... or I thought we were, until I learned he was behind the offers to buy me out.' She took another deep breath. Tell the truth, Cam had said. 'We first met briefly over thirty years ago, then again when he dined here. He invited me to dinner, and we ate out together a few times... as old friends do.' She paused, cautious of overdoing it.

'And did you ever have occasion to visit the motor cruiser, *The Odyssey?*'

'Once. We had lunch there.'

He wrote something down.

Poppy squirmed in her seat.

'You attended the town meeting?'

'Yes, along with most of the residents of Pelican Crossing.'

'Did you speak at the meeting?'

'No.'

The detective paused and glanced at his companion who gave him a brief nod. He closed his notebook. 'That will be all for now, Ms Taylor. We may require to speak with you again.' He rose.

His companion rose, too. 'Thanks for the coffee,' he said.

Poppy heard them speak briefly to Michelle as they walked through the restaurant, then heard the door close behind them. She let out a sigh of relief.

Michelle popped her head through the office door. 'They've gone now.'

'Thanks, Michelle.'

'Everything okay? Is there anything you need me to do?'

'Everything's fine. You don't need to do anything different from usual. I assume we're ready to serve lunch?'

'Of course.'

It would take more than a visit from two detectives to interrupt the routine in the *Crossings'* kitchen. Poppy walked out to stand in her usual place. Hopefully she'd satisfied her visitors and she wouldn't see them again.

Forty-three

To Poppy's relief, the two detectives appeared satisfied with what they'd learned in Pelican Crossing. By the end of the weekend, they had returned to Brisbane, and the latest news bulletin reported that the explosion was deemed to be a dreadful accident which had inflicted terrible injuries on Jordan Butler and his two crew members who were now in a critical but stable condition in a Brisbane hospital. Poppy had called the hospital and attempted to get more information but, as she wasn't a relative, she only learned what she already knew.

She decided she'd done what she could and determined to consign the entire episode to the past and focus on the approaching festivities and her future with Cam.

Everything was ready for Christmas, the beds in the spare rooms made up and waiting for her guests to arrive. The young couple weren't going to be here till Christmas Eve, but Gail would arrive the next day. Poppy was looking forward to seeing her old friend again. It had been too long since they last met.

'Maybe we should cool it when Gail's here,' she said to Cam on Monday morning as they were lying in bed after making love.

'Why?' Cam leant up to support himself on one elbow and stared at Poppy. 'She'll soon find out about us, may even know already. Scarlett and Lachlan do and may have told her.'

'It's not about her knowing. I just think I'd feel odd if you stayed overnight while she's here. The kids will be here too. It'll only be for a couple of weeks. They'll all be gone in the new year and things can go back to normal.'

'I don't see why, but if it makes you happy…'

'It doesn't make me happy. I'd much rather have you here. You do know that, don't you?' She reached up to kiss him, one hand tousling his hair. 'But I think it would be better. Maybe we can sneak off together… to your place.'

'So you're not going to cut me off completely?' He grinned.

'I could never do that, not now we've found each other.'

'You'd better not.' Cam began to tickle her, and they ended up entangled in the bedclothes before making love again.

By the time they emerged from the bedroom, Angus was whining for his breakfast.

'Sorry, Angus,' Poppy said, filling his bowls. But she couldn't keep the smile from her face. It was going to be difficult for her too, to survive without Cam sharing her bed over Christmas, but she remembered what Liz had said and had decided to avoid the possibility of any awkwardness.

'Busy day ahead?' Poppy asked Cam when they were eating breakfast of muesli topped with fruit and yoghurt and enjoying coffee.

'Busy time. We're fully booked right up to the end of January. It may tail off when the schools go back, but not all of our clients are bound by school holidays. I'll close the office between Christmas and New Year but will have to be on call for any emergencies.'

'Right.' Poppy was glad they'd at least have Christmas week together, the time when Scarlett and Lachlan were here.

'You?'

'I'm as prepared for Christmas as I can be here, but there are still a few things to iron out at *Crossings*. As we're open on Christmas Day, I like to give my staff some time off before then, so it's a matter of juggling the staffing for the next few days. Then we're closed for Christmas week too.'

'You're a good boss. I've always admired the way you handle both the restaurant and the staff. You're much more sympathetic to their needs than Jack ever was – not to criticise him, he had other qualities which made him a good restaurateur.'

'He did, didn't he? I always miss him more at this time of year. He loved it so much.' The memory of Jack walking into the restaurant dressed up in a Santa suit brought tears to Poppy's eyes. She brushed them away.

'I do too. Remember when the kids were little, and he spent an entire morning setting up a train around the Christmas tree?'

'And the rest of the day playing with it, while the kids moved on to other things?' Poppy laughed, her tears quickly drying. Then they threatened to start again at the realisation Jack would never have the opportunity to do that for his grandchildren.

'Hey, don't cry. Jack would hate that.'

'I know.' Poppy smiled through her tears. 'I was just thinking that he'll never see his grandchildren, and they'll never get to know what a ball of fun he was.'

They sat in silence for a few moments until Angus came over to nudge Poppy's ankles.

'Angus wants his walk,' she said.

'And I need to go. I'll see you tonight. We should do something special. With Gail arriving tomorrow, then Lachlan and Scarlett, it may be the last evening we have alone for some time.'

'Unless we sneak away,' Poppy said, grinning. 'But, yes, it would be lovely to do something special. What have you in mind?'

'Don't know yet. I'll work on it. See you then.' He kissed her, then was off, whistling as he let himself out.

'Okay, Angus,' Poppy said to the little dog who was jumping up and down. 'Let me load the dishwasher and we can be off. Then you'll need to be a good boy today as I have a lot to do at *Crossings*.'

*

Poppy was exhausted by the time she got home. She'd been tempted to stay at the restaurant, only the thought of Cam and what he might have planned made her take Michelle's advice and go home. 'We can manage without you tonight,' the girl had said, steering her out the door. 'You've done enough for today.'

Once home, she was greeted by Angus who was always excited to see her, whether she had been away for a day or only five minutes. She decided to have a shower, knowing a blast of cold water was exactly what she needed to re-energise her and recharge her batteries. She hoped Cam didn't have anything too energetic planned; she just wanted a quiet evening.

Unsure what to wear, Poppy decided on the loose multi-striped pants she'd bought on a trip to Bellbird Bay, teamed with a white top. Surveying herself in the mirror, she thought that she didn't look too bad for fifty-one, conscious she had another birthday coming up in the new year. She pulled her stomach in, aware of the extra kilos she'd gained, of what Cam called her sexy curves and grinned. He was such a lovely man. She was so lucky. Her musings were interrupted by Angus's bark followed by a knock at the door.

'Hello, gorgeous.' Cam greeted her with a hug and a kiss. He was dressed casually in a pair of jeans and a tee-shirt.

'What have you planned?' Poppy asked, wondering if she was overdressed for what he had in mind.

'I guessed you might have exhausted yourself today. When I peeked in around lunchtime, you were dashing around like crazy. I thought you'd want a quiet evening, so we're going for a picnic on the beach.'

Poppy stared at him. How could he gauge her feelings so accurately? It was the perfect ending to her day. 'Wonderful,' she said.

'Angus can come, too.'

'Better not,' she said, looking down at her pet who, seemingly having understood Cam, was wagging his tail furiously. 'I don't trust him not to run off, and we won't be able to find him in the dark.'

'Sorry, old man,' Cam said. 'The boss has spoken.'

Angus visibly drooped.

*

Cam unloaded a basket from the boot of his car and handed Poppy a picnic blanket. 'If you can carry this, I'll manage the rest.' Then, taking her hand, he led her down the path to the beach.

It was deserted at this time of night. The sea was still, the only sound the gentle lapping of waves on the shore. Overhead, the moon shone brightly, its beams glistening on the water. It was a perfect evening for a picnic.

Cam spread the blanket on the sand and placed the basket down. He held up a hand to Poppy. 'Join me?'

Poppy sat down, curling her legs under her, curious as to what might be in the basket.

First, Cam took out a bottle of wine and two plastic glasses which he filled, before handing one to her.

Poppy took a sip. It was a chilled chardonnay from her favourite vineyard.

Cam then produced a cooked chicken, several tomatoes, various cheeses, a packet of crackers, a container of strawberries and a bunch of grapes. There were also paper plates and napkins, and wooden cutlery. It was a fitting feast for a night like this.

When they had finished eating, and the wine bottle was empty, Poppy lay back on the picnic blanket, her head in Cam's lap, and gazed up at the stars. Lying here like this, she was struck, not for the first time, how insignificant she and everyone else was compared to the magnitude of the universe. She turned to tell Cam her thoughts, but he was gazing at her.

'Penny for them?' he said, gently stroking her forehead and sending shivers of delight through her.

'I was just thinking how unimportant we are in the great scheme of things. When you look up at the sky, at everything up there. And we get caught up in our petty issues.'

'They're important to us. Right now, you're the most important thing in my life.' He bent his head till their lips met, sending all thoughts of the universe out of Poppy's head as she became lost in a tumult of desire.

When they finally drew apart, Poppy became aware that tiny drops of rain were beginning to fall.

'We should get back before we get soaked,' Cam said, rising and beginning to pack the hamper.

Realising he was right, and the rain was becoming heavier, Poppy rose too and folding up the blanket, took his hand to climb back up to the house.

By the time they got there, they were both drenched, but they were laughing.

'We need to get out of these wet clothes and have a shower,' Poppy said, managing to ignore Angus's demands for attention.

'Mmm, a shower sounds good.' Both removed their wet clothes, dropping them onto the floor as Cam followed her into the bedroom and into the shower, where they laughingly clung together under a cascade of water.

Later, when they were lying together on Poppy's bed, Cam took her in his arms. 'Now, where were we?' he murmured, as their passion mounted again.

In heaven, Poppy thought as he kissed her.

Forty-four

Next morning, Poppy was awakened by Angus scratching at the bedroom door. Checking the time, she realised they'd overslept and there was only time for a quick cuddle before fixing breakfast. It had been some time before they had fallen asleep the previous evening; Poppy glowed as she remembered their lovemaking.

After their cuddle, Cam jumped out of bed and headed into the shower, while Poppy pulled on an oversized tee-shirt and went to the kitchen.

After breakfast and listening to the news bulletin on the radio which reported that Jordan Butler was making good progress in hospital and would soon be moved to Sydney to be closer to his family, Cam rose to leave.

'I wish I could stay,' he said, pulling Poppy into his arms. 'I'm going to miss you.'

'I'll miss you, too, but it's not for ever,' she said, stroking his cheek. She was tempted to tell him she loved him, but he hadn't mentioned the L word, and she didn't want to be the first to say it. Perhaps after Christmas was over... 'Now, you'd better go.' She shooed him out of the house, watching from the doorway as he got into his car and drove off.

Gail's flight was due in at nine-thirty so once Cam had left, there was just time for Poppy to shower and get dressed before she had to leave for the airport. 'Walk later,' she promised an unhappy Angus.

The drive to the airport was one Poppy had always enjoyed, but this morning her emotions were mixed. On the one hand, she was looking forward to Christmas and to seeing her old friend, on the other, she wished it was all over so she and Cam could be together again. We're not being parted, she reminded herself, it's only that we won't be spending our nights together – and probably not being as openly affectionate with each other as they'd become used to.

Poppy arrived at the airport to discover the plane had been delayed. She should have checked before leaving home; there might have been time to take Angus for a walk after all. She bought a coffee and settled down at one of the small tables to check her phone. There was another article about the explosion on Jordan's boat. Poppy read it avidly to discover that one of the crew members who wasn't as badly injured as Jordan or the other crewman, had been interviewed. His account confirmed it had been an accident, the explosion caused by a build-up of gas fumes in the fuel compartment.

Her phone pinged with a text. It was from Cam.

Love you. See you tonight. Cxxx

Poppy's heart leapt. He'd said it; he'd said it first. Bursting with happiness and wanting to shout her joy to the world, she replied.

Love you too. Pxxxx

The Christmas carols which had been playing in the background suddenly stopped to be replaced by an announcement that the plane from Sydney was about to arrive. Poppy put her phone away and finished her coffee, before heading to the area where passengers would disembark and joining the crowd of people waiting for their loved ones to arrive for Christmas.

The passengers dribbled out in twos and threes, till Poppy finally recognised her old friend. Gail looked older than she remembered, but it had been a few years since she'd seen her, and she'd recently lost her wife. Grief could be aging.

'Gail, it's so good to see you.' Poppy hugged her, noticing how thin she had become, and how her hair seemed to have lost its lustre. Gail had always been proud of her appearance, but now she appeared drab and indifferent to how she looked, dressed in a pair of loose pants and a creased linen shirt.

'Good to see you too, Poppy.' Gail returned her hug. 'Thanks for letting me spend Christmas with you.'

'Of course. What are friends for? Let's get your luggage.'

'There's only this.' Gail gestured to the small carry-on case sitting at her feet. What had happened to the woman who couldn't go anywhere without a large case full of clothes?

'Okay, let's go.'

Gail didn't talk much on the way back to town, leaning her head back on the headrest and closing her eyes. She didn't open them till Poppy stopped the car. 'Sorry, I haven't been able to sleep much recently. It's good to be back in Pelican Crossing,' she said, getting out of the car and looking up at the sky. 'I love the air here. It's different. I've missed it.'

Poppy knew what she meant. The Queensland air *was* different. She always felt that way too, when she returned from visiting other parts of Australia. It was difficult to describe it; it just felt like home. But it wasn't home to Gail any longer. It had been over ten years since she left to make her home in Sydney with Judy. 'I'm so sorry about Judy,' she said, wishing she'd said it before – though she had said it on the phone.

'Thanks. It doesn't get any easier, but I hope... being here...' She sighed.

'Lachlan and Scarlett will be arriving on Christmas Eve,' Poppy said, 'and there's our grandchild to look forward to.'

'You're right. A new life.' Gail smiled, but it seemed forced.

'Tea?' Poppy asked when they went inside to be greeted by an excited Angus. He always loved visitors.

'I'd love one, thanks.' Gail dropped into a chair as soon as they reached the kitchen.

Poppy busied herself making two cups of ginger and lemon tea and popped some of the gingerbread cookies Rachel had sent home with her onto a plate. 'I didn't bake these,' she said, placing them on the table along with the tea, and taking a seat, too.

Gail looked shattered, Poppy thought, as if a slight breeze would blow her away. 'I thought we might take a walk on the beach,' she said. 'Angus likes one in the morning, but if you're too tired...'

'No.' Gail seemed to rouse herself. 'That sounds lovely. I've missed the Pelican Crossing beach too. We all had such good times here.' She sighed again.

Poppy was puzzled. She had expected Gail to be sad, grieving for Judy. All this talk about missing Pelican Crossing was unexpected, but maybe it was just the result of coming back after so long.

Angus, excited as usual at the mention of a walk, was standing below the hook which held his lead, wagging his tail with anticipation.

Once on the beach, Poppy forgot her confusion as her customary enjoyment of the beach took over. It was difficult to be anything but relaxed, walking along with the sand between her toes and the sea air filling her with a sense of wellbeing.

Gail seemed more relaxed, too, swinging her sandals in one hand while she picked up pieces of sea glass with the other. 'I'll take these back to Sydney,' she said, 'to remind me...'

Meanwhile, Angus ran back and forth chasing the seagulls ever out of reach and making both Poppy and Gail laugh.

Back home, Poppy prepared a light lunch of salad with spinach, beetroot, orange and goats cheese, then Gail said, 'I think I'd like to have a rest.'

'Of course. I'll show you to your room. I'd planned for Cam to join us for dinner – perhaps at *Crossings* – if you feel up to it.' She hadn't counted on Gail being so fragile. The Gail she remembered had always been full of energy. She and Jack had been the drivers of the four, with Poppy and Cam following their lead. But she recalled how she had been after Jack's death. She'd have been lost without *Crossings*. The restaurant had saved her, given her a reason to live.

With Gail lying down, Poppy went out to the deck intending to spend a few hours reading. Angus followed her, plopping himself down at her feet and curling up. Poppy opened her book but found it difficult to concentrate on the Scottish crime series she'd been enjoying. Gail's lack of energy worried her. She had arranged to meet Cam at *Crossings* where she could keep an eye on things while they ate. Maybe she should reconsider, have dinner here, where she and Gail could have an early night.

While she was wondering what to do, her phone rang. Seeing Megan's number, she answered quickly. 'Is everything all right?'

'Keep your hair on, Mum. I'm only calling to see if Aunt Gail arrived and how she is.'

'Yes, she's here. We had a walk on the beach, then lunch, and now she's having a rest. I'm worried about her, Megan. She's a shadow of her former self and seems to have lost all her get up and go. I know I lost it for a while after your dad passed, but... and she's talking a lot about missing Pelican Crossing.'

'How weird. I never thought she was particularly attached to the place. But I was in my teens when she left. What do you plan to do with her?'

'I intended for us to have dinner at *Crossings* with your Uncle Cam tonight, and laze around and catch up with things in the next few days, though I'll have to spend some time at the restaurant. But now I'm not sure if she's up to it.'

'Dinner at *Crossings* is a good idea. She does know about you and Uncle Cam, doesn't she?'

'I assume Lachlan will have told her.' Poppy bit her lip. What if Gail didn't know? Should she bring it up? How could she?

'Why don't Gav and I join you there for dinner? I'm getting a bit fed up sitting at home. I feel like a whale. This baby can't come soon enough.'

Poppy laughed. 'You don't have long now, then you won't know what's hit you. It would be great to see you and Gavin tonight.' The presence of the young couple should take off any pressure she might feel with Gail seeing her and Cam as a couple.

'Good. We'll see you there. Seven?'

'Seven,' Poppy agreed.

It was another couple of hours before Gail emerged looking more refreshed. She'd applied some makeup and changed into a dress, making her appear more like her old self, albeit thinner and more strained. 'Sorry I conked out,' she said 'I felt like a wet rag when I arrived. I feel better now. What's the plan for this evening?'

'I thought we'd have dinner at *Crossings*. Cam's going to join us, and Megan and Gavin.'

'That sounds lovely. It'll be nice to see Megan again. Lachlan told me about you and Cam,' Gail said, coming over to give Poppy a hug. 'I'm glad. You'll be good together. I always thought he'd be the one you'd choose.'

Poppy stared at her in amazement. Did she mean now, or back when the four of them did everything together, before she and Jack became a couple? She decided not to ask, relieved Gail knew they were together now, and she didn't have to be the one to break the news.

*

The restaurant was buzzing with the sound of chatter when Poppy and Gail walked in. Poppy glanced around at the full tables, the staff delivering meals, and inhaled the familiar aroma emanating from the kitchen.

'Full house,' Michelle whispered. 'Lucky I saved you a table.'

'Megan and Gavin are joining us. Can you fit five?'

'No problem.' Michelle dashed off to organise it.

Gail looked around at the busy restaurant, the tables filled with happy diners. 'You've done well,' she said. 'I saw *Crossings* featured on *Weekender* but I didn't realise...'

'It's a bit different to when Mum and Dad ran it,' Poppy said, proud of what she'd achieved. 'Take a seat.' She gestured to where Michelle was organising two more places at a table in a prime position. 'I just want to check the kitchen.'

When she returned Cam had arrived and was chatting to Gail. Seeing Poppy, he rose to give her a platonic kiss on the cheek. 'Hey, you,' he said so quietly only she could hear. The warm glow she always got when Cam was near, unfurled in her stomach again.

'Mum!' Megan and Gavin arrived and, after hugs and kisses all round, they took their seats around the table.

'Not long now,' Gail said to Megan who was clearly finding it difficult to find room for her baby bulge at the table.

'Thank goodness, Aunt Gail. The sinker can't come soon enough.'

'The sinker?'

'It's what she's been calling the baby. I've told her to be careful the name doesn't stick when it's born,' Poppy said, frowning at her daughter.

'No chance,' Megan said. 'We've already decided on names – Hazel if it's a girl and Noah if it's a boy.' She smiled at Gavin and took his hand. 'That's right, honey, isn't it?'

Gavin nodded.

'I like them,' Poppy decided. 'You didn't want to call a boy after your dad?'

'We did consider it, but it's so old-fashioned.'

The waiter arrived with menus and listed the day's specials.

'What do you recommend, Poppy?' Cam asked. 'I saw you come out of the kitchen. You must know what looks good.'

'Everything on the menu will be delicious, but I'm going to order the saffron croquettes with paprika aioli, followed by...' – she read from the menu – '...grilled swordfish with lemon myrtle and caper butter sauce, saffron potatoes and asparagus.'

'That sounds yum. I'll have that, too,' Megan said.

'Gail?' Poppy asked.

Gail stared at the menu as if seeking inspiration. 'Maybe the octopus with limoncello and pepper and a garden salad,' she said at last.

Poppy looked at her with concern. It was a tiny meal, but at least she'd ordered something.

'I think we men need something more substantial,' Cam said, giving Gavin a wink. 'What about a half dozen oysters followed by the pork loin?'

'Sounds good to me,' Gavin replied.

'And I think this evening deserves a celebration. We'll have a bottle of prosecco and one of sparkling mineral water,' he said to the waiter with a smile in Megan's direction.

'Thanks, Uncle Cam,' she said with a grimace. 'I can't wait to be able to have a glass of bubbly again. I was sorry to hear about Judy, Aunt Gail,' she added. 'It must have been dreadful for you.'

'Yes,' Gail said, her eyes moistening, 'but Cam was good. I'd have been lost without him.'

Poppy gave her a quick glance. It was the second time she'd said that. She was beginning to wonder exactly how big a help Cam had been.

The conversation turned to the forthcoming birth and the preparations for Christmas and the moment was lost. But it stuck in Poppy's mind.

When they left the restaurant, Megan and Gavin went straight to their car, leaving Poppy standing with Gail and Cam. She wanted to kiss him properly to tell him she'd miss him tonight but felt awkward in Gail's presence.

'Shall I walk you two ladies home?' Cam asked.

'Yes, please. That would be lovely,' Poppy said, as he linked arms with both her and Gail to walk towards the house on the clifftop.

Once there, to Poppy's relief, Gail seemed to sense her desire to be alone with Cam.

'See you inside,' she said, opening the door with the key Poppy had given her.

Left with Cam, Poppy stood still for a moment before wrapping her arms around his neck and wishing she hadn't made the crazy decision not to sleep with him while Gail was here. But it was too late to change her mind now.

'It was a lovely evening, but I wish…' Cam said, before crushing her to him in a passionate kiss that sent her senses reeling.

'So do I,' Poppy said, unable to stem the rush of desire she felt at the touch of his lips.

'We'll work out something. I can't wait till after Gail leaves.'

'Mmm.' Anything Poppy wanted to say was stifled by Cam's lips on hers again.

'Tomorrow,' he said. 'You'll be in *Crossings* at lunchtime?'

'Yes.'

'I'll see you then.' He gave her one last kiss and hug and was off, striding down the slope, Poppy's eyes following him till he was only a speck in the distance.

Forty-five

By Christmas Eve, Poppy's house had suddenly gone from being practically empty to being full of people. Although Gail had already been there for a few days, it wasn't till Scarlett and Lachlan arrived that it became filled with the sounds of loud voices. Even Angus seemed to have sensed the excitement and was making more noise than usual.

When all the hugs and greeting were over, and Scarlett and Lachlan had disappeared into their room, Scarlett claiming she needed to rest and Lachlan reluctant to leave her, Poppy looked at Gail. 'I think you and I need a cup of tea.'

'Yes please. I'd forgotten how loud these two could be together. When they were in Sydney, they were more subdued, probably because of Jude.' Her eyes clouded over as Poppy had noticed they did from time to time, usually when she thought no one would notice. It must be hard for her. Poppy remembered her first Christmas without Jack… and the next… and the next. She'd had her three girls to help her. Gail only had Lachlan who was too wrapped up in Scarlett and the baby to worry about his mother.

'Remember when they were seven…' Poppy said, in an attempt to cheer Gail up, '… how they would hide and play tricks on everyone until we begged them to stop?'

'Jack encouraged them. He was like a big kid himself.'

'Yes.' It was Poppy's turn to relive the past. 'They were good times. And now these two are about to become parents themselves.'

'They'll be good parents.'

'And you'll make a good grandmother.'

'You, too.'

'I hope so.'

'When's Megan due?'

'January. Not long to go.'

By this time the kettle had boiled. Poppy dropped two of the peppermint teabags she knew Gail liked into mugs and carried them out onto the deck. It was still hot out there but shaded. Angus followed them out, dropping down at Poppy's feet.

'How are you bearing up?' Poppy asked.

'So, so. I have good and bad days. Cam was a wonderful help after… I don't know what I would have done without him,' she repeated. 'I was completely spaced out for days. Coming here for Christmas has helped. Thanks, Poppy. I couldn't face spending Christmas in the Sydney house without Jude. It was always such a special time for us.'

'So you said.' Poppy put a comforting hand on Gail's arm, trying to ignore her reference to Cam's help yet again. 'I'm happy to have you here.'

'I hope I haven't spoiled things for you. Lachlan said you and Cam…'

'Of course not,' Poppy lied. She was missing Cam. She'd only just become accustomed to sharing her bed with him. Now she was there on her own again. Seeing him in the company of others wasn't the same, wasn't enough.

'You're coming to the carol singing tonight?' she asked, to inject a more cheerful note into the conversation.

'Of course. I wouldn't miss it for the world. It's so much part of the Pelican Crossing Christmas I remember. Being here brings back so many happy memories. They were good times, weren't they? When we were all young and together.'

'Yes, they were. And you'll have good times again, Gail. I know that, right now, it's difficult to believe. I didn't believe it either when people told me time was a great healer, but Jack's been gone for five years now, and it does get easier with time.'

'You've moved on.' There was a note of wonder in Gail's voice.

'I have… and you will, too. Not yet, maybe not for a few years. But the time will come when you decide to pick up your life again.'

'I wish I could believe you.' Gail looked down to where Angus was lying, his eyes partially closed, but ready should any titbit appear.

*

Poppy had arranged to meet Cam, Amber, Chris, Megan and Gavin outside *Crossings* so they could all go to the carol singing together. As in previous years, it was to be held at Pelican Plaza. When Poppy and the others arrived, the area was already crowded, only the early arrivals having managed to find a seat, many of them having been there for hours.

'Will you be all right standing?' Cam asked Megan. 'I can fetch a chair from the marina.'

'I'll be fine, thanks, Uncle Cam, but I may not last till the end.' She smiled up at Gavin whose arm was around her shoulders.

'You have a good man, there,' he said.

'I know.' She smiled at her husband again.

Seeing the interchange, a bubble of happiness bloomed in Poppy's heart. All was well with her world.

It was a perfect evening, the stars sparkling in the clear sky, the moon's beams shining down on the water like strands of tinsel, and the large Christmas tree behind them with its twinkling lights adding to the festive atmosphere.

A cheer went up when the mayor appeared to open the proceedings, then his place was taken by the musical group and choir from the local high school.

It was a cheerful group who joined in the singing of a collection of traditional carols and some not so traditional. During the evening, several other schoolchildren moved through the crowd collecting for pelican rescue, some of the money from which would go to old Agnes's refuge, and the rest to the wildlife organisation which conducted the regular tourist sessions at Pelican Plaza.

The service had been going on for some time, and the crowd had just finished a rousing rendition of *Hark the Herald Angels Sing*, when Megan said, 'I think I've had enough.'

'Me, too,' Scarlett said, cradling her baby bump.

'Can I catch a lift with you?' Gail asked. 'I'm beginning to wilt. There's no need for you to leave,' she said as Poppy started to join her. 'I'll be fine with these four.'

'If you're sure?' Poppy asked, her voice almost drowned out by the musical group beginning to play *Silver Bells*.

'We're sure,' Gavin said. 'See you tomorrow.'

They all hugged, and Gail and the two young couples left.

Once they had gone, Cam moved closer to Poppy and snaked an arm around her shoulders. It was as if he felt free to do so now Gail had left them, Poppy thought, dismissing the notion as soon as it arrived.

The carols continued for another half hour, concluding with *We wish you a Merry Christmas*. As the crowd began to disperse, Poppy hugged Amber and Chris, with promises to catch up again next day.

Left alone, Poppy and Cam looked at each other. Poppy could see her own desire mirrored in Cam's eyes. His apartment was only a short distance away.

'My place?' he asked and, without waiting for an answer, grabbed her hand and, like a couple of teenagers, they ran across the way together, arriving at Cam's apartment block laughing and out of breath.

'I guess this may have been what you meant when you spoke of sneaking away,' Cam said when they were inside, the moonlight shining through the large window. 'I feel like I'm eighteen again, though I didn't have a pad like this then,' he chuckled, before they were overtaken by passion, divesting themselves of their clothes and falling onto the king-sized bed.

They were still locked in a passionate embrace when they heard the clock in the town centre chiming midnight, heralding in Christmas Day.

'I should go,' Poppy said regretfully.

'Must you?'

'Yes, I wish I didn't, but I have a busy day ahead.' In her mind she started to itemise all the things she had to do on Christmas Day.

'Before you do. I have something for you.' Cam opened a drawer on the bedside table and took out a gaily wrapped box. 'Merry Christmas.' He kissed her.

'Merry Christmas. Your present is under the tree.'

'I can wait. I wanted to give you this when we were alone.'

'Did you plan to come back here tonight?'

'Not plan, but I hoped.'

Poppy kissed him again then tore off the wrappings. 'Wow! Thank you so much, Cam.' Poppy slipped on the two-toned gold and silver bangle with a dual knot which was a perfect match for the necklace Jack had given her. She held up her wrist. 'It's perfect. How did...?'

'I wanted to give you something special, something to make you remember the time we found each other.'

'Oh, Cam!' Poppy threw her arms around him, kissing him again and again. 'I don't have anything special for you.' She thought of the two shirts she'd lovingly wrapped and were now lying under the Christmas tree in her living room.

'That's okay. I have another gift for you, too, one I'll give you in front of everyone else. This can be our secret.'

'A lovely secret.' Poppy gazed at the bangle admiringly again, knowing it would be just as precious to her as the necklace Jack had given her.

'Now, I'll take you home.'

When they reached Poppy's house, they embraced one more time before Poppy quietly opened the door and tiptoed into the silent house, careful not to disturb anyone as she crept into her bedroom, her heart overflowing with love for Cam.

Forty-six

Christmas Day dawned, a day which had always been chaotic in Poppy's life with the restaurant serving Christmas lunch. Nothing had changed in the past five years and, for Poppy, the buzz in *Crossings* had always gone some way to filling the empty spot where Jack should have been.

This year would be different. Scarlett, Lachlan and Gail were with her, and there was Cam… Poppy looked at the bangle Cam had given her and was again enveloped in the glow that had never been far away, ever since their first kiss. Last night had been special, and she hoped they wouldn't have to wait till her house guests were gone before they could repeat it.

She struggled out of bed, aware she had a house full of family – she had always counted Gail as family – for whom to prepare breakfast. Cam was joining them for breakfast, partly because Lachlan and Scarlett were there. She hoped he'd had a better night's sleep than she had. She'd lain awake for what seemed like hours reliving their lovemaking and wishing Cam was with her.

The sound of Christmas carols met her ears before she reached the kitchen where she found Scarlett and Lachlan were already preparing breakfast. 'Merry Christmas,' she said. 'You're both up bright and early.'

'Merry Christmas, Mum.' Scarlett hugged her. 'I don't get a lot of sleep these nights, and it's so much hotter here than Canberra, but I'm not complaining. It's good to be home.' She shot Lachlan a look which puzzled Poppy.

'Merry Christmas, Aunt Poppy.' Lachlan hugged her, too. 'We fed Angus, and Dad texted to say he's on his way. I've cut up several of the mangoes that were in the bowl, and Scarlett's making pancakes. Hope that's okay. I looked in on Mum. She was still asleep, and I didn't want to wake her.'

'That sounds wonderful. I'm glad your mum's having a good sleep. I don't think she's slept much since Judy's death, probably not even before that. She needs a good rest.'

Poppy was glad she'd showered and dressed before coming through to the kitchen. She was wearing a shocking pink, sleeveless maxi-dress she'd had for years and which she knew suited her, and her often unruly hair had behaved itself. She laughed to see Angus capering around the kitchen with a tinsel bow attached to his collar, no doubt Scarlett's doing.

Cam arrived, and Gail appeared, looking rested and more elegant than she had since she arrived, and suddenly the kitchen was full of people. When the newcomers had finished wishing and being wished Merry Christmas with more hugs, Scarlett sent the three older members of the group out to the deck with glasses of mimosa, the sound of carols following them out. Angus followed, too, in the hope of more food.

When breakfast was over, it was time for Poppy to go to the restaurant. In a pattern which had grown up over the years, she'd go to *Crossings* to supervise the lunch. It was one of the busiest days of the year for the restaurant, almost rivalling Melbourne Cup Day, and she was always there to greet their guests.

Their family Christmas celebration would wait, as usual, till the evening when Amber, Chris, Megan and Gavin would join them, and she'd be able to relax. There was always plenty of food left over from the Christmas lunch prepared in the restaurant kitchen, so no need for her to cook.

When she reached the restaurant, Poppy was greeted by more Christmas carols and Christmas wishes from the staff who had given up this part of Christmas Day with their families to serve others.

The tables were all set with tiny Christmas trees and crackers and, as she expected, when she entered the kitchen, everything was prepared for the set Christmas lunch. It was to be a four-course lunch including the traditional roast turkey with a seafood option for those who'd prefer it, and Christmas pudding to finish.

Satisfied everything was in place, Poppy went back into the main part of the restaurant to wait for their customers to arrive.

*

It was late afternoon before Poppy arrived home. As she unpacked the eskies of food from the car, she heard the sound of laughter, then Scarlett and Lachlan appeared at the top of the cliff path, followed by Angus.

'Let me help,' Lachlan said, taking the esky from Poppy. 'You go inside. I've got this.'

'Thanks, Lachlan. Been for a swim?' she asked Scarlett as they went inside to the cool house.

'We have. It was glorious. I've missed living so close to the ocean,' Scarlett said, throwing her arms in the air. There was a sense of excitement about her that Poppy couldn't identify. Perhaps it was Christmas.

The house was silent.

'Where's your Aunt Gail?' Poppy asked.

'She said she wanted to rest. Do you want me to check?'

'No, she'll come through when she's ready.' Poppy would have liked to rest, too, but there was a lot to do before everyone arrived for dinner. She felt tired but knew she'd be better after a cold shower.

'You need to rest, too,' Scarlett said, as if reading her mind. 'Why don't you put your feet up for a few minutes while I make you a cup of tea? Camomile?'

'That sounds wonderful, darling.' Poppy went through to the living room and dropped onto the sofa to be joined by Angus, pleased to see her back.

'Where would you like these?' Lachlan popped his head through the door.

'Put them in the kitchen. Everything should be right in the eskies.'

'No worries.'

Poppy put her head back and closed her eyes, one hand lying on

Angus's soft coat. There was the sound of voices coming from the kitchen, but the words were indistinct. She was almost asleep when a voice close to her said, 'Mum?'

Poppy's eyes flew open. Scarlett was standing there, holding a cup of tea, a gingerbread cookie balanced precariously on the saucer. 'Thanks, sweetie. You going to join me?'

Scarlett shook her head. 'I'm going to have a bit of a lie-down, too. I don't want to fall asleep during dinner.'

When Scarlett had left, Poppy sipped her tea and nibbled on the cookie. It was lovely to have her youngest daughter home again. She'd missed her since she moved to Canberra. She'd make the effort to visit there in the coming year, Poppy vowed, especially when the baby was born. She had no desire to miss seeing this grandchild growing up. Two grandchildren. This time next year, she'd have two grandchildren. She fingered her necklace with her free hand wishing Jack could be here to see them. Then she looked at the bangle on her right wrist, the bangle she hadn't removed since last night, and smiled, knowing Jack would approve.

'You're back.' Gail was standing in the doorway. 'Did I hear Lachlan and Scarlett come back, too?'

'Yes, Scarlett's having a rest, but I don't know where Lachlan went to.'

'I expect he's having a rest too.' She made quotation marks with her fingers around the word rest. 'Remember what it was like when we were first married? We didn't want our parents to know we were having sex in the afternoon, so we snuck away and tried to be very quiet.' She laughed.

Glad to see Gail looking and sounding so much better, although suspecting it was only temporary, Poppy laughed too. 'We were so young,' she said, thinking how much she wished she could sneak away with Cam right now, despite feeling tired after a busy session at the restaurant. It had nothing to do with age.

'I'm glad Lachlan and Scarlett finally got together,' Gail said, taking a seat next to Poppy. 'It brings our two families together. Remember how we planned it when they were toddlers?'

'And we almost ruined it with all our expectations,' Poppy said.

'But it's turned out well, and now we get to share a grandchild.'

'In Canberra.' Poppy grimaced.

'It could be worse. They could have gone overseas.'

'True.' Poppy remembered how, at one point, it had been Scarlett's ambition to live and work in London. Thankfully, it hadn't lasted.

'What can I do to help with dinner?' Gail asked.

'First, I need a cold shower,' Poppy replied, then, seeing Gail was already dressed for the evening in a green and white dress, added, 'Maybe you could set the table while I do that. You'll find the Christmas placemats in the top drawer in the dining room, and the cutlery...'

'I think I can remember where you keep it.' Gail smiled.

'Thanks.' Poppy drained her cup and took it through to the kitchen. Scarlett had been right. The tea had refreshed her. She'd feel even better after a shower and when she was dressed in the red dress with a row of white reindeer prancing around the hemline which she planned to wear that evening.

*

The house was filled with music and laughter with everyone gathered for Christmas dinner, and Poppy was pleased to see Amber looked happier than she had for some time. She put it down to the festive spirit.

Dinner was a fun affair, as they all donned the paper hats and read out the jokes from the Christmas crackers. As expected, the food was delicious. Poppy was glad she hadn't had to cook the turkey herself.

She was about to rise to clear away the plates, when Lachlan held up a hand. He looked at Scarlett who was smiling. 'Scarlett and I have some news,' he said. 'Well, actually two pieces of news.' He took his wife's hand. 'First,' he said, gazing proudly at Scarlett, 'We're having a boy – Taylor Mitchell.'

The others all cheered, and a tear began to form in the corner of Poppy's eyes. Jack would have been so proud. She looked across the table at Cam, knowing he was thinking the same.

Lachlan cleared his throat. 'Our next news may come as a surprise. We've both missed Pelican Crossing and everyone here, and with Taylor on the way, we've made a decision. We're moving back home.'

For a moment, there was a stunned silence, then it seemed as if everyone was talking at once. Poppy felt her heart was going to burst. She'd have all her girls home again and she wouldn't miss out on Scarlett's baby growing up. He'd be right here in Pelican Crossing.

'How?'

'When?'

'Where?'

The questions came thick and fast.

Lachlan held up a hand again. 'As I said, we've missed Pelican Crossing, missed all of you guys. Sorry, Mum,' he said to Gail, 'I know you're not here anymore. We decided we wanted our son to have the same sort of happy childhood we had, to grow up surrounded by his family. I applied for a job with a local firm of architects, was interviewed via Zoom, and was offered a position.'

'Congratulations, son.' Cam was the first to find his voice.

The others all echoed his words.

'When…?' Megan asked.

'I start on the fifteenth of January, so we have a lot of packing to do before then.'

'Where will you live?' Poppy asked. 'There's plenty of room here, if…' While she'd love to have them stay with her, it would cramp her and Cam's style, but she couldn't let that stop her.

Lachlan grinned. 'We're working on that. My old school mate, Miles Connor, is working with a local realtor. He has one of those new apartments by the river coming vacant in the new year and has offered to show it to us before we go back to Canberra. With a bit of luck…' He held up crossed fingers.

'Aren't the realtors closed over the holidays?' Chris asked.

'He's willing to make an exception for an old mate.'

Poppy couldn't keep the smile off her face. This was the best Christmas gift she could have had… though her bangle from Cam came a close second.

'Isn't this marvellous. We're all together again,' Megan said. 'One big family, like we used to be.'

Poppy glanced across to where Cam was sitting next to Gail. They were laughing, looking so… natural together. She was pleased to see how, after all Gail had put him through, he'd been able to forgive her, that they could all move forward, now that they'd be sharing a grandchild.

Then, suddenly, her heart plummeted. She remembered what Gill had suggested, what Megan had said before she knew about Poppy and Cam. She remembered all Gail's comments about how helpful Cam had been, how she would have been lost without him. Were they looking too comfortable together?

No, she was imagining it... but... She looked at them again. She swallowed hard. 'That's wonderful, Lachlan. We must have a big welcome home party when you guys move back,' she said, trying to force an upbeat note into her voice.

'Good plan,' Cam said, but he was looking at Gail, not Poppy.

After dinner, they all decamped to the living room to open their presents. Lachlan, still buoyed up with his announcements, refilled the glasses of everyone except Scarlett and Megan with bubbly, and they all found seats around the tree.

There were lots of exclamations of surprise and pleasure as they opened their presents. Cam proved to be delighted with Poppy's choice of shirts for him, and she had to smile when she opened the bundle of books he gave her.

'I don't know when I'm going to have time to read them all,' she said, 'But I'd better read this one first.' She held up one entitled *Becoming Grandma,* laughing, despite the tiny niggle at the back of her head which refused to go away. She kept looking across the room to where Cam and Gail were sitting together again, trying to tell herself she was imagining things. But was she?

Finally, it was over. The gifts were packed up, the paper thrown in the bin, and there were hugs and goodbye kisses as Amber, Chris, Megan and Gavin took their leave. Cam was last to go, giving Poppy a warm hug and kiss. 'Something wrong?' he asked, perceptive as ever, when she drew away. Poppy shook her head. 'Just tired,' she said.

'See you tomorrow.' They had planned to meet at the marina where Cam was going to take everyone out into the bay for a day of fishing, swimming and relaxing on the water.

'Tomorrow,' she agreed.

Poppy couldn't wait to go to bed, to be on her own, to think carefully about what she had seen, or thought she had seen. Megan's words rang in her head. 'One big family like we used to be.' Only Jack was missing. Poppy had been so thrilled with her new closeness to Cam, she'd forgotten everyone else. Had she been selfish? Should she have considered Gail more?

It had been a happy day, wonderful to hear Scarlett and Lachlan were moving back home, to know there would be a new baby with Jack's name. But for Poppy, Christmas Day had been spoiled.

Forty-seven

Poppy didn't get much sleep. She lay awake tossing and turning till the early hours, worrying, till she managed to convince herself that the kind thing, the most thoughtful thing for her to do was to allow Cam and Gail to be together again. Now they were to be grandparents to Scarlett and Lachlan's baby, to Taylor – her lips curved into a smile at the name – and the young couple were returning to Pelican Crossing, surely it made sense for Gail to return too. And now Judy had died, and Gail was alone in the world, she and Cam could… It was at this point that Poppy's reasoning broke down, that she began to weep.

But she forced herself to continue her line of thought, heedless of what Cam might wish. Gail was her friend too, and Poppy knew how it felt to lose the one person you loved. It made sense for her to turn to the other person she'd loved, the father of her son, the grandfather of her grandson. Gail needed Cam more than she did. By the time she fell into a restless sleep, she had it all worked out.

Poppy awoke to the ringing of her phone.

'Good morning, sweetheart. The sun's shining. It's going to be another lovely day. Ready to go sailing?' Cam asked.

The temptation to agree, to act like before, was so strong Poppy almost gave in. But she remembered the decision she'd made in the early hours and, instead of responding as she knew Cam expected, she said, 'I'm going to cry off. I'm not feeling too well. I think I should stay home.' It wasn't really a lie. The lack of sleep and the wild thoughts whirling around in her mind were giving her a headache, and she felt nauseous. She just wanted to curl up into a ball and forget everything.

'Do you want me to come round?' Cam sounded concerned.

'No, it's nothing much but I don't think I can face a day's sailing.'

'If you're sure…' Poppy could hear the disappointment in his voice. She was disappointed too, but she was determined not to change her mind, no matter how much it hurt.

Without taking time to shower or brush her hair, Poppy pulled on a pair of shorts and an oversized tee-shirt, and went through into the kitchen where the others were having breakfast. All three looked up when she walked in.

'Breakfast, Aunt Poppy?' Lachlan asked.

'Just a cup of tea. I'm not feeling too good this morning. I think I'll go back to bed.'

'Oh, no, Mum! It's such a glorious day,' Scarlett said.

'Would you like me to stay with you?' Gail asked, her face etched with concern.

'No, you go. I'll be fine on my own. I'll have Angus.'

At the sound of his name, the little dog gave a tiny yelp.

'We'll miss you,' Scarlett said.

'You can tell me all about it when you get back.'

'You'll take care, won't you? I don't remember you ever being sick,' Scarlett said.

'I'll be fine,' Poppy repeated. She picked up the cup of tea Lachlan had poured her and carried it back to bed, staying there till she heard the door close and was sure they had all left.

Angus pushed open the door of the bedroom with his nose and jumped up onto the bed. 'Oh, you darling,' she said, a break in her voice. Knowing it was her decision didn't make it any easier, but the hurt would ease over time. As she'd told Gail, time was a great healer. Though she knew it would be doubly hard seeing Cam and Gail together, having to spend time with them as a couple, knowing it could be her by his side.

*

Cam couldn't work out what was wrong. Ever since Christmas Day, Poppy had seemed to distance herself from him. He'd tried to think of what he might have done or said to offend her but hadn't been able to come up with anything. Christmas Eve had been so wonderful, He had felt rejuvenated, as if he was twenty years younger, as if his life was about to begin again. Then, sometime between then and Boxing Day it was as if a light had gone out. Poppy had changed.

In the lead up to Christmas, before Gail, Lachlan and Scarlett had arrived, Poppy had been full of plans for all the things they'd do together, just like in the old days, the things Jack would have planned if he was here. Then there had been Lachlan's big announcement.

Thinking back, it was around then Poppy had seemed to change. But that was crazy. Surely she was as happy as he was that the young couple planned to live in Pelican Crossing? It was more than they could have dreamed, to have their grandson growing up right here with them. He was already looking forward to doing Grandad duty, to teaching young Taylor to swim, to sail, to fish.

It had been three days since then, and all the activities they'd planned together had taken place, but it was as if Poppy had retreated into a shell. No matter what he did, what he said, he'd been unable to coax her out of it. The others hadn't seemed to notice, Lachlan and Scarlett too wrapped up in their own happiness, and Gail in her grief. Megan hadn't taken part in all the activities, blaming what she was still calling the sinker, and Gavin chose to stay with her in case the baby decided to come sooner than anticipated. But Amber and Chris had been part of the group which had gone swimming, played beach cricket and argued over whose catch was biggest. They'd all come together again for a beach barbecue the previous evening, where Poppy had again been more subdued than usual and seemed to be trying to avoid having contact with him. He hoped it was only a reaction to the hectic pace Scarlett and Lachlan set, and everything would get back to normal when he and Poppy were on their own again.

Forty-eight

'What's happening with you and Cam?' Gail asked.

Scarlett and Lachlan had gone to meet his old schoolmate to inspect the apartment for rent, and Poppy and Gail were sitting on the deck with coffee and the last of the gingerbread cookies. Angus was lying at their feet as usual, hoping some crumbs might fall his way.

'What do you mean?'

'When I arrived, you seemed to have difficulty in keeping your hands off each other, but these past few days... since Christmas... you've been acting differently towards him. Have you argued?'

Poppy flinched. It had been so hard to keep her promise to herself. Every time she was near Cam, she wanted to reach out and touch him. It had taken all her will power to resist the urge to respond to his kisses the way she had before. It was lucky she still had a houseful of guests. There had been no more sneaking off like they had on Christmas Eve, and although it devastated her to think they would never make love again, she was sure she was doing the right thing, for him, for Gail, for everyone. Everyone except her.

'No, we haven't argued. Maybe we aren't right for each other.' She took a deep breath. 'Are you thinking of coming back to Pelican Crossing too, now Lachlan and Scarlett will be here?'

Gail stared at her as if she was mad. 'No, I need to go back to Sydney, to the house Jude and I chose together. Like you stayed here when Jack died. It's what I want, what Jude would want. It's where I feel closest to her. I'll come back to visit, to see Lachlan and Scarlett, to get to know my grandson – gosh, that makes me feel old. But my home in Sydney now.'

'I see…' was all Poppy could say.

'You see?' Gail said, 'Is there something you're not telling me?'

Poppy took a breath. 'It's just… I thought maybe… you and Cam…'

'Oh, Poppy,' Gail laughed. 'My feelings for Cam are those of a friend, a very good friend, but a friend, nevertheless. You still care for him, don't you?'

Poppy flinched again. Was she that transparent? 'I thought, maybe… now you're on your own…'

Gail laughed again. 'No, I won't be going back to Cam… or Pelican Crossing. As I said, my life's in Sydney. We… I… have friends there, friends who knew Judy and me together, friends who understand me, the person I am now, not the person I was growing up in Pelican Crossing. It's been lovely spending Christmas here, seeing everyone again, being part of a family, but it's not how I want to spend the rest of my life. If you have feelings for Cam, and he has for you, then my advice is to act on them. It's what I did when I realised how I felt about Jude, and I'll never regret it. We had fifteen wonderful years together, made wonderful memories, memories I'll treasure for ever.'

'Oh, Gail.' Poppy gave her a warm hug. She'd been such a fool, imagining… She knew what Jack would say if he could see her now. He'd tell her to get real and enjoy the second chance at love she'd been given. She could almost hear his voice.

'Have you said anything to Cam about this?'

Poppy shook her head. She'd been trying to pluck up the courage, but there never seemed to be the right moment – or the right words.

'Thank goodness for that.' Gail gave a sigh of relief. 'It's easy to see he's besotted with you. He's already had his heart broken once, and I'm not proud I was the one to do it. He doesn't deserve to have it broken again. He loves you, Poppy, and I'm pretty sure you love him too. Stop trying to be a martyr, it doesn't suit you. Life's too short. We both know that.'

Poppy winced. Gail didn't mince her words. She never had, and she was right. Poppy had been trying to be a martyr, to put other people's happiness before her own, regardless of what they might want for themselves. She'd been wrong on so many counts. Had it been her way of trying to protect herself from being hurt? But Cam would never hurt her. She could only hope she hadn't turned him off with her crazy behaviour, and that he still wanted her.

'Why don't you go to see him?'

'Now?'

'There's no time like the present.'

'What if…'

'Poppy!'

*

Poppy only took time to drag a comb through her hair and add a touch of lipstick. A glance in the mirror showed the fear in her eyes. Was it already too late?

As she drove across town to Cam's apartment, Poppy thought about all the times she'd spent wishing Cam would see her as more than a friend. Then when he did, when everything was going so well, she had to behave like an idiot and imagine things that weren't there, try to arrange others' lives for them. Jack used to warn her about her tendency to act first and think later. This was a prime example, and if it ended up in her being hurt, she had no one to blame but herself.

She reached her destination before she was ready, before she'd worked out what to say. Taking a deep breath, she made her way to Cam's door and knocked.

'Poppy, what are you doing here? Did I forget…?' But the welcoming smile on Cam's face was encouraging.

'Can I come in?'

'Of course.' He hugged her but his kiss was the same peck on the cheek she'd received for years, before they became lovers.

Poppy walked in. There was a mug on the coffee table beside an open laptop.

'Just catching up on a few things,' he said, closing the laptop. 'Is something wrong?'

Poppy stood in the middle of the room twisting the bangle on her right wrist, the bangle Cam had given her, the bangle she'd thought would be the only reminder of their time together. 'It's me. I'm sorry

I've been so distant these past few days. I was trying to get something sorted out in my head.'

'Is it sorted now?'

'Very sorted.'

'Good.' He gave her a quizzical look. 'Are you breaking up with me? Something happened on Christmas Day. You changed. Did I say... do... something to offend you?'

'No, it was nothing you said or did. It was me, all in my mind. I'm sorry,' she repeated.

'As long as it's okay now. It is, isn't it?'

'Oh, Cam!' Poppy began to weep, to weep for all she had nearly thrown away, all because of some misplaced idea of loyalty. 'I do love you.'

'And I love you.' Cam pulled her into his arms. 'I know you miss Jack more at Christmas and I thought, with all the family there, you were regretting...'

'No, never. Jack was Jack. I'll always love him. What I feel for you is different. It's a more mature love. You're special.' Gail was right, she thought. Cam was a good man.

'I don't deserve you,' Poppy sobbed, 'but I promise never to be so silly again. I... I love you so much, more than you could imagine.'

Cam silenced her with a kiss.

Forty-nine

2 weeks later

The phone rang, wakening Poppy from a deep sleep. She and Cam had spent the previous day helping Scarlett and Lachlan settle into their new home, a lovely three-bedroom apartment overlooking the river, not far from where old Agnes had her pelican rescue centre. Scarlett was considering offering to volunteer there until the baby was born, claiming she'd be bored if she didn't have something to fill her days. Then they'd celebrated the news from Gavin that the police had arrested a group of youths who'd admitted to the vandalism, revealing they'd been paid by Jordan Butler to create the damage. Butler himself was improving, but would be in hospital for months to come and would prove no threat to Pelican Crossing.

'What time is it?' Cam muttered, as Poppy picked up the phone.

'The baby's coming. We're at the hospital.' Gavin's excited voice almost deafened Poppy.

'We'll be right there.'

'What is it?' Cam asked, suddenly sounding more awake.

'Megan's in labour. We need to get to the hospital.'

Throwing on the first clothes that came to hand, Poppy and Cam tiptoed out of the house, careful not to waken Angus who was snoring away in his bed in the kitchen.

'I must look a fright,' Poppy said, checking herself in the mirror on the sun visor and running a hand through her hair. 'I'm going to be a grandmother. I can scarcely believe it.'

'Believe it,' Cam said, chuckling.

'It seems like it was only yesterday that Jack was driving me to the hospital to give birth to Megan. Mum and Dad were looking after Amber. It was in the middle of the night then too. I hope it all goes well.' She bit her lip. Her baby was about to give birth.

It was easy to find a parking spot, and Cam took Poppy's hand as they hurried in and made their way to the maternity ward. Gavin was nowhere to be seen. Poppy's heart was pounding. What if...?

'Mrs Taylor?' A nurse came out of a nearby door. 'Megan's mum?'

Poppy nodded.

'Gavin said he'd called you. They left it rather late to come in. It was a very quick labour and...'

Poppy held her breath.

'... you have a lovely, healthy granddaughter.'

Poppy exhaled. She turned to Cam, who took her hand and squeezed it. A daughter. Megan had a daughter. 'Can I see her?'

'I don't see why not, but only for a few minutes. She needs to rest.'

'I'll wait for you here,' Cam said.

Poppy threw him a grateful glance, then pushed open the door.

Inside the room, Megan was sitting up in bed holding a small white bundle. Gavin was seated beside her, looking very proud.

'Mum!' Megan beamed at Poppy. 'Come and meet your granddaughter.'

Poppy walked across to the bed and peeped at the tiny bundle, at the little face of her first grandchild. 'Oh, Megan, she's beautiful,' she said.

'Isn't she,' Gavin said. 'I still can't believe she's actually here.'

'And her name? You said Hazel for a girl,' Poppy said.

'We changed our minds. We're going to call her after Dad. This is Jackie,' Megan said, gazing down at her daughter, her face filled with love.

Poppy's eyes filled with tears. 'It's a lovely name. He'd be so proud.'

*

Poppy had planned a special celebration in *Crossings* to mark Jackie's birth, following the naming ceremony on the beach which Megan and Gavin had decided on instead of a more traditional christening service. It was reminiscent of Scarlett and Lachlan's wedding, another family event in which Jack would never take part. But his name would live on in Megan's daughter and Scarlett's son.

And this time, Cam was by Poppy's side, not only as a friend, but as her partner.

The family were all seated around the table. The meal was over, the toasts had been drunk. Amber stood up. 'I know this is Megan's celebration,' she said, 'but Chris and I have some news.'

Poppy looked at her eldest daughter, remembering the glow she had noticed in her on Christmas Day. It was still there, and Amber was beaming.

'We're pregnant too!' she announced, to be greeted by loud cheers from the entire table, causing the other diners in the restaurant to turn and stare at them.

'Oh, Amber! I'm so glad,' Poppy said, rising to hug her. She'd almost given up hope, afraid to ask Amber about her treatment lest she upset her. She had become so sensitive about her failure to fall pregnant.

'How wonderful, Amber,' Scarlett said. 'Our children will be able to grow up together. When…?'

'July,' Amber said, grasping her husband's hand, 'and the doctor says it's going to be twins.'

'I think this calls for another toast,' Cam said, as a waiter appeared to refill their glasses.

'What a day!' Poppy said, when she and Cam were back home. She had kicked off her shoes and collapsed onto the sofa. 'I'm so pleased about Amber. I was so afraid… when her sisters…'

'There was no need. Nature just needed a little nudge.' Cam joined her on the sofa. 'Now you can concentrate on being a doting grandmother.'

'It sounds strange, doesn't it? Me, a grandmother. It's the beginning of an era, a new generation. I wonder what they will grow up to be like.'

'We'll have plenty of time to find out. In the meantime, why don't we concentrate on the present.'

'Mmm.' Anything else Poppy wanted to say was muffled as Cam pulled her into a passionate embrace.

The End

If you've enjoyed Poppy and Cam's story, a way you can say thank you to me is to leave a review on Amazon and/or Goodreads. A few words will suffice, no need for a lengthy review. It will mean a lot to me and help other readers find my books.

It's been exciting for me to start this new series set in Pelican Crossing and I hope you're going to fall in love with the new location and the characters who live there. As promised you'll meet some old friends from Bellbird Bay as the series progresses.

The second book in the series, *Secrets in Pelican Crossing* is Liz's story.

A heartwarming tale of family, friends, and second chances.

Divorced, frustrated by her daughter's matchmaking, and resigned to staying happily single, *Liz Phillips* thinks she has her life all figured out... until she meets *Finn Hunter*.

Having moved to Pelican Crossing twelve months earlier to support his daughter after a family tragedy, Finn finds himself juggling family obligations and a demanding job as the editor of the local paper. He has little time for romance.

When Liz and Finn's paths cross, there's an undeniable spark between them. They quickly form a connection which neither of them anticipates.

Amidst the whirlwind of their relationship, a secret from Liz's past resurfaces, threatening the closeness she shares with her daughters. Having Finn to lean on is a godsend, but Finn is concealing a secret of his own. A secret that once revealed could undermine the trust and understanding they share and destroy any chance of a future together.

Can Liz find her happy ending or is she destined to face the future with only her family for company?

You can order it here: https://mybook.to/secretsinpc

From the Author

Dear Reader,

First, I'd like to thank you for choosing to read *The Restaurant in Pelican Crossing*. I hope you've enjoyed visiting Pelican Crossing as much as I've enjoyed creating it.

I'm really enjoying starting this new series in another fictional town in Queensland and populating it with characters who I hope you will come to love. As book one in my new series, I'm hoping you will fall in love with the characters as much as you did with those in Bellbird Bay. Like all my other books, although it is part of a series, it can be read as a standalone.

If you'd like to stay up to date with my new releases and special offers you can sign up to my reader's group.

You can sign up here

https://subscribe.maggiechristensenauthor.com/readersgroup

I'll never share your email address, and you can unsubscribe at any time. You can also contact me via Facebook, Twitter or by email. I love hearing from my readers and will always reply.

Thanks again.

MaggieC

Acknowledgements

As always, this book could not have been written without the help and advice of a number of people.

Firstly, my husband Jim for listening to my plotlines without complaint, for his patience and insights as I discuss my characters and storyline with him, for his patience and help with difficult passages and advice on my male dialogue, and for being there when I need him.

John Hudspith, editor extraordinaire for his ideas, suggestions, encouragement and attention to detail, and for helping me make this book better.

Jane Dixon-Smith for her patience and for working her magic on my beautiful cover and interior.

My thanks also to early readers of this book – Helen, Maggie and Louise for their helpful comments and advice, and a special thanks to Maggie for helping me with the description of the Melbourne Cup Lunch.

And to all of my readers, reviewers and bloggers. Your support and comments make it all worthwhile.

About the Author

After a career in education, Maggie Christensen began writing contemporary women's fiction portraying mature women facing life-changing situations, and historical fiction set in her native Scotland. Her travels inspire her writing, be it her trips to visit family in Scotland, in Oregon, USA or her home on Queensland's beautiful Sunshine Coast. Maggie writes of mature heroines coming to terms with changes in their lives and the heroes worthy of them. Maggie has been called *the queen of mature age fiction* and her writing has been described by one reviewer as *like a nice warm cup of tea. It is warm, nourishing, comforting and embracing.*

From the small town in Scotland where she grew up, Maggie was lured to Australia by the call to 'Come and teach in the sun'. Once there, she worked as a primary school teacher, university lecturer and in educational management. Now living with her husband of over thirty years on Queensland's Sunshine Coast, she loves walking on the deserted beach in the early mornings and having coffee by the river on weekends. Her days are spent surrounded by books, either reading or writing them – her idea of heaven!

Maggie can be found on Facebook, Twitter, Goodreads, Instagram, Bookbub or on her website.

https://www.facebook.com/maggiechristensenauthor
https://twitter.com/MaggieChriste33
https://www.goodreads.com/author/show/8120020.Maggie_Christensen
https://www.instagram.com/maggiechriste33/
https://www.bookbub.com/profile/maggie-christensen
https://maggiechristensenauthor.com/

Milton Keynes UK
Ingram Content Group UK Ltd.
UKHW010814300424
441987UK00005B/381